THE BATTY INVENTOR

THE
BATTY
INVENTOR

ALEXANDER LOTEN

Copyright © 2023 Alexander Loten

The moral right of the author has been asserted.

Apart from any fair dealing for the purposes of research or private study, or criticism or review, as permitted under the Copyright, Designs and Patents Act 1988, this publication may only be reproduced, stored or transmitted, in any form or by any means, with the prior permission in writing of the publishers, or in the case of reprographic reproduction in accordance with the terms of licences issued by the Copyright Licensing Agency. Enquiries concerning reproduction outside those terms should be sent to the publishers.

This is a work of fiction. Names, characters, businesses, places, events and incidents are either the products of the author's imagination or used in a fictitious manner. Any resemblance to actual persons, living or dead, or actual events is purely coincidental.

Troubador Publishing Ltd
Unit E2 Airfield Business Park,
Harrison Road, Market Harborough,
Leicestershire LE16 7UL
Tel: 0116 279 2299
Email: books@troubador.co.uk
Web: www.troubador.co.uk/matador

ISBN 978-1-80514-102-0

British Library Cataloguing in Publication Data.
A catalogue record for this book is available from the British Library.

Printed by Printed and bound in Great Britain by 4edge Limited
Typeset in 11pt Minion Pro by Troubador Publishing Ltd, Leicester, UK

Matador is an imprint of Troubador Publishing Ltd

This book is dedicated to all those clever guys that ought to take a little thought before inflicting some bright new idea on us. What about the long term consequences?

PREFACE

Have you ever wondered about the scientific advances being made in our times? Some of them have been distinctly helpful; others have been quite disastrous. One wonders if the clever inventors actually do stop to think of the medium to long-term consequences of their clever ideas.

Let me introduce to you a certain very clever crackpot, by the name of Dr. Lawrence Robinson, known to the few friends that he had, as Larry. He has a lovely habit of dreaming up a stunningly clever idea, but has no thoughts about the mayhem that it is likely to cause.

This story is obviously a grand exaggeration, which staggers belief. Even so, we have to ask ourselves, how much of this is actually happening in our own times, even if it is on a more modest scale? We face an uncertain future. There are all sorts of breakthroughs going on in laboratories all over the world; the possibilities becoming available are massive, but also frightening. One wonders where it will all end.

An important substratum to this story is the urgent need for World Peace. This includes harmony and understanding between peoples of different opinions and traditions. This applies particularly to religion but also political dogmas. These matters are not impossible where genuine love and caring are allowed to rule the day.

THE CAST LIST

Sally Wilkins	Kuku
Larry Robinson (Lawrence)	King Chu-chu
Kevin Kerry	Mr. Chom
Mrs. Curran	Mr. Flam
Sergeant Muldoon	Constable Julie Mayfair
Charles Nonkwhistle	James Whitlock (Jimmy the Whizz)
Mr. Ivanov	Professor Donald Drakeworthy
Arthur Richardson Maudsley	Betty Marston
Captain MacDonald	Prince Baba
Jed-jed	Derek Normbrain
Mi-mo	King Jaja
Seamus Kerry	Jemima Robinson

CONTENTS

1.	In the Laboratory	1
2.	A Strange Visitor	8
3.	Troubles Developing	15
4.	The Coppers	23
5.	Strange Meeting	31
6.	The Police Station	39
7.	Success	49
8.	The Expert	59
9.	More Experts	69
10.	Kevin's Romance	79
11.	Another Offer	89
12.	The King of Oogie	97
13.	The King of the Widgeys	105
14.	The Homecoming	113
15.	The Republic of Whipplitude	121
16.	The Republic of Chiploddy	131
17.	Precipitous Summit	139
18.	Government Intervention	147
19.	Right Sort of Tone	157
20.	The Negotiations	165
21.	New Quarters	173

22.	The Peace Talks	183
23.	Disarmament	191
24.	Wedding Day	201
25.	Reproduction	209
26.	Another Official Visit	219
27.	Another Discovery	227
28.	The Escape	237
29.	Evacuation	245
30.	Citizens of Oogie	255
31.	In the Long Term	268

CHAPTER 1
IN THE LABORATORY

Sally edged her way into the laboratory. She had in her hand a mug of coffee which she assumed Larry would appreciate. A young man was stooping over a funny sort of gadget which kept making oogley noises. In his hand was a soldering iron and he kept giving the gadget a quick jab and a joggle.

"Nearly there!" he breathed, hardly being aware of Sally's presence. Still less was he aware of the collection of coffee mugs, some half consumed at the end of his bench.

"Here's your coffee," ventured Sally, "you haven't finished the others."

"What? Oh!" he was miles away, only just realizing that his assistant had crept in. Not that he really needed an assistant, since she had no idea of what he was on the verge of discovering, and could hardly have offered any advice on the matter. She had gained an A in both Physics and Chemistry at A level and was a bright lass, but with this business she was way out of her depth.

"Wouldn't you like to take a break, Larry?" she suggested gently, "you haven't had a decent meal for three days."

"I suppose you're right," he yawned, advertising the fact that he had hardly had any sleep in several days. "You see, it's important that I keep the thread of what I'm doing. Nearly there!" he proclaimed as if it were the greatest discovery ever found in the history of scientific blunderings. He picked up the coffee and took a couple of mouthfuls. Then he put the mug down and turned his attention afresh to the gadget. "Now is the big moment!" he waggled his hands. "Let's see if this works." The goofy look on his face had Sally somewhat apprehensive of the next eventuality.

"Larry!" she issued caution, "What is supposed to happen?"

Larry produced a square of sheet metal and placed it carefully two feet away from the gadget. He then proceeded to switch on and twiddle some of the knobs on the control panel. The gadget began to make some more googley noises and a reasonable imitation of a donkey's fart.

"Now watch that piece of steel," he pointed, goofily, as he made an attempt at running his fingers through his tousled hair, "this is the moment of truth." It was a proclamation of some kind of clinching gospel; it had Sally full of expectation. But nothing seemed to have happened! The piece of steel appeared to have undergone no alteration. Sally frowned and issued a remark that was suggestive of Doubting Tomasina.

"Now look!" he snatched up the sheet of steel and shoved it under her nose. "It may look like steel, but just try to bend it… go on." he challenged.

Sally gingerly held the piece of steel in her hands and began to flex it! Crack! It snapped asunder just like a potato crisp! She knew that steel, three millimeters thick would never behave like that, normally. But this was nothing normal. The steel had lost its strength and was completely brittle with no strength at all. Even then, it still had the appearance of steel.

"WHOOPPEE!" yelled the scientist, "it's a breakthrough."

"It's a break-something," frowned Sally, staring with astonishment at the fragments of what had been steel. "What on earth have you done to it? You must have messed up the atomic structure of the metal."

"This is fantastic!" the scientist jiggle-joggled up and down in ecstacies, "I've managed something that the sages of the ages never managed to do."

"Does this trick work on any metal?" she frowned apprehensively, "I mean, how about copper and tin… and nickel?"

He interrupted with gusto. "Why not?" He was full of self-congratulation, "anything that's got metallic bonding ought to behave in the same way. I shall try them all out and see if they behave in the same way. I know," he pointed vigorously, "down in the shed is a chunk of tungsten carbide, on my lathe. If my gadget can jigger that up, that will be really something. Pop down and fetch me one."

Sally almost retorted, "fetch it yourself, you nitwit," but recalled that he was paying her to be his assistant and keep house and lay on meals. This was all a bit of an approximation since Larry kept no regular hours, was totally unpredictable and not at all cooperative on household matters.

A few minutes later she returned with a couple of lathe cutting tools made of tungsten carbide, about the toughest metal that mankind had ever devised. Larry snatched them off her and placed them before the wonderful gadget. After a few more funny noises the chunks of metal had all the appearance of being the same, but when Sally tried to bend one, it just went snap like a carrot.

"Blimey!" she stared in astonishment. She knew full well the characteristics of tungsten carbide. The specimen was now no use as a lathe tool; it was just crumbling into tiny particles. "Larry!" she expostulated, "what have you done?"

"I've come a lot nearer to completing the work of the ancient alchemists," he announced as if this were the greatest advance since the invention of the wheel.

"Come a lot nearer to wrecking the entire civilized world," she murmured sourly.

Larry ignored this deep truism. "You see, our old friends, the alchemists were convinced that you could fabricate gold from base metals. They had all kinds of clever ideas for achieving this, but they never managed it. That was because they didn't have any idea of the atomic structure of metals, or of how to alter the atomic structures of them. If they had, they might have managed it. But now, we know how metals are formed with atoms in a lattice."

Sally nodded, since she had learnt that in her Physics and Chemistry courses.

"In theory, if it were possible to alter the atomic structure of one metal to become another, it would stand to reason that we could fabricate gold from any old rubbish, like a tin can…"

"But all you've done is to destroy the composition of the metal, so far…" she carped.

"Ah! But that's the point," he wagged his finger meaningfully, "if we can destroy something, we can also reconstitute it as something else." Came the superior smile on the stupid face. "I'm on my way, All I need to do is devise a gadget that does the reverse and turns steel into another metal. It's only a matter of time before I get the formula right, and turn it into gold. Our ancient alchemist friends would have been thrilled to bits." He jazzed around the room in triumph. Sally was not so sure. She watched him try it on another chunk of metal, this time an old frying pan. She watched him twiddle the knobs and listened to the crazy noises emitted. This time, the frying pan collapsed asunder under its own weight, leaving an assortment of something not even metallic.

"Done it!" he trumpeted around the room. "A real breakthrough!" It was significant that while the metal had disintegrated, the plastic bit, the handle, was unaffected. Larry picked it up and tested it. "Doesn't work on plastic," he puzzled.

"I'm glad to hear something might survive," Sally reassured herself. She began to pick up the collection of half-drunk coffee mugs on her tray and began to head for the door. "Now that you've had a double breakthrough, Larry, why don't you have a decent meal and a good night's sleep?"

"You know?" he nodded his wobbly head in agreement, "I might take you up on that. I'll come down to the kitchen in a few minutes. He stared at her in admiration, not for the fact that she was indeed a beautiful young lady, but for the fact that it had never occurred to him to take a breather.

Sally arrived at the door and made as if to pull it open by operation of the handle. But the handle was not to be found. She stared in consternation at the hole in the door, where that handle was supposed to be. The door was actually open a crack, so it was not difficult to pull it open. But just as she tugged on it, the whole thing swayed over, hit her on the head and induced the tray full of mugs to slosh all over her dress. She emitted a short scream!

"Help!" she yapped, "what's happening? Larry, this door has come away and hit me on the head." She began to wrestle with it, dropping the crockery on the floor and causing an almighty disturbance.

But the hare-brained inventor was already miles away, fiddling with his pet project again. "A – what?" he emitted dreamily, "Make it a hour, could you? I've just spotted something else that needs an adjustment…" He turned and noticed her discomfiture… "oh dear!" he sniffed, "you in a spot of bother? I say?" he stared goofily, "what's happened to the door? Seems to be in disagreement with its framework."

"And I'm in disagreement with you," sobbed Sally, "just look at my dress, all messed up."

"Should wear a lab coat like me," he suggested inoffensively. "Now let me see," he ignored the fact that Sally was sitting on the floor, clutching her head, "what's become of the hinges? And the lock? Well, blow me down!" he was staggered, "they've all gone. Disintegrated! What a shame I shan't be able to keep this work secret any more. Still, never mind, I can rely on you to keep people out of the house, can't I, Sally?"

"You can rely on me to keep myself out of the house,"

she stormed, scrambling to her feet. "You know something? You are crazy. A full blown crackpot. I tremble to think what will happen if this idea ever leaks out. Do you realize that the whole of civilization will be blown apart if this doofer ever gets to be known about?"

"Oh! I suppose there may be something in what you say," he remarked vacantly, "But we shan't let everybody fiddle about fabricating gold from old frying pans..." It was like a child playing with his pet toy.

Sally stalked off down to the kitchen. "Give me patience," she trembled on the edge of despair. "He has no idea of what he has latched on to. He is a complete nutcase, even if he is brilliant."

But how true of life this is?! Sally, the innocent but intelligent young lady, was learning that being brilliant is not always the same as being sensible; still less, the long term ramifications of the bright ideas that some people have, can be quite earthshattering. She sat considering for some time, that there was great potential in Larry's bright idea as long as it was used carefully and ethically. In the wrong hands, with someone who was unscrupulous and self-seeking, it could be a total disaster for mankind. She decided she would not walk out on him after all, but attempt, somehow, to steer this lunatic into some kind of rational course.

CHAPTER 2
A STRANGE VISITOR

For some time Sally sat at the kitchen table, trembling with apprehension about the new-fangled gadget that Larry had developed. It was deeply worrying. She set to work to make a mental list of all the essential things that were made of metal and which potentially could be vapourised just at the flick of a switch. Even if plastic goods were exempt from this scourge, how much of civilization would survive? Anything made of wood, fabric, and just plain muck would assume a much greater importance. And what about gold? If Larry did manage to find a way of fabricating gold, a process which might now be highly possible, what would happen to the world economy? It would be like when the Spaniards discovered masses of gold in the Americas, and made a complete disturbance to monetary values all over the known world. Her nerves became all jangled up. She knew how to calm herself down. She went into the front room and pulled out her violin. It was a musty old thing which could hardly be seen as a prized antique. But she loved it. It was a family heirloom and one of the things she most valued in life. She began to play and the soothing sounds exerted their usual magic on her troubled soul.

After a few pages she became aware of someone else who found her music irresistible. Larry had drifted in from his laboratory and was leaning against the doorpost, completely carried away by the sheer poetry of it. That was one of the reasons why he had engaged her as his personal assistant, for not only was she knowledgeable about scientific matters and efficient about the house, but she was a talented musician who would reach out to the soul of mankind. Not many people could claim to be of such qualities. But like all exquisite ointments, there had to be a fly in it. Both of them became aware of a scuffling sound outside in the garden. Larry's immediate reaction was to bolt back into his laboratory and make a botched attempt at reinstating the door. Sally at first tried to ignore the scuffling sound, but had to stop, as there was a furtive knocking at the door. This was reinforced by another spate of tapping, now louder and more demanding. She had no idea who it could be, since Larry never had any visitors, still less herself.

At last, she put down her violin and went through the kitchen to the back door. "Who's there?" she called gently.

"Please, please, let me in," came a desperate voice. It was that of a young man, exhausted, terrified, urgently seeking help.

"Who are you and what's the matter?" she hissed through the letter box.

"Please, please," came the supplication in an Irish accent, "if they catch me, they'll kill me. For the love of

Mike, would yer save my life? I'll do anything to help you, if yer just let me in."

It was a young man with a straggly beard and unkempt appearance. He was clearly exhausted and terrified. He checked that the kitchen door was locked, pulled the curtains over the window and collapsed into a chair at the table. He put his head down on the tablecloth and shuddered, whimpered and wept. Sally stared at him in amazement, words failing her.

After some time, he calmed down to some extent. "That was yourself playing the violin," he stared in wonderment. "I thought to meeself, anyone that can play like that, must be a wonderful soul, a kind person, someone who could show mercy. So I took a chance and tapped on your door."

"Who on earth are you, and what's this all about?" Sally managed to croak, as fear gripped her artistic soul.

The heavy Irish accent made an attempt at continuing. "Moi name is Kevin Kerry," he lilted, now rather more engagingly, "Oi come from County Kerry, yer knaw, in the Emerald Oile."

"Well this is middle England," Sally replied, "you are a long way from home. You can feel safe in this country. Are the Police after you?" Her tone became slightly suspicious at this point.

"No…no…no," he wafted it off as some sort of irrelevance, "I'd feel a lot happier if it was just them. No… no, far worse than that. Nasty people who'd give me a really nasty time of it. You don't realize how horrific it can get. I need to go into hiding, change my appearance, reinvent myself. Can yer help me do that? I know yer a kind lady.

Just look at that lovely face you've got. You wouldn't hand me over to that lot."

"I don't know what to say, Kevin," her voice wobbled, "for one thing, this isn't my house, and I don't know what the owner would say… I mean, I don't know what he would say to harbouring… a criminal… is that what you are? Have you done something dreadful?"

"Can you find out for me, please?" came the supplication, "is he a hard man? Has he got any sense of mercy? I really dare not go out into the streets again and take the risk of being spotted by them… " he tailed off, as terror clouded his face.

"I think it's fair to say, he's a decent chap who wouldn't want to land anyone in trouble," she speculated slowly, "but he is so immersed in his work, that it might be a problem to get him to apply any thought to hiding a fugitive. Can I trust you to stay put while I nip up and ask him? I'll try not to be too long. Hang on, Kevin."

•

"Larry!" she called furtively from the door which had every intention of interrupting the conversation.

"Um!" he remarked in a dazed voice, totally absorbed in tinkering with his gadget. He was miles away. He might as well have been on another planet, far from the troubles of this world.

"Larry!" she hissed, "there's a bloke arrived downstairs…"

"Best not bring him up…" he nattered as he twiddled with his knobs.

"Larry! He's on the run. What shall I do?"

"Show him to the lavvie," came the abstracted remark, miles away.

"No, you dope," she was despairing, "I think he might be in serious danger. Can he stay with us? Can we hide him?"

This was met with a nil response as the crackpot continued with the twiddling. "Shush!" he cautioned, waving his hand at her. "Just about to try something else. Here's a silver bracelet. Now just watch. This could be a major breakthrough. This could be history in the making."

Sally sighed with apprehensive impatience. He was clearly not engaging with the real problems of this world. The gadget was induced to make some more funny noises, terminating with a belch not unworthy of a dyspeptic elephant. The chunk of silver slowly began to change colour. Can you guess what that colour was? It was not red, or blue, or black, but a colour that is the fascination of all instinctive responses in the human soul; it was GOLD!!!

Larry was totally overwhelmed and in ecstasies. "I knew it! I knew it! It can be done!" he shouted at the top of his voice.

"Shshshshsh!" Sally tried to shush him down, "we've got company. Calm down, Larry. Anyway, how do you know it's real gold as opposed to something that just looks like gold, you know, fool's gold?"

"Yes, yes," he palpitated, "the acid test. Let me get on with it."

"But what can I do about this visitor?" she urged.

"What?" he blurted, clearly having no idea of what she was talking about, as he applied the acid to the artifact.

"This bloke that's turned up… what must I do about him?"

"Oh yes, I remember," he gurgled in a self-congratulatory splurge, "he wanted to use the lavatory. Fine; as long as he doesn't think my laboratory is a lavatory." The clumsy pun was not calculated to reassure Sally at all, but she made an attempt at laughing, not very convincingly.

"Can you let me deal with this matter?" she begged, "he is in desperate need of help."

"Why? Is his zip stuck?" came the goofy reply from the one who had a one-track mind.

"Oh I give up!" she sighed, as she had a renewed wrestling session with the damaged door.

•

"For the time being, Kevin, you can hide here," Sally handed him a cup of tea.

"Have yer nothing stronger?" he gasped, "even a drop of the hard stuff."

She poured out a gill of whisky into his cup and stared at him, calculatingly. "It's only fair if you tell me what this is all about," she insisted, "if you are a criminal, I should really call the Police."

"Would yer judge for yerself," he pleaded, "someone like yourself, with a face like the Holy Virgin herself, all I can ask for is mercy on a poor tortured soul. Yer violin itself is enough ter bring healing ter my soul. I could listen to it for hours. But first; I must tell ye me story."

The story began ten years before, in the depths of Southern Ireland, as Kevin had been induced to join the IRA. "I was full of fervor for the unification of the Emerald

Isle, and how dreadful the Brits were. I became involved in framing a plot to blow up a Police Station. My friends were convinced that this would induce the Brits to go home. Then it came to the day of the attack. My job was to observe and report any developments that could mess things up. My friends planted the bomb and ran off. It was a timed device. Would you believe it, just at the wrong moment, a crowd of people including children walked past the Police Station, and the device went off. I was frantic, for even though I tried to alert my colleagues, this made no difference. Many people were injured and two people were killed. I thought to myself, that was a bunch of Protestants, so that would teach them a lesson. Imagine my feelings when I discovered later that that crowd of people were a group of Catholics on their way to church, and one little girl…" His face creased up…"who had lost a leg. . was actually a distant cousin of mine. Oh God!" His face went down on the tablecloth and he wept in despair. "To think, that little child, will have to go through life with a leg messing…no fault of her own… poor little soul. I felt sick right to the depth of my soul. I knew I had to get out of this organization. But how? They don't take kindly to anyone backing out. I told them they were crazy. I received threats. I knew I had to get away… Away from Ireland… away to England, perhaps, keep out of sight… Change my identity… hide… Oh God!" he spluttered, "is there any forgiveness?"

Sally put her hand on his, squeezed gently and sighed. "You can stay, Kevin."

"How long?" he juddered.

"As long as it takes.

CHAPTER 3
TROUBLES DEVELOPING

Sally stared at Kevin with something between disbelief and deep distaste. She had never had any time for terrorism, and the troubles in Ireland had simply appalled her. To come across someone like Kevin, who was clearly implicated in the terror programme but was riddled with guilt over it, was a major eye-opener. At length, she decided she would try to redeem this tortured soul.

"If you want to hide here, Kevin," she stated firmly, "you need to clean yourself up, shave that beard off, wear smart clothes and get rid of that Irish accent. Hopefully we can re-invent you so that your friends, so-called, will hardly recognize you. Are you with me?"

"You are so kind," his voice vibrated, "and I will do what you say. Only please don't hand me over to the Police. They might be quite lenient, but once my friends find me, since it will probably get into the media, I may as well shoot myself."

"Go to the bathroom and make a start," she ordered, pointing aloft. "A good bath and a shave to start with and I will see if Larry will lend you some clothes. I might manage to grab his attention for a few split seconds," she pulled a wry face.

•

Dr. Lawrence Robinson was found sitting back on a chair in his laboratory, clearly full of self-congratulation with regard to his latest breakthrough. The few friends that he had, one of which was Sally, called him Larry. He might as well have been entitled Heath, after that crackpot inventor, of the same surname, to wit, Robinson. But Larry was almost certainly in a different class to Heath Robbo. After all, it is not every inventive scientist who can convert silver into gold. At least, that is what he felt confident about.

As Sally approached him, the draught from the damaged door stimulated one of the sashes in the window to part company with its framework, and crash down into the garden below, decapitating one or two cauliflowers. A quick examination revealed that the handle and the hinges on the sash had also perished away to nothing.

"We are all set to make a fortune!" he announced in great confidence.

"What? With all the metal fittings in the house going kaput?" Sally complained, "Larry, have you any idea of what the consequences will be? It will produce pure chaos in the modern world."

He was clearly quite carried away by his own success. "It did turn into pure gold," he enthused, "it wasn't just in appearance. I've tested it. It's pure gold right through," and he waved the erstwhile silver bracelet in front of her face. We can be as rich as kings."

"I can't."

"Yes you can. I will share it with you."

"I'm a woman, silly, so I can't be a king. A queen more like. Seriously, Larry, we must keep this business under wraps."

"I suppose you're right," he admitted sourly, the daft face just attaining a little more common sense. We need to concentrate on the positive developments of this idea. Just destroying things, like bits of metal, is… well, it has its place, but you are right. It could ruin all sorts of things."

"At last, you're beginning to see sense," she sighed. "Now listen carefully, Larry." She tugged at his arm as he began to fiddle with his gadget again… "pay attention please."

Larry let go of the knobs, just for a moment or two.

"We have a visitor."

"Oh! Anyone I know?" he quizzed with his eyebrows, not that he knew many people anyway. "Somebody from the family?"

"No, listen! This bloke is in a real mess. He is being hounded by wicked people…" she tightened her face as his attention was clearly straying away from the matter and the gadget was occupying the centre of his thoughts… "Larry! Don't fiddle."

"Oh!" he jerked, "wicked people. You mean Communists, Nazis?"

"Worse than that. Let's make a deal. One secret for another. I'll keep your secret. You keep mine. Agreed?"

"What? Have I got a secret?" he was plainly miles away.

"Yes Larry. Your invention. You don't want some rotter to pinch your idea, do you?"

"By crikey, no," he blurted. "I want the credit for this, and the royalties and the profits. OK. You keep my secret; I'll keep yours. What is it? You got a boyfriend or something?"

"Much more serious than that, Larry…" and she quickly explained about Kevin Kerry.

•

While this was going on, a woman in the street had noticed that the sash had fallen out of the window frame. It struck her as most odd, especially as no one seemed to have pushed it, still less appeared in the garden to retrieve it. Consternation was the word, as a cast iron drainpipe fell off the wall and crashed down on the fence. There was no apparent cause. The woman stared in amazement. She was about to approach the house in a neighbourly spirit, to report the matter. Imagine her being staggered as a boy on a scooter drew near to the house and the aforesaid vehicle came to pieces and the boy found himself careening into the fence, beside the remnants of the drainpipe. The boy could be forgiven for uttering a very naughty word, such as those of a junior time of life ought not to express, at least, not in the hearing of ladies. He stared at the remnants of his scooter and could think of no explanation for this disaster. The lady approached him and took his arm.

"You all right, young man?" she steadied him. "What's happened to your scooter?"

The boy shook his head in amazement and could offer no comment. The lady decided to tap on the door of Larry's house. This exploit began well, but deteriorated into an uncertain exercise, as the knocker, made of brass, fell to pieces. She immediately assumed it was her fault and felt obliged to apologise in full to the householder. Sally opened the door and stared in amazement at this strange lady.

"Hello! Can I help you?" she asked gently, "Do I know you? Are you Mrs. Curran from number 10? You look a little perplexed."

"Yes, I am, dear. I just wanted to say… this is very strange, but your drainpipe has collapsed off the house… and your window has just fallen out… and…" she noticed the puzzled look on Sally's face, "and I'm sorry to say, your door knocker has… erm…"

It was beginning to dawn on Sally what all this destruction meant. It was brought home even more as a passing car shed a wing mirror, which crashed into the gutter, leaving bits of mirror minus its metal framework. A mixture of anger and frustration stimulated her to close the door as quickly and as tactfully as she could, shot up the stairs and into the laboratory.

"You'd better switch that blessed thing off at once," she snapped. "Larry, do you hear? You are causing mayhem in the street." She quickly explained what had happened.

The expert twisted his face in puzzlement and declared, "Well I never did!" He twiddled with some more knobs. "It seems to work through solid walls. Did the doorknob turn into gold?" he questioned in all seriousness. "Cor blimey, this is interesting!"

"Larry!" shouted Sally, "switch that blooming thing off at once. Completely off, before you wreck anything else. I insist. Do it!" she snapped angrily. "Remember; secret!!??" and she wagged a bossy finger at the gawping face.

•

"Ye know, it's a funny thing," puzzled Kevin, as he shovelled his first decent meal for some time down his throat.

"What? Cottage pie?" Sally served her own portion up, "normal thing in England."

Kevin was quite transformed all in the space of an hour. He was wearing a smart suit, borrowed from a scientist who was hardly aware of actually owning one, his face was clean-shaven and his hair was decently cropped. He was now an entirely presentable young gentleman. Sally was full of admiration and might have begun to harbor romantic notions for him, were it not for her knowledge of his curriculum vitae.

"No, no, no, for the cottage pie is excellent," he grinned in congratulation. "The funny thing…I don't know how to describe it. When I was in the bathroom," he began to snigger…"you'll never believe this… one of the taps went all woggly." He watched her face for a reaction.

"How do you mean?" she asked, trying not to give too much away.

"It bent in me hand," he blurted, forgetting to minimize the Irish accent. "And when I tried to turn it off, it went like plasticine, but I managed to stop it spurting water all over the place." He studied her face for some kind of reaction, but there was no reaction.

"Is there water all over the bathroom?" she asked in a neutral voice.

"I think it all stopped," he breezed as if it were a mild shower of rain.

Sally darted off upstairs to check on the bathroom. The tap in question was clearly a funny shape but was actually watertight. A feeling of renewed panic shot through her mind. She darted into the laboratory, only to find that the great inventor was having another twiddling session with those knobs.

"Larry, for Pete's sake, switch that damned thing off," she yelled. "It's just going to land us in more and more trouble."

"Must just let me finish this test," came the abstracted reply as if from planet nine, and then in a more chummy tone, since he liked Sally, "come on, don't be such a spoilsport."

"Spoilsport!" she protested, "at this rate you'll not just spoil everyone's sport, but just about everything else." She hesitated as through the gap in the window she could hear raised voices down below in the street.

"Now what's this all about?" came a voice of authority. Sally was immediately on her guard; Larry was totally absorbed with metal-mongery and fiddle-twiddling. Sally peered out to spot a Policeman chatting to Mrs. Curran and the father of the boy whose scooter had descended into chaos.

Downstairs, the same voice of authority had drifted into the kitchen as Kevin was finishing his dinner. He was immediately on his guard; fear shot through his body. He peeped out of the kitchen door to catch a glimpse of the English Garda in the exercise of his duty. His frantic brain indicated that a hiding place would be the best expedient. As Sally rumbled down the stairs she was met with a terrified Irishman seeking a more secure lodging place.

"The coppers!" he rasped, "where can I hide?"

"Under the stairs, quick!" She yanked the sloping door open, half expecting the hinges to be non-existent. Mercifully, as Kevin bolted down the steps into the cellar, Sally ascertained that the door fittings were intact. Phew! Safe for the time being, at least.

CHAPTER 4
THE COPPERS

There came an authoritative rap on the front door. Sally knew it would be the policeman, but she hesitated to open the door just in case the metalwork on it had gone through some sort of metamorphosis. She decided to slip out of the back door and through to the street. The policeman was staring in consternation at the remains of the drainpipe, draped over the hedge. He was totally mystified.

"Good afternoon, Constable," she piped as innocently as was possible, trying to simulate a naïve schoolgirl. "Is there a problem?"

"Madam, I have had reports of strange goings on in this street. These people inform me that there have been weird incidents happening. No one knows what to make of it. Have you noticed anything peculiar happening?"

"Has a crime been committed, Constable?" she managed to sidetrack.

The notebook landed back in the official pocket, but the law-worthy finger pointed to the remains of the drainpipe and the scooter. "What would you say has happened here?" he frowned, in total mystification. "And this," he pointed at the oddments of a scooter, "and this," he picked up the shards of mirror from the gutter.

Sally stared at the pieces in amazement, while she considered what to admit to. Clearly there was going to come a point at which someone in authority would have to be acquainted with Larry's invention. That was unavoidable. On the other hand, she had two awkward secrets lurking about in the house. It was a dilemma for a young girl, intelligent, but barely into her twenties. She decided that she had better invite the bobby into her kitchen and disentangle him from the onlookers in the street.

•

"Cup of tea?" she offered, as she tried to shuffle Kevin's empty plate away to the sink.

The standard 'no thank you' came out smartly. The Constable sat at the table and pulled out his notebook. "We have some very strange goings on in this street, Madam," he intoned, "do you think you can help us with our enquiries?"

"First things first," she sipped at her cup, "you are here at my invitation. This is not my house. I am only… what shall we say. . for want of a better word, the servant. The owner may appear at any time and ask you to leave. Do you have a warrant to search these premises?"

"Can I ask, who is the owner? I do not have a warrant, but I could get one."

"On what grounds? I think you said there had been no offence committed. The owner is Dr. Lawrence Robinson. He is very busy at the moment, and you may find he's rather a strange person to talk to. What is the substance of your enquiries?"

"I'm not at all sure what this is all about," began the constable, a gentle smile on his face. He found Sally an engaging young girl, without a hint of guilt on her face. "We have had reports of things just collapsing… or. erm. descending into dust. I don't know what to make of it. That Mrs. Curran, who tried to work the knocker on your door, she says it just fell apart in her hands. I don't know what to make of it."

"You mean, the door just fell apart?" Sally tried to look amazed, "it's still there, in place."

"No, I mean, knockers don't just fall apart, Miss."

"Knockers!" she expostulated, "you being personal, mate?" She grasped the opportunity to swing the discussion in her favour. Sally was quite well-endowed. She managed to blush; it was a fair pretence.

"No offence meant, Madam," came the profuse apology, "I mean, the door-knocker did something very strange. I am beginning to think someone has been hallucinating." He decided to curtail his visit, and rose from his chair. As he reached the door, he failed to notice that the metal numbers on his shoulders had mysteriously melted down and dribbled all down his sleeve. Sally did notice, but managed to stifle a gasp.

"What's the matter, Miss?" he frowned, "you in pain?"

"Sort of," she wheezed, theatrically, "I might call a doctor. Good bye, Constable."

•

Shortly afterwards, Kevin emerged from his hiding place under the stairs. He had obviously over heard all of that conversation and was clearly intrigued.

"So what's going on, Sally?" he teased, "are the leprachauns playing their tricks again? I thought they only messed folk about in dear old Ireland."

"It might as well be," sighed Sally, "I think we are heading for big trouble."

"Is that a polite way of telling me to clear off?" he almost choked on it.

"No, no, not you. We do have funny goings on in this house."

"Would you tell me what it's all about? I think I'm beginning to guess. I promise I will not tell a soul, not even my dear old sainted Mother." He slapped the table with some force.

Sally set to work to explain what was going on upstairs and the extraordinary effects that Larry's invention was already having. She impressed on Kevin the importance of keeping the old mouth shut at all costs. Kevin sat there, his eyes growing wider and more astonished with each revelation. Sally waited for the expected outburst of disbelief and ridicule. But it never came. Kevin clearly believed every word of it. It was like telling a little child a fairy story; he was taking the whole thing completely at face value. Sally was clearly confused within herself, for she herself was only just managing to give the lunatic inventor a modicum of credit.

"And if he can turn silver into gold," he remarked in a matter of fact way, "can he do it in reverse… I mean turn gold into silver?"

"I have no idea," she despaired. "All I can say is that if this idea gets out, it could wreck the whole of civilization. Everything metallic will be at risk."

"And what about other things?" he scratched his head, "like plastic and fabric? And wood?"

The uncertain look on Sally's face was at that moment in receipt of clarification. From out in the street came an almighty clanking and yelling. A passing car, which was mercifully doing only about 20 mph, suddenly disintegrated, leaving the driver still seated in his chair intact, but not really attached to anything else except perhaps the remnants of the steering wheel. Sally and Kevin raced to the front room window and peered out from behind a curtain. Providentially, the curtain was suspended on plastic runners.

"My God!" she gasped in astonishment, "that bloke's car has completely come apart."

"The Saints and the Holy Virgin protect us," gurgled Kevin, "what are we up against in this road?"

"In this house," she chipped, trembling with fear, "that policeman will be back again in no time. You had better hide. He might have a warrant to search the place. You'd better go right down to the back of the cellar, Kevin."

"What puzzles me," began Kevin, "why didn't that car turn into gold? That would have been the start of a mega gold rush, like California." It was as naïve as the loony Doctor upstairs.

They continued to peer round the curtain to view the developing situation in the street just outside. That policeman had now returned, with a Sergeant. They were talking to the car driver, who was clearly in a state of shock. They lifted the car seat up against the fence and let him sit down, to recover his composure. There were bits of car parts strewn about the tarmac, and tail pipe and a spare tyre, chunks of plastic and upholstery in complete disarray. The constable, who had clearly not yet noticed the disaster to his metal numbers, was inspecting a puddle of petrol and oil smeared all over the road.

"This is all very strange," he muttered, "I think we shall have to close the road. This petrol could easily catch fire. The fire brigade ought to be called out…"

"That is the giddy limit," exploded Sally, "that idiot upstairs has got to be stopped before someone gets killed. I must have a word with that policeman again."

"Ah now, just a minute," cautioned Kevin, "before you blow the gaff for the entire world to find out what's going on…" They slid off into the kitchen… "Let's not rush it. I can see that there's a great potential in an invention like that. I know it looks like destruction on a massive scale, but it could also be a great factor in world peace, don't you think?"

"World peace," she objected, "World Chaos, more likely. If this gets into the wrong hands, heaven help us all."

"Steady on, Sally," he begged, "why don't you at least let me have a chat with this guy upstairs? Clearly this idea is in its infancy and he hasn't worked out how to use it under control, or responsibly. There is so much potential in this gadget. I know, in my soul, how clever gadgets can cause pain and suffering, in the hands of someone who is evil. I've seen it for myself. It needs someone who is bent on solving problems, not inventing more problems. Let me talk to him. I might knock some sense into him. Please!"

"Very well!" came the despairing response, as the expected knock on the door commenced, "go up and see if you can hide in the laboratory, if they decide to search the place."

•

Sergeant Muldoon took a seat in the kitchen, while his Constable stood behind.

"Constable," he frowned, as he eyed the man's uniform, "there's something missing, I think. Where are your numbers?" He pointed to the man's shoulders.

The Constable began to realise the non-existence of his numbers. "Where on earth have they got to?" he snatched at his jacket. "Hey, Sarge, what's happened to yours?" he pointed out in an et tu brutus gesture.

Sally was near to tears and trembling like a leaf. She decided she would tell all, in spite of her obligation to keep a secret. After all, Larry was in intent on inflicting his clever idea on all passersby. She bid them listen carefully. She went into detail about the invention upstairs; how it could transmogrify anything metal, and more sinister, turn silver into gold. The two policemen eyed each other and gave a very slight shake of the head. Clearly they did not believe a word of it.

"And do the pixies come out in the night and pinch the gold?" asked the Sergeant gently.

"Perhaps they know where the rainbow ends and then

you can get that crock of gold," teased the Constable, a little less politely.

"You can be forgiven for thinking I'm completely nuts," she sobbed, "but I really think you should contact somebody in the Government, someone scientific, and at least stop this crackpot before he causes any more mayhem. What government department would that be?"

"I don't rightly know, Madam," Muldoon considered, "I suppose they might not know what to make of all this. What do you think, Ted?" as he turned to the Constable.

"Department of mental health," he muttered sourly, if unadvisedly.

"Is it possible to inspect this gadget you're alleging can destroy metal, Madam?" came the Sergeant. "Can we take a look round your premises?"

"I can't really say without the property holder giving permission," she blurted, "since you haven't got a search warrant, the answer will be no… for the time being."

The two policemen headed for the door, muttering to each other. "She's clearly bonkers," whispered Ted, "what a shame, a lovely girl like that."

"A fine tale," murmured Muldoon, as he pulled at the door to leave the premises. Neither of them had any idea of why the door suddenly fell down and hit them on their helmets!

CHAPTER 5
STRANGE MEETING

While the Law was conversing with Sally downstairs, Kevin of the Emerald Isle had infiltrated Larry's laboratory. This was not difficult since the door had long since given up any hope of retaining the secrets of the room of great experimentation. Larry, as usual, was totally absorbed in adjusting his gadget and oblivious to his uninvited guest. He assumed, from the gentle footsteps that this was Sally with another cup of tea.

"Just put it down there," he murmured, "I'll drink it later."

Kevin's eyes roved over the room, with bits of wire, valves, chemicals, and bits of paper with elaborate formulae inscribed thereupon. He coughed deferentially in the hopes of gaining Larry's attention.

"Sorry to intrude. I assume you are Dr. Lawrence Robinson."

"Yes, of course, Sally," he nattered impatiently into a box of bits and pieces, "I can't stop now, this is another big moment in the history of science." This was reinforced by a funny noise which terminated in an almighty

POP!! Augmented by a most interesting pong. "Well by Jimminy!" his face was a picture of self-admiration, even if it was smeared with smoke. "That's another amazing breakthrough!"

"Dr. Robinson, we are into an awkward situation. I would ask you to listen and take action."

At last, Larry turned and beheld his strange guest. "Oh hello! I thought you were Sally. You must be my unscheduled guest. You had a problem, I think. Yes! I remember. Did you manage with your flies?"

"Flies?" stared Kevin, "I'm quite good at swatting them."

"Strange fellow," blinked Larry, "Not heard of that sort of thing before, still, you never know. Oh wait a minute; yes, yes, it was your zip. Did you manage to get it down… oh I see you zipped it up again OK." The daft look was glancing down at Kevin's trousers.

"Dr. Robinson…" began Kevin politely but urgently.

"Just call me Larry. Are we related?" he had picked up the impression of an Irish accent…" All I ever get is the occasional relation call in to see me. Are you a cousin of mine? I don't seem to recognize you."

"Larry," Kevin recommenced, "we have big trouble downstairs. The Police have been round, twice now. Sally is fit to scream. That invention of yours is causing mayhem. Can you please switch it off?" He was as insistent and firm as an Irishman ever can be.

"I say…" remarked Larry in a modicum of delight… "that accent… you must be Irish. Am I right? You know, my great grandparents were from County Sligo." He put on a slight imitation brogue. "Yer know, we might just be distant cousins, would ye not think so?"

"Larry, there's a car down in the road, and it's collapsed into tiny pieces."

"Typical of modern manufacture," the boffin sighed, "never the same quality as in days of yore."

"Your clever gadget, Sir," emphasized Kevin. "Anything metallic just falls apart. The Police are going to fetch a search warrant. They will find out what you've been up to. May the Saints protect you. Can't you hide the thing quickly and give up wrecking everything?"

The gadget made another unscheduled squawky noise, not unlike a demented howler monkey and another sash fell out of the window, crashing down into the garden and marmalising a couple of sticks of rhubarb.

"Oooops!" remarked Larry, "funny things going on at Robinson Towers." At that moment, the metal clasps on two pairs of trousers melted into nothing, and two pairs of underpants sizzled into view. "Hey!" pointed Larry with a goofy look on his face, "you don't have to take them down in here. The lavatory is just round the corner. Oh well, I'm a broadminded bloke. I don't mind really, if you're desperate. Look; here's bucket." And he handed him a plastic bucket.

Kevin grabbed at his bags and heaved them up. Larry had clearly failed to notice that his own bags had descended in the general direction of Australia. "I think it might be yourself in need of a quick on, Dr. Robinson," he pointed.

"No, I'm fine," came the reassurance, "look, this way to the toilet," and he stepped towards Kevin with the intention of showing him the way. But with his trousers fully at bottom mast, so to speak, he tripped up and fell headlong, landing with his head stuck in the plastic bucket. "Ooooops!" he googled from within, "what happened there? Have I been transmogrified into outer space?"

"That's the best idea you've had yet, Doc," whispered Kevin, as he helped him off with the bucket. "Pull your bags up and prepare for trouble."

"What trouble would that be?" came the imitation brogue.

"The Police are coming round, Doc," he shouted in despair. "You might get arrested."

"What?" he stared down at the descent of his bags, "you think they might think I'm one of those peculiar people… you know, kinky, eh?"

"They might indeed, Doc, and what will Sally downstairs be saying if your knickers are on show? But more serious than that; the coppers will want to know why anything metallic goes all peculiar in this street. It's only a matter of time before they find out what you've been up to. I think you ought to switch that thing off and hide it in the attic or some such place."

But it was a little late for that subterfuge. A police car pulled up outside in the road and three bobbies emerged, one them of the female persuasion. None of them managed to observe that some of the handles on their car had disintegrated, but they had other matters on their minds. They headed for the front door, which strangely was still occupying the same space as it had done for many years before, even if the knocker had done a Houdini. Sally appeared from the back and had a warrant waved in her face.

"Come this way, gentlemen," she beckoned, "and can I

ask you; if you find anything of interest to you, you must keep it confidential. Is that a promise?"

"Of course," replied Sergeant Muldoon with great self-confidence. "I would like to introduce you to Constable Mayfair." He pointed out the third person in blue. "She is very good at counselling."

"Excellent!" sighed Sally, "the bloke upstairs is certainly in need of something like that."

"No dear," Muldoon's voice was full of apology, "she's here to help you…"

•

As the boys in blue went from room to room, attempting to explain the extraordinary happenings outside in the street, Sally and Julie Mayfair sat in the kitchen and chatted cautiously.

"I have been so worried," Sally began, "that bloke upstairs. I'm convinced he's completely crackers."

"Which bloke would that be, dear?" Julie asked gently. "We are more concerned about you. What was all that about a machine that could ruin any metal? Have I got that right?"

"Yes, and you must keep your mouth shut about it. I did ask your men to find someone from the Government, you know, an expert, to come and assess this gadget. If it gets into the wrong hands, it could cause mayhem in the modern world. Perhaps a government scientist could talk some sense into him. I've tried, but he just won't listen."

"Of course, dear," came the sympathetic drawl, laced with disbelief. "You say he can make metal go all funny? Are you sure that is quite so? I mean, isn't that impossible?" Julie was smiling gently at Sally, across the table. She seemed such a sensible, well-balanced girl, not the type of person given to flights of fancy. However, strangely, Sally's frontage seemed to lurch into a state of imbalance. Julie had never observed a well-endowed woman with her bosom pointing it two directions at once, up as well as down. She could see through the girl's blouse that her bra had come apart on one shoulder strap, but not the other. Julie had no idea of what to say. Sally began to become aware of the problem, as the rest of her bra on the other side did the same thing. Now she was restored to a balanced state of affairs, only rather unsteady in general effect.

The metal clasps on her bra had disintegrated!

In the meantime, the Sergeant and the Constable had worked round to the laboratory, and encountered the boffin who was still fiddling with some kind of control knob. Kevin Kerry had donned a lab coat and was pretending to be experimenting with some chemicals.

"Good afternoon, gentlemen?" Muldoon stared in amazement, "and what have we here?"

Ted waved the warrant at Kevin, who pointed to Larry and stated, "his house. Tackle him, Constable. I only follow instructions." It was a passable English accent.

Muldoon approached Larry and tried to gain his attention. "Sir!" he tried to sound important, "I have a warrant to search your premises."

"Found anything yet?" came the abstracted remark, "feel free, Inspector. Why don't you tell me what you are looking for and I will help you as much as I can?" Larry went on twiddling and fiddling, and operating the on-off switch in a distracted manner. "Now why won't it do that again?"

Muldoon stared around the room and was overwhelmed by the multiplicity of equipment, bits of wiring, chemicals and mixtures of fantastic colours, and papers covered with elaborate calculations. He realized that he was completely out of his depth, and since he had no idea of what he ought to find, he sighed and began to head for the door. From down below, he could hear the strains of a beautiful piece from Handel, played on the violin. Julie Mayfair was totally captivated by it as Sally gave herself solace in the front room. Julie quickly forgot that she was a lady in blue and began to question in herself how and why her colleagues had dubbed Sally as off her rocker.

"That sounds absolutely lovely," she piped, "is that a Strad?"

"No, it's Handel," Sally replied.

"Oh! I thought it might be Bach."

"The only bark here, comes from upstairs; he's barking mad." Sally emitted a sigh.

"No; I mean the violin. Is it a Stradivarius? You know, really valuable. The tone is superb."

"Come off it," laughed Sally, "what would a bog-standard fiddler like me be doing with a Strad? No, it's just a plain ordinary production fiddle."

Muldoon appeared in the doorway. "So while he twiddles upstairs, Sally fiddles downstairs," he grinned. "I think we can leave these dear people alone, Mayfair," came the reassuring order, "we seem to have found nothing suspicious in this house. I wouldn't be surprised if it's that fiddle that's distracting people and making them have a bit of an accident," he joked, rather inappropriately.

"Sarge," the lady copper objected, "she's brilliant. Can't you appreciate excellence when you hear it?" The conversation continued down the passage. "She can hardly be raving mad," stated Julie, "my opinion is that she's highly intelligent. You know she's got an A in Physics and Chemistry?"

"Come off it, Mayfair, there's no such thing as a machine that can change metal into rubbish, still less turn silver into gold. That is pure fiction… fantasy… moonshine."

They discovered that re-entering the car was a bit of a problem, since all the handles on the nearside had vapourised. They were even more mystified, but still there was no obvious solution to their closed minds.

Upstairs, Kevin was feeling mightily relieved that neither of the coppers had taken a close look at him and recognized him. Larry, as ever, was tweaking his gadget and emitting remarks such as, "by gum, nearly there," and, "just look at that," and, "I wonder if I shall be getting a Nobel prize." But Kevin, under his breath, confided in himself, "no prize for you, mate, except maybe the Clanger Booby Prize for complete lunacy."

CHAPTER 6
THE POLICE STATION

Sergeant Muldoon and his colleagues arrived back at the Station to find that a certain gentleman had just been arrested. It was James Whitlock, often known as Jimmy the Whizz; this was because he was highly accomplished at pick-pocketing. Somebody had managed to make a citizen's arrest, catching him red-handed. Jimmy, as clever as ever, was in the process of talking his way out of it.

"Oh! Not you again," sighed Muldoon, "what was it this time, the Crown Jewel's you were trying to pinch?"

"More likely some poor unsuspecting lady's bottom," teased Julie Mayfair.

"I never done it, mate," protested Jimmy, "I ain't got nuffink off some uvver blighter, and yer carn prove a darned fing. You can just lemme go."

While Jimmy was waiting in the interview room, he could overhear Muldoon and Ted joking in the corridor.

"A gadget that can turn metal into nothing," joked Muldoon, "what a load of codswallop."

"Go on, Sarge," replied Ted, "if we got the right side of that boffin bloke, he could fix us up with gold earrings, and

Mayfair with a gold nose ring. We'd better chat him up and get the right side of him."

"What a load of baloney," chortled Muldoon, "mind you, we could have gold numbers on our shoulders. When did you carve those numbers of, Ted?"

"I never did," the Constable protested, "and anyway, Sarge, what about your numbers?"

Muldoon examined his shoulders in an attempt at explaining the missing numbers. "Well no one's snipped them off with scissors," he puzzled, "the threads are intact, but the metal has all gone. That is very strange. Best get them back on before someone notices."

Julie Mayfair appeared, now about to go off duty. "That business is very strange," she frowned, "there are too many odd coincidences going on here. It's all very well you laughing, Sarge, but you haven't explained what's happened to the handles off that car. I have a funny sort of feeling that that girl, Sally What's-its-name, is telling the truth. She is not completely barmy, as you think. I suggest we get somebody scientific in to find out what's going on. Anyway, good night."

While Muldoon and Ted were still pouring scorn on the matter out in the corridor, Jimmy the Whizz was taking all this in. It is a strange thing about people. When something of this nature happens, they either swallow it, hook line and sinker, or refuse to give it any credit. Jimmy, who was always on the look-out for a new idea to perpetrate a fiddle, was inclined to take the matter seriously. The mention of gold immediately had him thinking. If this boffin, so-called, could manufacture gold, the possibilities would be massive.

Jimmy put on his best little innocent act and managed to talk his way out of the police station, much to the disgust of Muldoon. Later that evening, Jimmy was wandering down the road to encounter a road block on Venture Street. It immediately occurred to him that this was the scene of what Muldoon had been talking about earlier on. But which house would be the target of his enquiries? He encountered Mrs. Curran on the corner.

"What's all vis in aid of mate?" he waved a prestidigious paw, almost managing to invade her handbag.

"Bit of a crisis, young man," she replied, "there's a car fell apart and the road is smothered in petrol and oil."

"What? You mean a crash?" He stared at the wreckage.

"No one knows how it happened," she frowned, "it wasn't two cars colliding. Just the one car that fell to bits outside that house. And a boy's scooter fell to pieces as well. It's a total mystery."

But Jimmy the Whizz was already beginning to put two and two together, not that his arithmetic was anything spectacular, but something more impressive than four was hovering in his crafty grey matter. He could speculate on millions, and that would be lovely as he would be able to give up being a cheap sneak thief cum pick-pocket. He managed to circumvent the men on the barriers and sneaked up to the house of one Dr. Lawrence Robinson. Jimmy decided to pose as a window cleaner. He tapped with his knuckles on the front door, since he could not find the knocker. Sally appeared from round the back. She was immediately on her guard.

"Fancy 'aving yer winders cleaned, Miss?" a fag dangling from his mouth.

"What at this time of night?" she sounded indignant.

"I'm a winder cleanah, and I notice that yer winders are a bit mucky."

"Where are your ladders, and bucket and cloth?" she riposted, "go on, don't kid me."

"I don't mean just nah, Mate," he shrugged his shoulders, "in ver mornin'. Ay-up, yer've got two winders missin' " he pointed.

"So there won't be so much work for you, will there?" cheeked Sally, "go on, push off and mind your own business."

"I'll mend 'em for yer," he persisted, "I see they've fallen inter ve garden. I'll bring some tools and a ladder and fix it for yer in ver mornin'."

"Clear off!" ordered Sally, as firmly as she could. "And mind your own business." She did not like the look of him, and doubted that he was a real window cleaner. After all, she had never seen him in Venture Street, as an odd job man or anything else.

The effect on Jimmy was simply to confirm his earlier suspicions. There was clearly something strange going on in this street, and it had something to do with metal. He considered what Muldoon had been saying, words that he was not supposed to have overheard. He considered how he could infiltrate that house and find out what was going on. Sally's attitude reinforced his impression that there was something being concealed in there. He would think out a plan of action to gain access to that house, even with people inside it.

The next morning, Jimmy appeared with overalls

on and a bag of tools. He tapped on the back door. Sally appeared and told him to go away.

"Ah Miss," he insisted, with a note of authority in his voice, "we have a report of a gas leak somewhere round here. I had better inspect your premises."

"You're not coming in here," she snapped, as she noticed Kevin Kerry making a bolt for the cellar.

"I can insist," came the pestilential reply, "if there's a gas leak, I can force an entry and you can't prevent me. Come on, let me in."

He was now elbowing his way into the kitchen. He was just in time to see the door under the stairs closing. He decided he would investigate that first. Ignoring Sally's protests, Jimmy opened the door to the darkened cellar. He could just hear the last of Kevin's footsteps in the dark.

"Is this where you keep your meter?" he demanded, "most people do."

"I don't know," shrugged Sally, "I don't think I've ever seen a gas meter in this house." She noticed Larry descending the stairs. This was a rare sighting and probably betokened augmented hunger. "Ah Larry!" she besought, "any idea of the meter?"

"I don't think I'm going to meet her," he responded stupidly, "or indeed anyone… or perhaps I am," as he spotted Jimmy, "I say, is this another long-lost cousin of mine?" He beamed at Jimmy. "Nice to meet you. It's a case of meet him, rather than meet her."

"It's the gas meter," explained Sally with heavy emphasis, "this gentleman thinks there is a gas leak and he wants to inspect your house. Can you smell anything?"

43

Larry sniffed thoughtfully and pronounced that the breakfast he was in hope of devouring might be a little overdone. "Bacon's burning," he intimated to his assistant, "still, I like it overdone."

"No, Larry, " she emphasized, "can you smell gas?"

The boffin sniffed thoughtfully and stated with the Wisdom of Solomon, "Gas? Not the sort of thing you smell. Normally you have to listen to it from ladies with no sense of economy of loquatiousness." He pulled a stupid face. Jimmy thought that was really quite fun, but Sally was reaching the limit of her patience.

"Just a minute," the expert waved a thoughtful finger. "Gas? You mean that stuff that comes through pipes? Ah, no, young man. We haven't got any in this house. I remember now. We never had it installed. We haven't got a meter, nor any pipes. Sorry to disappoint you."

"So how do you manage with your Bunsen burner, Larry?" came the objection from Sally.

"Oh! I have bottled gas upstairs. They are not leaking. Never mind. Why don't you have some breakfast with us? I like finding lost relations. Are you from the Robinson side of the family, or the Cursons? You look a little like that other cousin that turned up yesterday, that Irish chappie. Now where is he?"

All this time, Sally was shaking her head in dismay. It occurred to her that this interloper could be sidetracked by tempting him with comestibles, so she steered him to a chair at the kitchen table and put on a few more rashers of bacon. The issue of the gas, which was non-existent, was quickly forgotten, as Larry and Jimmy quickly palled each other in. Jimmy was quick on the uptake to realize that this worthy proprietor was living in a little world of his own, was an easy target for con-artistry, and was a complete cuckoo. Larry, who was intent on taking a little social breather from his researches, was eager to fit Jimmy into the Robinson family tree, somewhere, even if it were to be something of a stretch of the imagination.

"So have you come far?" the clever chap nattered on, almost tripping over the bag of tools.

"All the way from County Kilkenny," Jimmy did his best imitation of the brogue, even if Cockneyisms managed not to intrude over much. "Me dear old mother, said ter me, she said, why don't yer try ter find that Larry of ours, that went missing years ago.' And now I've found him, so I have, the cheeky little leprechaun, so it is."

"Well by Jingo!" enthused Larry, "after all these years. And you will be delighted to know, only yesterday, another of my cousins turned up, and he's interested in science, and wants to be my lab assistant. Sally; where's Kevin got to? He's from County Kerry, you know? Quite a gathering of the clans, don't you think?"

Sally decided it was like trying to reason with a soggy lump of jellyfish. She edged towards the cellar door, waited for them to be engrossed in conversation and eased Kevin out into the passageway. "I think it's all right," she whispered, "they're both managing to kid each other. That so-called gas man is nothing of the kind, neither is he really Irish. Let's see if you can work out what he's up to."

Kevin infiltrated the kitchen as Sally began to serve up an augmented breakfast. The three men nattered on about the Robinsons, and the MacNeiles and the Kilroys and the Kiljoys and all manner of funny families that might have kissed the Blarney Stone, or possibly not, if they had had any sense (which was quite unlikely). But never mind, it was all great fun; at least it was for them, but not for Sally. She could have cheerfully bashed all three of them over the head with the frying pan, especially the big brain in the white coat, but then she recalled that he was actually paying her something called 'wages', at least sometimes. However, it occurred to her that this was what Larry needed most, a break from fiddling about in the lab.

The gas leak motif, now well and truly displaced by the excitement of renewed family connections, gave way to heated conversation on the subject of Robinson-it-is. The temperature rose slightly as the subject of religious commitment reared its ugly head.

"Now my father," invented Jimmy, "he was a full-blown, rip-roaring Protestant."

Kevin's face did a curious concatenation of careful declutching. "A Proddy," he lamented in an undertone. "Dear me!"

"And what about yerself, Larry Robinson?" quizzed the so-called gas man, "are ye a proddy?"

Larry shoveled more bacon into his concrete-mixing mouth. "I occasionally take a prod at the garden," he stated uncertainly, "you know, weeding and digging."

"No, you nitwit, he means are you a Protestant?" explained Sally.

"Oh… ah! I see what you mean. I suppose I am," he chomped. "All my family were. But I'm on good terms with everyone, no matter what religion they espouse." Kevin looked quite confused at that; Sally smirked.

Trying to keep out of it, she stated rather uncertainly, "I think I'd say I'm a Buddhist." It was not the truth, but she hoped it would confuse them a little.

"Well that sounds interesting," Kevin piped innocently, "would that be a Protestant Buddhist or a Catholic Buddhist?"

Trying not to sound confused, she stated with some invented conviction, "we don't have that sort of problem. Buddhists are peaceful people and they don't have the need to chuck bombs at each other, even if they have their trivial disagreements."

"There's nothing trivial about Catholics versus Protestants," snapped Kevin, as his inborn prejudices frothed up from his early indoctrination.

"Oh come now," Larry interposed, "it's the same God and the same Jesus. What's the point of blowing each other up? Can't you just accept that you have minor differences of opinion? I mean, just think of the scientific world. Us scientists have different ideas and have terrific arguments, but we never think of blowing each other up."

"No, but you're quite happy to blow yourselves up with some crazy new invention," whispered Sally into her tea mug. "Hey! Just a minute," she startled, "that's a funny smell coming from upstairs. Larry? Don't you think you ought to…"

This was interrupted by the most enormous bang from upstairs, shaking the house even to the extent that more windows fell out into the garden and the front door fell out of its framework and swivelled over into the street. The three men hurtled upstairs to investigate. Sally had the presence of mind to remove that bag of tools to a place of concealment.

CHAPTER 7
SUCCESS

"That's it! I've got it!" cried Larry as he poked at the smoky outside of his gadget. "Just the thing!" As the smoke cleared, largely helped by a through draught from the absence of various windows, he proddled his invention and jumped for joy. "My friends, this is it!" he trumpeted.

"Would yer have it perfected, Dr. Larry?" came the astonished stare from Kevin.

Jimmy eyed the entire laboratory for something that might be pinched, but there was nothing that he could see would be worth taking down to the pawn shop. "You one of those clever geezers?" he gasped, the pseudo Irish accent mostly diminished.

"Just watch this," Larry held up a piece of metal, "this is carbon steel, very hard. Now watch," as he placed it in the right spot, and pressed a button. The machine hummed and gurgled, then made an abrupt noise not unlike a belch from a bronchial giraffe. To their astonishment, six eyes beheld the steel slowly collapse into dust on the table. They were speechless, except for Larry who was full of congratulations for his own skills.

But the collapse of the front door had again drawn the attention of the Law. Sergeant Muldoon ambled up to the newly formed opening in the house and peered inside. "Hello!" he called, "anyone in? Is Sally in there."

Sally came through from the kitchen and was lost for words. Muldoon helped her to heave the door up, back into its aperture. He followed her round to the back and into the kitchen. She was still trembling all over from the explosion. They sat down at the table and he tried to calm her down. He could not fail to notice there were four plates with half-finished breakfast upon them.

"You have company?" he asked, not realizing the implications in that question.

"No, no," she tried to make herself say, "I mean, well, sort of," she juddered, "Larry's got two Irish cousins landed on him, or at least he thinks they are. I wish they'd go away."

There were six feet clumping down the stairs, with Larry in the lead. He was quite easy with the idea of another chat with Muldoon, but the other chaps, of supposed Irish origin, on catching a glimpse of a big gentleman with a flat cap on, decided that discretion was the better part of invasion, and suddenly went into reverse. Larry found himself encountering Muldoon without any male backup. Sally listened to the retreating footsteps and did not need to speculate on the motivation thereof. Muldoon turned his head just at the right moment to catch a split second glimpse in that direction and immediately recognized Jimmy the Whizz.

"Good morning, Sergeant," enthused Larry, "back so soon?"

"Your front door fell out. It could have injured someone, Sir," Muldoon stated somberly. "On inspection, I noticed that the hinges and a lock were missing. Did you take them off?"

Larry looked genuinely puzzled. "How strange!" he frowned, "I hope the door is not damaged."

"No, but someone could have been hurt, I must point out. Why don't you make sure your door is properly secured?"

As Larry went off to investigate the door, Muldoon decided to confide in Sally. "You've got two blokes upstairs, haven't you?" he pointed. "There's no point in denying it. I saw them, and they saw me. That's why they scuttled back out of sight." He eyed the plates on the table.

"Yes. These are the cousins I was talking about…"

"I'd better tell you. One of them is trouble. His name is James Whitlock, known in the underworld as Jimmy the Whizz. He's a highly accomplished thief. What's he doing here? Up to some sort of mischief, I'll be bound."

"I thought he looked a bit dodgy," she was near to tears, "he appeared last night, pretending to be a window cleaner and today he's posing as a gasman. Tried to make out there was a gas leak. Larry's got this idea he's a long lost cousin from Ireland. Absolute nonsense. Don't believe a word of it. Can't you arrest him, or something?"

"Not until he actually does something illegal. And the other feller; never seen him before."

Sally wanted to say nothing, but realized that the policeman could hardly help her if she did not come clean.

"He's another cousin, called Kevin something-or-other. He might be a real one, at least Larry thinks so. Larry's family did originate from Ireland."

"I can see you're in a right state, Sally," he came the gentle advice. "I would say, before you get mixed up with characters like that, you need to get clear out of this place. Jimmy is nothing but trouble, I can promise you. He's been to goal about three times and he's only 25."

"Oh heck!" she trembled, "but I can't leave Larry. I'd have no job and he'd probably starve to death. I like him, in a funny sort of way. He's very clever, but a complete nitwit. Does that make sense?"

The answer to that was swept aside by the reappearance of Larry from the front of the house. "I say," he blurted, "that thing…" he noticed Muldoon, all ears… "very strange. The hinges and lock have disappeared. Did you take them off, Sally?"

"No of course not, Larry," she expostulated, fighting for words not to be spoken. Muldoon was not slow to appreciate she was holding something back. He recalled what he had already been told and compared it with his recent experiences. But the closed mind was still incapable of giving credit to the claim that a funny machine could marmalise metal.

"I thought the hinges might have changed into gold," he teased, pulling a face at Larry.

"No, no, they'd have to be silver to do that," came the incautious blurt, which he tried to cover up with a spasm of giggles, "come on, Sergeant, this isn't Willie Wonka land. Is it actually illegal to have a front door with no hinges?"

"No, I suppose not."

"Have we actually broken the Law this morning?" Larry was slightly more serious now.

"No, but you might have done if that door had actually injured someone. I would advise you, Dr. Robinson, to secure your property against any further mishaps which might endanger life and limb, and I'll go further..." He rose to depart... and say, "do please be careful of the company you keep. You could land up in very hot water."

"Sally?" he expostulated, "I know she's hot stuff, but there's nothing wrong with her. She's a lovely girl and just the person I want to keep house for me."

"No, no, no, I mean the other guys that are hiding upstairs. I think you've got a problem there."

"My cousins from Ireland?" Larry chaffed, "they're excellent fellows. I've been checking on my family tree and it's all wonderful, how long lost relatives turn up out of the blue." He was clearly miles away from reality and totally taken in by both characters. Sally shook her head in dismay.

Muldoon sighed as he reached the kitchen door. "Have it your own way," he waved his notebook. "But I would suggest that you listen carefully to what this young lady will advise you with. I know she's young and inexperienced, but she has got a lot of gut common sense..." The innuendo was not lost on Larry, just for once. As the door closed, Larry almost managed to take on board the implied insult, to wit, that he was an idiot, but it did make him start to think, just for once, and for a moment or two.

"Now Larry!" she waved a cautionary finger, "will that make you calm down a little? We need a council of war.

Already too many people know about that invention of yours, and it's a wonder Muldoon still thinks it's all a lot of nonsense." She went to the bottom of the stairs and called up. "Kevin; Jimmy! Safe to come down now. We need to sort things out."

As four feet clattered on the stairs, Sally decided that backing out was not realistic. She would grasp the thistle and try to knock some sense into these chaps. Larry stared at her in amazement. He had never seen this young girl take control of the situation quite like this, but he was full of admiration for her. Being willing to admit to his own hare-brained mentality, he decided that someone with an atom of common sense ought to take charge of the matter.

The four of them sat round the kitchen table and looked disconsolate that their breakfasts had gone cold. Sally reassured them that a renewed repast would be provided after the conference.

"What's this about Jimmy?" demanded Kevin.

"This gentleman here," Sally pointed bossily, "is called James Whitlock, otherwise known as Jimmy the Whizz."

Jimmy tried to come the innocent, but it was a waste of time.

"How many times have you been to prison, Jimmy?" she asked, "is it two or three?"

"I never done nuffink," he wheedled, the Cockney accent firmly in control now.

"That policeman told me all about you. You are a con-artist, a thief and a pick pocket. Don't waste our time trying to talk your way out of it. Why don't you just admit it? If you come clean and play along with us, I shan't call the Police. Aren't you fed up with the clink?"

"You 'ain't gonna grass on me, mate?" the Cockney accent was palpable.

"Shut up and listen, " Sally snapped, "we have a very important matter to sort out. Like it or not, all four of us are in it together. Larry has invented a machine that can marmalise metal. Is it perfected yet, Larry?" she demanded forcefully.

"Not quite," he admitted, like a child with a broken toy.

"If I can speak," cut in Kevin, "it's a brilliant idea, but not properly under control. Can't you get it to focus on what you want to ruin? When you switch it on, it wrecks all sorts of things that you don't want to wreck. I think you need to do more work on it, Dr. Robinson." The attempt at on English accent was showing much progress.

"Only too true," Sally felt for her bra straps. "Can't you develop it a bit further so that it can bust only the thing you want to bust?" She regretted the double entendre, but amazingly the three men failed to see it. "It's a brilliant idea but in the wrong hands it could cause mayhem. In the right hands, it could solve all sorts of major problems in the world."

"Absolutely right," cut in Kevin. "Just think, all the guns and tanks and weapons of war could be destroyed. We could have world peace. Away with violence and cruelty! Why can't we all live together like good neighbours?"

James Whitlock was curiously silent during all this; his devious mind was trying to see the financial possibilities in it. He had not forgotten about silver being turned into gold.

"I think we need to call in a government scientist as soon as possible," Sally nattered on, "someone who can talk to the right people at the top. Larry; have you any idea who we might contact? Surely you must know someone like that?"

Larry was staring vacantly out of the window, in a little world of his own again. He noticed some of the nails holding the garden fence, had given up on the task, thus allowing the wooden panels to fall down over the bluebells. "What me?" he came to realize his opinion was needed. "Oh yes, erm… shame the bluebells have got squashed."

"Larry!" she shouted. "Who was your old professor at University?"

"Oh, erm…" as he tried to recall. "Old Donald Drakeworthy," he murmured, half-abstractedly, "he was a jolly old boy. He could always take a joke."

"Larry!" she blasted, "this is not a joke. We are talking about wrecking the entire modern world. Do you really want to go back to the Stone Age? Flint axes and bow and arrow? Go back to your lab and get it right. We need a pocket-sized version of that thing, and which can be trained on what you really want to destroy. Not door knobs and certainly not bra catches. Go on!" she shooed him off upstairs.

"We could make a fortune out of this," hissed Jimmy in Kevin's ear. "No need to nick anything at all. Just hold all the governments of the world to ransom."

"All you can think of, is yourself, Mr. Whitlock," sighed Kevin. "Have you no consideration for other people? I've learnt my lesson and I'm desperately sorry for what I've done. I'm on the straight and narrow now, and no mistake. Take my advice and go straight."

"Faw!" uttered Jimmy, in derision.

"Listen you," Kevin demanded, "can you honestly say that your fiddling has never injured anyone at all? Come on, be honest for once."

Jimmy sniggered dismissively. "I once nicked a bloke's car while he was 'avin' a pee behind a tree. He'd left the keys in the ignition. He came running out, doing up his flies, tripped up and banged his 'ead on a kerb stone." Jimmy chortled self-defensively. "That taught 'im."

"I don't think that's funny," Kevin shook his head solemnly, "did you go back to find out if he was all right?"

"Nah! I didn't wanna get nicked," came the slightly less amused reply.

"So you don't know what it's like to feel really guilty?" challenged Kevin. He went on to describe his activities in the IRA and how it resulted in a little girl, one of his distant relatives, being seriously injured. Jimmy was curiously silent. Kevin had just managed to make him stop and think about the consequences of his actions. They listened enchanted, as Sally commenced to play a sonata from Handel. It wafted all through the house and into the street, through the missing windows.

"Vat's lavlie," remarked Jimmy, "'oo put the record on?"

"That's not a record, Jimmy, " Kevin steered him along to the front room. There they stood, in total awe of Sally's skill.

"In case you're thinking it's a Strad, Mr. Whitlock," Kevin breathed in his ear, "it is not. It is no Stradivarius, so there's no point in pinching it." The thought had occurred to Jimmy, but then it also dawned on him that it was far more lovely just to listen to someone playing it really well, rather than taking it off down to the local antique shop.

" I admit it, Mick," he murmured, "I've been on the fiddle. Let the girl do the fiddling, and I'll go straight. You 'elp me, Mate."

"There's a time and place for everything," came the Wisdom of Solomon, "and a bit of crafty-crafty can come in useful, as long as it's for helping people. And you needn't call be Mick or I'll call you two-timing Limey."

The two men shook hands and decided that they would work together for the good of mankind, as opposed to purely seeking their own ends. Larry, as you would expect, was upstairs, fiddling with his gadget, miles away, and totally absorbed in modifying his brain-child.

CHAPTER 8
THE EXPERT

It was a few days later that Larry had managed to contact his old Professor, Donald Drakeworthy. He had had a lengthy chat on the telephone to the University and had received a promise that someone from the Ministry would be coming along to assess this new development.

Larry put the receiver down and informed the other three. "There's a bloke coming tomorrow," he stated in great triumph, "an expert from the government. Recognition at last! Watch out for a Mr. Frederick Wallitude, who knows all about metals. Mind you, I've heard this chap before, and I have to say, we have to wonder about the state of his marbles."

"You mean the Elgin Marbles, Doc?" teased Kevin.

"No, dear cousin," Larry pointed to his head, "this kind of marbles. Grey matter."

There was no need for anyone to comment on that.

•

The front door, which was still held in place with bits of

string and parcel tape, received a polite knock the next morning. The two 'cousins' vanished into the cellar, but kept within earshot of the kitchen. Sally fetched the boffin round through the back door and introduced him to a cup of tea. She stared at him in an attempt at assessing this new visitor. He was late middle aged, exceedingly smart, polite, efficient and gave the appearance of being highly intelligent. As Larry came down from his development area, Fred arose and offered a hand.

"Mr. Wallibrain," Larry was as confused as ever, "nice to meet you."

"Wallitude," came the correction, "and you are Lawrence Clobinson? I think we have a lot to discuss." Sally decided it was going to be one of those conversations, and resolved to make an attempt at hanging on to a bit of rationality.

"We are on the brink of a major breakthrough in science," began Larry, as if it were the invention of the wheel. "I have discovered how to dematerialize metal… any metal."

Fred stared at him in total disbelief. "Not possible," he shook his head dismally, "you are obviously working under an eginigomous, fandolacious, wiggling delishipump. Nothing can dematerishitize; that includes all metals. You, my friend, are clearly livifying in a clouditious, gooney-bird, territory." Sally managed to keep a straight face, but she wondered how long that endurance test would last.

Larry stared at the boffin with a look which contained derision with a trifling of confusion. "My dear fellow," he decided to give as much as he was being handed, "the whichy-keediness of the eginigometry is charfully integratitudiness with the atomish structitude. Now listen carefulatiously."

The look on Fred's face was as institutionally stolid as ever, even if he was blinded by some kind of high level analysis. He nearly blurted out, 'yer whot?' but managed to rephrase it as something like, "atomishal conconcorrity is, or might be, or possibly was, at one time, epidonkeytatious. Are you going to show me the evidentitude of this whopping great claim you seem to be makyfying?"

"Can't you two talk plain English?" sighed Sally, knowing full well that this was all scientific gobbledegook. Fortunately for her, and all us readers, she knew enough to be able to realize that the two of them were just throwing sand in each other's eyes.

"And who are you?" demanded the Wallitude, archily.

"I'm Sally Wilkins," she insisted, "Larry's keeper," this was in an undertone." But Larry was quite relieved to hear it, knowing full well that he had no idea of how to deal with some kind of cranky boffin from the Ministry.

"And what are your qualifications in this field?" snorted Fred.

"What? That field out there?" she pointed to the extensive garden, "I'm quite good at horticulturetudenatiousness," she tried it on, "I've got a suggestion for you."

"Go on then," Larry grinned hopefully.

"I'll put on a video of Star Trek. That's got lots of pseudo-scientific jabber in it. The difference is that you can almost make sense of it. This lot here," she waved a place-mat at them, "is totally incomprehensible. Why don't you just call a spade a spade?"

"You mustn't say things like that," expostulated Fred, "that's politically wrong. My suggestion to you, is, Madam, just keep out of these things and let us experts assess the matterterialisation of it." He pulled a superior face which was intended to intimidate Larry as well.

Larry decided to make another assault on the closed mind. "Why don't you just have the patentatiousness to permit the old auriculisers to give a smatterofatory of luggyology?"

Sally noticed the confused look on Fred's face. "He means, why don't you just shut up and listen carefully?" she translated, with a canny degree of accuracy.

"Listen carefulatiously? To choppitudinous scientofortry like that? To put it crudely, Madam, in terms that even you might apprecitude, codswallop! Do you know what that means?"

"It is nothing of the kind," stormed Sally, as she checked her spare bra for continued stability, "I am a witness to these matters. I have actually seen it in action. He has a machine that can destabilize metal. Are you listening to me? Tungsten carbide; you know what that is?"

"Oh that sort of rubbishometry," Fred snorted, "a bit out of date, I suppositude. Well, what about it?"

"Larry can render it down to powder, at the flick of a switch," she emphasized, doing a snap of the fingers.

"Madam, you are clearly fantisitatious," came the closed mind. "Impossible! Lawrence here has clearly managed to create for your innocent young mind, a state of illusitoritrociousness. How could you, Chobinson, I mean Robinson, pull the wool over this young lady's…"

"I am not pulling any wool over anything," shouted

Larry, now growing angry. "Before you sneer, Wallibrain, why don't you let me demonstrate the machinatical gadgetratiousness of this new evolutionary development?"

Fred stared with widening wonderment. "Development? Evolution?" he enthused with almost a frothy face, "you mean evolution in action? Did it EVOLVE!!!!????" he watched Larry gently nodding his head in a suggestive mode. "My word," he breathed, almost choking with enthusiasm, "Evolution in action, in our own times! How wonderful! This is one to tell the boyfulnesses. Come on Chominson, show me how it works." The closed mind, it would seem, did have just one portal with a door slightly ajar.

They rattled upstairs, to find the two 'cousins' were in their lab coats and doing a bit of remedial work. The sash windows were now freshly ensconced albeit with the aid of elastoplast and bits of string.

"These are my two cousins, over from Ireland," breezed Larry, in great confidence.

"Well I haven't all day," Fred fiddled with his watch, "come on, Chobinson, give us a demonstatitude of this great evolutionary what's-its-name."

"Now watch carefully," Larry waved a chunk of tungsten carbide under Fred's nose, "no hands," as he placed it carefully in the right spot. "No tricks." He pressed the switch and the gadget began to hum and finally emitted a snort not unlike that of a hippopotamus objecting to a hot summer's day. The experiment was a complete success, but Fred was failing to notice the result. He was fiddling with his watch, as the tungsten carbide squattered away into tiny grains of something or other.

"There, you see!" pointed Larry with a wobbly finger, "will that convince you?"

"What? Oh!" the expert came back to realities. "Never!" he passed off as a triviality, "obviously sleight of hand. I haven't time to waste this morning. Best be on my way." He turned to go but became aware of a slight impediment. His trousers were half-way down his legs. The two 'cousins' sniggered at each other.

"You weren't even watching," cried Sally in despair, "I thought you wanted to see evolution in action. Now do it again, Larry, and this time, this boffin must pay attention." She caught hold of his arm as he was attempting to hoist his bags up.

"Let me help you," came the Cockney pickpocket, as a couple of fingers removed something from Fred's apparel.

The experiment was done once more. "See! How about that?" cheesed Larry.

"That can't have been tungsten carbide," came the excuseful objection.

"It certainly was," emphasized Kevin, "and here's another to try. See for yourself. It's a lathe tool. Larry will marmalise it for you. Go on, Dr. Lawrence."

Five pairs of eyes focused on the metal sample as the switch went on. Another buzz and a belch not unlike a gorilla in high dudgeon, and the metal disintegrated. Fred stared with a strange look and decided he would have to make some kind of constructive comment.

"That looks very clever," he remarked in a neutral voice. He wondered if the high-flown conversation would cut any ice now, but he decided to try a little. "The prestidigitatiousness of that evolutionary experiment is somewhat of a mystificatious conglomeration."

"Can't you see; it works," Larry jazzed up and down.

Fred thought hard for some kind of put-you-down. "Can't see what use it would be," came the offhand remark. "I think," he pondered, "can't you devise a machine that will do that with plastic?" The plain talk began to surface. "You realize that we are inundated with bits of plastic that we can't get rid of? That would be far more use."

"Just have a whopping big bonfire," Kevin remarked coldly.

"A bonfire!!! My dear fellow, that's outrageous. Just think of the environmental implicatiousness of such a perpetratetude of such an outrage!" Fred turned to go, as he assured himself of his ability not to trip up over his trousers. "And how many of these gadgets have you got?" he demanded.

"I've been working on a small portable one," gestured Larry, as he pointed to several little boxes stacked in the corner.

Fred took out a notepad and wrote something down. "I say, isn't that an aeroplane coming rather low?" came the plain but panicky voice, as he pointed to the window in the opposite corner. Jimmy, who was used to that kind of tactic, was the only one not to crowd round the window in the expectation of spotting an aeroplane in distress. It was only Jimmy that managed to notice Fred furtively remove one of those small gadgets and hide it in those trousers that were noted for a certain element of instability. Disappointed at failing to notice the aeroplane, the other three began to follow Fred and Jimmy down the stairs.

"I must go now," came the imperious parting shot, "keep trying Blobinson, dear fellow. One day you might latch on to something really worthwhile. Good morning!"

As he reached his car, in the street, Jimmy called out, "thieving b…d!"

"That's ripe coming from you, Jimmy," Sally chimed in, "shall we let him have his wallet back?"

"Oh I can't win with you, young lady," he sighed, as he handed over Fred's wallet to her open hand. "Try and get him to hand back that gadget that he nicked from upstairs."

"Typical!" snorted Kevin, "must be a Proddy."

Sally caught up with Fred outside his car. There seemed to be a problem. He was trying to locate the door handle prior to entering his car.

"Try the other side," Sally indicated. "I think that one's OK."

Fred, in high dudgeon, entered the car via the passenger seat, and refused to admit that he had sat rather awkwardly on the handbrake. "Ouch!" was the word that he managed not to expostulate, as it came out as a murmuratious, "Ooooooh!"

"Can we have that gadget back, that you've removed?" demanded Sally, curtly.

"You accusing me of stealing?" he snapped angrily.

"If you want your wallet back, Mate, let's have the gadget. You don't fool us."

Fred went red in the face. "My wallet!" he blazed, "give that to me," and he tried to snatch it off Sally. She was ready for that and whipped it away just in time.

"All right, if you don't want it, good morning," and she headed back for the house.

Fred scrambled out of the car, by the perilous passenger route but was prevented from catching her by two cousins who were blocking the passageway.

"Some kind of scientist you are," sneered Kevin, "totally dishonest. Hand it back at once. Fancy nicking someone else's invention."

"I don't know what you're talking about," Fred snapped, "and I want my wallet back."

At this moment, Larry appeared to back up his cousins. "You wretched, thieving cretin," he waved an admonitory finger. Hand it back at once or I shall report you to higher authority."

"Dream on, Flobinson," came the rude retort, as Fred turned to go to his car. But the weight of the gadget hidden in his trousers induced them to descend once more, rather more precipitately. He staggered over again, colliding with his car, and the gadget fell out on to the pavement with an accusatory 'clank'.

"Left us with a deposit, have you?" Kevin sneered, "I can tell you a joke about that. Do you want to hear a joke?"

Fred managed to steady up to a certain amount of equilibrium. "Go on then, Paddy."

"There was a Protestant lady had a dog that was not properly housetrained. She had a clever chap, a scientist… a proper one… and a Cotholic too, called in to see her. On the floor in the hall, there was a puddle of something nasty. The Proddy lady in a very clever voice, pointed down and said 'H_2O'. But the Catholic scientist replied, with a wink, "no, no, Madam, K_9P. And you know what, she couldn't get the joke."

Everybody else burst out laughing, but Fred stared in utter bewilderment. "K_9P," he muttered in stunned amazement, "I wonder what that is… Gosh a new idea."

"See, you can't get it either," teased Kevin, as he picked up the gadget, "I knew from the start, you're not a proper scientist, come on, admit it."

"Do you want your wallet?" called Sally in the distance.

"I don't think he ought to get that either," Kevin roared with laughter.

CHAPTER 9
MORE EXPERTS

Miss Betty Marston sat at her desk, as she eyed the coterie of scientists, discussing Frederick Wallitude's findings. He was quite dismissive about Larry's gadget but full of intrigue about K_9P.

"Obviously that idea of Crobinson's is some sort of conjuring trick," he breezed, "quite impossible to dematerialise metal. Anybody with any common sense should know that."

"But did the bloke actually show you this method?" asked Dr. Normbrain, who had an inkling of credibility for this claimed development.

"Oh yes, he showed it me," Fred emphasized with a scornful voice. "It was a piece of tungsten carbide, a lathe tool, and he made it just go down to a funny sort of powder. Obviously some sort of contrived stunt. Quite impossible, of course."

Miss Marston smiled to herself but withheld any comment. She knew how their minds worked, or in some cases, did not work.

"But the interesting thing is," blathered on Fred, "there

seems to be a new chemical formula going round. I got that from a little Irish chap. Mind you," in a dismissive tone of voice, "he was a Roman Catholic, but never mind."

"So what's wrong with being a Roman Catholic?" came a heavy brogue from somewhere.

"Roman Catholicism and science don't really gel together, do they, Charles?" Fred sounded so sure of himself. "Anyway, this new chemical. They have termed it K_9P. Have you heard of that before, chaps?"

Miss Marston managed not to snort with laughter, took out her handkerchief and applied it to her nose, but could not suppress a snigger.

"Gosh! That sounds interesting," remarked an aged boffin. "What sort of thing is that?"

"Very smelly," whispered Miss Marston into her hanky.

The entire room of boffins all nodded wisely and made remarks which would indicate that they had full prior knowledge of K_9P. But not one of them would admit to not having heard of it before.

"It would seem that this Irish chap knows where to find it. Probably in Blobinson's lab."

"More likely in an Irish lav," Betty Marston could hardly restrain her mirth.

"If it's K it must be related to Potassium," speculated a young boffin, newly qualified.

"But what would P stand for?" puzzled another expert.

At that Betty failed to restrain her mirth. They all turned and glowered at her.

The expert frowned at her. "This could be very important. You should go back and question this gentleman of Hibernian extraction. We would all like to know more about this. Fantastic; a new development. Evolution in reality in our own times. My word, Fred you could become famous. You could get to be a TV high profile scientist."

The telephone shrilled, but the boffins were too busy speculating to notice. Miss Marston lifted the receiver and got into a conversation with Sally in her kitchen.

"You've got a chap called Frederick Wallitude there, I assume?"

"Oh yes! What's it about?... his wallet... He left it behind... silly man. I'll just fetch him for you." Miss Marston approached the expert who was deeply engaged in a discussion about K_9P, without any admission that he had no idea of what it really was, but then none of the others gave any hint of such ignorance either.

"Not now, Miss Marston," he huffed, self-importantly.

"There's a lady on the phone, says she's got your wallet. Is that true? My word, what have you been up to?" she winked at old Normbrain.

"Later... later," came the flustered reply, "I'm very busy now. This could be a breakthrough. Take her number and I'll ring back." Fred fluffed her away to her desk.

•

From his private office, Fred Wallitude rang Sally as she was just about to serve lunch to the hungry house-keepers. "Is it Sally?" he muttered, "you have something for me?"

"Don't you want your wallet, Brainstorm?" she teased.

"You thieving blighter," he snapped, "let me have it back at once. How did you get this number?"

"Fortunately for you, Clever-clogs, the number was in your wallet. Don't you want it?"

"Yes, I do," he raged nastily, " just put it in the post to me, will you, and we'll say no more."

"Why don't you come and fetch it, after all, the postman might be a thieving blighter too," she teased. "In any case, the wallyficatiousness of the Wallitude wallet is a way to all wonderfulatious speculatiousness. Do you follow my meaning?"

"Oh yes, yes!" he admitted, slightly confused, "of course, of course, now please be a sensible girl about this…"

"I am a sensible girl," she piped, "and so is Miss Marston. Why don't you send her along to fetch it? I reckon she's got more common sense in the end of her little finger than you have in your entire carcass." Sally grinned at the men folk, who were chortling away.

"Come on, I want my lunch," sighed Larry.

The conversation dragged on a little longer, with Sally barely managing not to laugh her head off. The receiver went down and she announced that a Miss Marston might appear a little later on.

"Kevin, he is really impressed with our new chemical formula," she planted a Yorkshire pudding in front of him. "All the boffins in the research institute are totally captivated by it. They want to know more about it. I assume you can enlighten them?"

"Not the half of it," Kevin chomped at the roast beef, "I knew that he was an idiot, that guy."

"No doubt about it," Sally plonked a brussel sprout on Jimmy's plate, "here's an extra one for doing the right thing, just for once, Jim. But don't you dare slide into a life of crime again, do you hear? Or I shall get Larry to boot you out."

"We can't do that," chewed Larry, "he knows too much. K_9P!" he laughed, "he's such a clever-clogs, that Fred, that he can't admit to not hearing of it before. Anyway, I suspect we haven't seen the last of that bloke. We must keep an eye on things in this house, things that ought not to go walkies. Mind you, it wouldn't have been any good to him, since it didn't have a battery installed."

"Yes, but he could have taken it apart and found out how it works," muttered Kevin.

"That means you really ought to get it patented as soon as possible, Larry," Sally waved a spoon at him, "before some geezer pinches the idea and you won't get the credit."

•

It was later that day that another car pulled up outside the house in Venture Street. A very smart, purposeful young lady called Betty Marston stepped out and helped another visitor out on to the pavement. This was an elderly gentleman called Professor Normbrain, someone well-seasoned in years but well endowed with experience and a generous dash of common sense. He had the philosophy that one should never dismiss any claim, however far-fetched it might be, until it was definitely discredited. In other words, he had a smattering of rationality; something that he had in common with Betty Marston.

It was clear from the start that Betty and Sally were going to hit it off. Old Normbrain was content to sit and just listen, as he waited for a chance to discuss matters with Larry.

"So you've come for Fred's wallet?" grinned Sally, waving it about temptingly, "we shall want an undertaking that he will never again attempt to purloin any of Larry's gadgets."

"He actually tried to pinch…?" stared Betty.

"Yes. He poured scorn on the whole thing, but didn't hesitate to nick one of our machines. Fortunately, my friend Jimmy spotted him in the act and tipped me off."

"Can you tell me?" requested Normbrain gently, "what all this is about? I hear it's a machine that can de-materialize any metal. I know that sounds totally impossible, but then, the impossible has been shown to be possible, in the course of scientific progress. Can you enlighten me, dear?"

He was so humble and non-judgmental that Sally decided to explain something, but not all. "My boss, Dr. Lawrence Robinson, has devised a gadget that can wreck any metal, render it down to powder, or lose its strength. He has not quite perfected it yet, but he is working on it right now, with two helpers upstairs."

"Can you explain how it works?" the old boy was intrigued. He clearly was prepared to give it credit, which was in contrast to the attitude shown by many others.

"I must not go into too many details," continued Sally, "after all, Larry has not got it patented as yet, and that is something urgent, as you will appreciate. However, he has found that vibrations of a certain frequency… I don't know exactly what… can cancel out the atomic bonding of anything metallic. I must ask you to desist from spreading this about. It ought to be top secret."

"Absolutely right," chimed in Betty Marston, "I mean you can see the implications in this…" She clearly had no problem of credibility… "it means, in essence, we could all finish off back in the Stone Age. Am I right, Professor?"

The old man frowned and cogitated for a time. He could hear funny noises coming from upstairs. He stared thoughtfully at the light fittings and the electric appliances in the kitchen. His great and open mind were weighing up all kinds of variables.

"And the awkward thing is," continued Sally, "that machine has been busting all kinds of metal things that were not meant to be bust. I mean, the window catches, and cars out in the road, and drain pipe… and," she decided to confide carefully, "my bra catches." She did a check on her bosomworthy stability. Betty Marston began to snigger, but abbreviated it at the thought of her own bra coming apart.

"That is very interesting," the old man wobbled his sagacious head, "so has the electric wiring melted out as well?"

"Yes! That's got metal inside the plastic insulation," remarked Betty.

"And another funny thing," added Sally, "well not funny… I mean…strange… there's a tap upstairs in the bathroom… and it's gone, but it's gone wobbly and plasticiney, but it still holds water. Very odd!"

Normbrain nodded thoughtfully. "Can I ask?" he pondered gently, "this machine? Can it turn one metal into some other metal?" There was a certain glint in his eyes which made Sally come over all cautious. She was not going to spill the beans of silver being changed into gold. Her dilemma was cut short, as Larry appeared in his lab coat.

"Well, well!" he enthused, "and who have we here? Derek Normbrain, unless I'm mistaken. I used to attend your lectures. Lovely to have you come, my dear fellow."

"Robinson," came the cheery response, "what have you been up to? I think I'm going to learn a lot today." The two men headed off upstairs, leaving Sally and Betty to natter over a cup of tea.

"It's so nice to have a scientist with a decent slice of plain common sense," sighed Sally, "that Fred that came was a complete nutter, and downright dishonest."

"Oh my dear!" Betty chanted sarcastically, "you can't say things like that. All scientists are wonderful people. Honest to a fault! You can't criticize them. They hold the future of the human race in their grubby paws." She pulled a face which indicated deep scorn.

Sally spluttered into her teacup. "They aren't all like Fred, totally crackers, I hope?" she stated with some conviction. "My impression of your old pal is quite different. He seems to have a generous slab of common sense. Is he honest?"

"Oh I think so, dear," Betty confided, "in any case, I shan't let him walk off with one of those gadgets you're talking about. And I won't let him go blaring this thing all over town. Anyway, us girls should keep in touch. I can see so many possibilities in this idea, and those clever-dicks at the Ministry can't even get their heads round it. They are so narrow in their thinking."

The two young ladies carried on nattering away, forging an ongoing friendship that would be crucial to the outcome of future events. It was Kevin Kerry who came down the stairs and took a peek into the kitchen. He was intrigued at the sight of Betty Marston, and decided that a short visit could extend into an extended one. Betty's first sight of Kevin was not altogether different.

•

Meanwhile, upstairs, Old Normbrain was fascinated by Larry's new development. "A stunning new departure in the theory of atomic structure, it would seem. Are you going to tell me… well maybe not… what frequency those vibrations are working on? I don't think anybody has latched on to this idea before."

"Don't tell him," cut in Jimmy, "it's confidential as yet." Normbrain's wallet managed to relocate itself at an opportune moment.

"I had better not go into too many details," Larry excused himself, "but I can say that this vibration, on the strength of a simple twelve volt battery, is of a special modulation, and can destabilize any metal. By the way, you'd better check your trousers."

"Why?" the old boy grinned.

"That last expert, that Fred bloke, found himself debagged. The reason being that his steel clasp on his trousers, plus his zip, just disappeared. He was standing in the wrong spot, silly ass."

Normbrain burst out laughing. "Serve him right, the

stupid clot," he snorted, but then hastily inspected his own zip and clasp.

"Yes, do be careful," cut in Jimmy, "I see you've lost your bracers, old chap," and he handed them back to Normbrain, but omitted to return his wallet.

Normbrain stared at Jimmy in amazement. Words failed him.

Larry decided to explain. "Jim here is a highly accomplished pick-pocket, and Jim, are you going to let him have his wallet back… with all of the contents?"

"Oh all right!" sighed Jimmy in great reluctance, as he proffered the wallet, "sorry Mate, 'abit of a lifetime. No offence meant."

The three men dissolved into hoots of laughter; Normbrain especially, since there was nothing in the wallet worth stealing.

CHAPTER 10
KEVIN'S ROMANCE

It was a lovely afternoon in the park as Kevin and Betty Marston sat admiring the ducks. He slid his arm over her shoulder, but she made no objection. In fact, she was rather glad. She had had an instant attraction for him, and that lilting Irish accent simply reinforced her feelings for him. The attraction was mutual.

"He's a very clever chap, that Larry," he whispered in her ear. "That invention is a real stunner."

"I agree entirely," she replied, "and it could have massive implications for the future. Fortunately there is one person who is capable of taking it seriously. Old Normbrain has got a generous dollop of common sense. I get so fed up with these idiots in the office that keep on dogmatizing and trying to impress each other with some harebrained idea. They don't seem to realize what fools they are making of themselves."

"That one that came to us, Fred Wallibrain," he sniggered, "complete ass, if you ask me. I admit I don't know much about science, but even a complete idiot could see he was messing us about. Are they all like that in the office?"

"Some of them are, but not all of them," she grinned. It occurred to Betty that she ought really to be getting back, or at least, Normbrain might be thinking like that. It also occurred to her that she had actually found someone who had a degree of common sense and that she could relate to. "They drive me mad, sometimes, the idiotic ideas they come up with!"

"You don't have to rush back then?" he hoped, gently.

"Think of an excuse for me to hang on here for a bit," she whispered in his ear.

"It wouldn't be an excuse. It would be a perfectly good reason," he squeezed her hand. "We are on the verge of a major development not just in science but in the future of civilization. I think we should stick together and try to exert a modicum of rationality in this situation. Add to that, I don't want you to go away. I think you're fantastic!" He felt so pleased with himself for coming to the point. Suddenly they were embracing, to the amusement of anyone passing by the park bench.

•

Normbrain checked the stability of his trousers as he took a chair in the kitchen and gratefully received a slice of cake. "My word you have been busy," he enthused, "you made this yourself?"

"I do all the housework, the cooking and the gardening," Sally yawned copiously. "Never stop. When I said I was his keeper, I meant it. Not just a housekeeper, but keeper from starvation, exhaustion, and a few other nasties. Larry just has a one track mind, Prof."

"Oh call me Derek," he chomped, and pointed upstairs, "two very clever chaps up there."

"That Jimmy," she frowned, "we have to watch him. He's constantly in trouble with the Police. Thief! I'm letting him stay in the hopes that he can be taught better ways," she wagged a finger, "but time will tell. The Police know where he is and if there's an offence committed, they will be round straight away. Strange as it may seem, Larry has taken it into his head that Jimmy is a long-lost cousin of his, just like Kevin."

"I can see that that lad will have his uses," pondered Normbrain, "I would suggest you don't turf him out, at least not yet. Anyway, he knows about this invention, and we don't want that talked about all over town."

"The fewer people that know about it the better," Sally poured out another cup of tea.

"Now listen carefully," the common sense began to assert itself. "This invention, I believe, is a stunner. There is no doubt that it works, though how it works is beyond me, as yet. The fact is, that in the wrong hands, it could cause mayhem and even wreck civilization, more even than an outright nuclear war. In the right hands, and carefully controlled, it could usher in a new era of peace and international co-operation."

"The question is, how do we handle it?" Sally stared at him, dominatingly.

"I don't know," the wise head shook, "sadly, I am no politician, still less a strategist. Fortunately, at the moment there is one thing on our side. No one seems to give the idea any credit, which means that they are just refusing to accept the reality of it. I heard them in the office, this morning, crowing on about how impossible it was. Then they fastened on to that new formula, K_9P! That sidetracked them completely. Who thought of that one?"

"It was Kevin, our other guest, another of Larry's cousins," she flexed her eyebrows, "he's always coming out with a joke to confuse people."

"So it is a joke!" the old boy chortled, "I thought so."

"Don't you get it?" she put her head down on the table and roared with laughter, "K_9P! What doggies do when they're desperate. Canine pee!"

"Brilliant!" the old boy gurgled as the tea went down, "that just goes to show how these brain-storm people can be taken in and sidetracked. I love it."

•

"Would you like me to tell you another Irish joke?" teased Kevin, "one that the leprachauns told me, their very own selves." His arm tightened round her shoulders.

"Go on, silly!" she begged, "I love it. And those idiots just fell for it."

"Well now, it was like this. In Dublin's fair city, there was a tourist in his car, and he was trying to find the airport. But he was completely lost. So he stopped by a bloke on a bicycle and asked him, 'Hey Paddy, how do I find the airport? I'm going to be late for the flight.' And the answer he got was really quite simple. "Yer see that aeroplane comin' doon out the sky?' and he pointed aloft, 'well yer just foller that, and ye'll foind the airport, in the end.'"

"Complete with the little folk checking all the passports," teased Betty, as she burst out laughing. "I like your sense of humour, Kevin. You can tell me another one any time."

"Well here we go again," he squeezed her hand, "the little folk must have been up to their tricks by the tracks. This is a railway joke, this one. There was a railbuff riding along in a train, looking out for the mileposts, and you know what he said? He said, 'Ye know, on our railway, we've got moilposts, every quarter of a moile'!"

"Which should mean that Irish railways are four times longer than anyone else's?" she riposted, as she split her sides with mirth. "Oh Kevin, I love you!" she admitted.

"And I love you, my darling," he dared, "and what's more, you've got a face just like the Holy Virgin herself. I couldn't fail to love you."

"Kevin!" she was slightly startled, "are you a Roman Catholic?"

"Yes of course. We all are round our way."

"I think we'd better come to the point over this," Betty Marston spoke slowly, "I'm a Christian, but very, very Protestant indeed. In fact, I'm a full blown born again Evangelical… " it died away, as she expected him to explode. But he didn't, because love had taken over and surmounted all the prejudices on both sides. They both knew that they were faced with a situation which called for Christian co-operation and not disunity.

"We may have our differences of opinion, Kevin," she stated carefully, "but there's a lot more at stake here, than just some argument over religion."

"You're dead right, my darling, the essentials of

Christianity are about love and caring." Kevin dared not to start talking about his involvement in the IRA but he knew that he would have to come clean about it before long. It was a nasty guilt-glug hang-up at the back of his mind.

•

"I've given it some thought," Normbrain accepted another slice of cake, "and I just wonder. You notice the electric wiring seems not to be affected. Has Larry commented on this yet?"

"No, but then he doesn't comment on anything unless it's right under his nose, and even then, he often doesn't notice." Sally sipped at her tea thoughtfully. "Do you think the plastic insulation is preventing the wires from melting?"

"It could be," the old Prof nodded, "and that tap in the bathroom… the water may be preventing it from vanishing altogether… another kind of insulation. I must mention this to Robinson."

"And the water pipes…they are metal, but they don't seem to have gone wrong." A worried look crossed her face, at the thought of water squirting out all over the place. So far it had not actually happened. Whereupon a goofy face appeared in the doorway, and the boffin was enquiring about a cup of tea.

"Larry," she pointed to a chair, "your wonderful invention? Prof here has noticed that the electric wiring has not melted out. Is that because of the plastic insulation? Would that cancel out those clever vibrations you have dreamed up?"

Dr. Robinson sipped at his tea and spotted the cake. He made noises which would suggest his partaking of the same, to a generous degree. "Fantastic cook, this girl," he grinned dopily, "in fact I don't think I could do without her."

"Pay her a lot more money," Normbrain coughed.

"Ooooooh!" came a reply which could have come from a fully qualified Scotsman, fidgeting with his sporran, "better still, just marry her…" He tossed of the comment as if it were the quintessence of triteness.

Sally pulled a face which would be hard to describe, except that it betokened outrage intermingled with disbelief. "Pardon?" she exploded, "is that a serious proposal, Dr. Robinson?"

Normbrain made as if to make a hasty retreat, on the assumption that things were about to sink to a certain level of personal analysis. After all, popping the question in public is not quite cricket.

"No, hang on, Derek," she begged, "I think I might need a witness to this."

"Very wise, my dear," the old boy grinned, "and I want to hear Robinson's answer to the question he hasn't answered yet."

"What question would that be, Derek?" Larry stared vacantly. "I thought we were on about weddings and betrothals and all that lark." The dopey grin widened. "Well I can't afford to give you a pay rise, Sally, so I shall have to marry you."

"The cheek!" she expostulated, "was that a serious offer, Larry?" She had never really thought about it, on the assumption that getting romantically involved with a crackpot would be most unwise. But then it occurred to her that Larry was capable of manufacturing gold. That ought to mean he, and she, if she married him, could finish off rolling in money.

Normbrain made another attempt. "Robinson," he stated firmly, "do you think the plastic will prevent the wiring from going wrong?"

"What?" he was miles away, "what's that got to do with getting married?"

Normbrain sighed with slight impatience. "That machine of yours…it doesn't seem to mess up the wiring. Is that because…"

"Oh I see what you mean," grinned Larry, "well I suppose not. That could be the next round of experiments. Good thinking, old boy." The daft face had forgotten all about the proposed wedding. "You could help me there, Derek. Let's go upstairs and try one or two things. Thanks for the cake, Sally dear," he arose from his chair.

"I'll go up and check on Jimmy," chimed Normbrain, "I think you have a certain matter to sort out with this young lady." He gave Sally a look which indicated good luck and the Best of British. Normbrain extricated himself from the kitchen and closed the door firmly, one of the few doors in the house that had not collapsed, still less hit anyone on the head. The reason for this could have been, the use of plastic hinges and handles.

"Larry!" she challenged, "did you mean that or were you just kidding?"

"Well the water pipes seem OK," he breezed, evasively.

"No, Larry, you just proposed marriage to me. Did you actually mean that?"

"Oh I see," he dithered, "erm...yes, well, why not? I seem to be completely dependent on you, Dear. As you say, you are my keeper, and I'm sure I'd get into a complete mess without you."

"Larry. Marriage isn't about someone being a zookeeper or even a gamekeeper. It's essentially about love. You haven't said a word on that subject yet." She was near to tears.

"Oh I see," he had a realization penny just about to drop in the goofy brain box. "But of course. Obviously. I love you, Sally. You're a wonderful girl. Just my type. I want you to marry me. I promise I'll look after you..." This was met with a look of astonishment on her face..."I'll share everything with you. My Darling," he decided to go on bended knee by the kitchen table. "I want you to be my wife."

She stared into that daft look on his face, and wondered if he meant all that. She wondered if an immediate reply would be at all wise. "Larry!" she exhaled carefully, "thank you very much for the offer." She held his hands. "I want us just to take a little time and think it through. It's a mistake to rush into marriage. Let's just work things out a little."

"But we've been living together for three years," he bleated like a little lost lamb.

"Three and a half, actually," she corrected, "but not as husband and wife. Housekeeper, yes, but not wife, nor even mistress. Let's just not jump the gun too hastily."

Just as Larry was about to hoist himself up to his feet again, the door opened and in came Kevin Kerry and Betty Marston. "Hello guys!" came the cheery greeting, "hey Larry, what are you doing down there?"

"He's just proposed to me," Sally explained.

"Proposed what? To turn you into a chunk of gold?" teased Betty.

"No. Marriage," Sally murmured, as if it might be some sort of penal sentence.

"Well done," enthused Kevin, "that makes two of us in one day, you guys. I've just persuaded Betty here to change her name to Kerry. What do you think of that?"

"Well done!" nodded Sally, with a voice loaded with foreboding.

CHAPTER 11
ANOTHER OFFER

It was a lovely sunny day a few weeks later that found Jimmy the Whizz ambling along down Venture Street in time for his lunch. One could almost call him Jimmy the Wiser instead, since he had been a good boy and left ladies' handbags alone, and gentlemen's wallets in their proper place. After all, it was hardly worth pinching anything now, seeing that all was provided at dear old Doc. Robinson's abode. As he came in sight of the house, he spotted a gentleman from foreign climes, about to knock on the door. The gentleman was wearing fancy robes and a funny hat, which kept his nut-brown face firmly framed.

"Waste 'a time knockin' on vat door," remarked Jimmy.

"Why? Are they all out?" came the perfect English, with hardly any accent at all.

"The door will collapse if yer do. Vey are in, but not very keen on visitors, like. What's up, mate?"

"I would like to meet a gentleman called Lawrence Robinson," came the request.

"Oo's askin'?" demanded Jimmy, becoming a little suspicious. "Where are yer from, Mate?" Jimmy was beginning to sniff that unmistakable whiff of wealth, for which he had an undying instinct.

At that moment, Sally appeared in the alley and registered shock at this new arrival. "What's this all about?" she demanded. "You from some funny religion?"

"No, I am a Catholic Wesleyan Methodist, like most of my countrymen," he replied. "My name is Oogelly-oobaba. All my friends just call be Baba for short. Can I speak to Mr. Robinson, please?"

"Mr. Robinson is very busy," Sally emphasized, "but you can talk to me. I have his full confidence… that is," she murmured to herself…"rather more than most people." Then out loud, "I am his fiancée. We have no secrets, Mr. Baba."

The inevitable teapot did its duty in the kitchen. Noises from upstairs indicated that Kevin, Betty, Normbrain and Larry were getting close to some interesting breakthrough, even if it was unspecified. Sally closed the kitchen door rather pointedly and took her seat.

"Now, Mr. Baba," she inquired, "What can we do for you? Are you selling double glazing, or is it insurance? What country are you from?"

"You see it's like this," he began, "I come from Oogie-googie Land…"

"Where the dickens is vat?" frowned Jimmy.

"In the middle of Africa," came the reply, "you may have heard of it on the news." This was met with puzzled stares. "Anyway, our little country has been at war with the Widgey-widgeys for some time now. It is so stupid."

"All these wars are stupid," sighed Sally.

"Good for business, though," whispered Jimmy.

"Jimmy!" she snapped, "that's enough. How could you say such a thing?"

"True all the same," came the dismissive reply.

"Anyway, we all know it's completely pointless. Hundreds have been killed and there is no end in sight to it. No one can bring himself to call for an Armistice." The visitor shrugged his shoulders. "The hate on both sides goes back many centuries, and even if we have both accepted Christianity, we can't seem to apply it to ourselves. Peace on earth and goodwill to all men," he wiped his forehead, "some hope."

"What about the United Nations?" cut in Jimmy.

"Not working at all," came the sad reply.

"So what's this got to do with us?" frowned Sally, becoming somewhat suspicious.

"I hear this Dr. Robinson has developed a machine that can neutralize metal. Is that right?"

Sally's mouth dropped wide open with astonishment; Jimmy's somewhat less wide. "Where did you get that idea from?" she expostulated, "that's impossible, isn't it?"

"The idea is going all round Africa, Miss. I don't know for sure, but I think the idea originated in your Ministry of Defence. When you ask them about it, they just laugh like drains, saying it's ridiculous." Baba sipped at his tea and watched her reaction.

"So what makes you think it's got anything to do with us?" Sally managed to croak.

"A bloke in the ministry gave me this address," Baba let drop, "I can't remember his name. It was Fred something-

or-other…" he went vague, "very important chap, but he told me it was a complete hoax. An idea like that couldn't possibly work."

"So why bother us?" Sally tried to sound dismissive, but Baba was not convinced.

"It would seem that this Dr. Robinson… he may be on to something. Can I have a word with him? There is that old saying, I learnt at Eton, 'there's no smoke without a fire'. Mind you, that's not the only thing I learnt at Eton. I did A level Physics." He was slightly boastful.

"Then we have something in common," glowed Sally.

"To my mind, there is nothing inherently impossible about it, Miss Sally. I know these idiots in the Ministry. Anything they haven't thought of themselves, is automatically damned as nonsense. This idea could revolutionize war and peace. If this is true, it could mean that all the weapons of war, like guns and bullets, could be neutralized in a matter of a few minutes. That could end our stupid war at home."

"What happens if you go back to bow and arrow instead?" came the cynical comment from Jim, the street corner philosopher.

"It's what we need to bring both sides to the negotiating table," Baba continued, ignoring that remark. "My government is prepared to offer you a substantial sum for the use of this machine."

Jimmy and Sally stared at each other with mixed feelings; Jimmy could immediately see the financial advantages in it; Sally, who was less money-minded, could see the potential for peace in the world.

"How much?" demanded Jimmy.

"A million."

"A million what?" Jimmy sneered, "yen, roubles, Chinese dollars? No flannel with me, Mate."

"A million pounds," came the hopeful offer.

"Is that rental or an outright purchase?" probed Jimmy.

"Anyhow, how do you know this machine will work?" Sally frowned at him.

"I can tell by the evidence," Baba came over Sherlock-wise, "elementary my dear friends."

"You haven't even seen it working," snapped Sally.

"I notice that this house has all its windows and doors held in place with bits of string and elastoplast. The neighbours tell me that no one will drive a car down this street any more because they don't want it to dissolve into a puddle of petrol and grease. No child will play with his scooter along here since it is liable to fall apart. I notice this gentleman has his trousers help up with a piece of string. Something strange is going on, and you yourself have just admitted that it does work. Please, let me talk to Dr. Robinson."

•

It was some time later that Larry the boffin was persuaded to leave his experimentation alone and come down to the kitchen. He stared in amazement at Baba and for a few moments lost track of his scientific speculations.

"Mr. Robinson," declared Baba with great glee. "Just the man I want to see. Sally has told me all about you. You can help us so much. Please can we buy one of your machines, or at least rent one to us?"

Larry listened carefully to Baba's account of what was happening in Oogie-googie Land, and how a machine that could cause disarmament would solve the problem. Jimmy listened to all this with a kind of smirk on his face. He was waiting to hear the financial arrangements over it.

"Now Mr. Baba," the boffin sounded so reassuring, "I am quite sure we can help you. The difficulty lies in letting one of my machines out of my sight. How will I know that you are going to use it responsibly? After all, you could go all round Africa busting all sorts of things. Also it could get into the wrong hands, such as a government that is bent on causing trouble, rather than bringing about peace." Sally stared in amazement at Larry; this sounded so responsible and far-sighted for someone who was usually away off in cloud-cuckoo land. Her reaction for him was all the more strengthened. This was going to be a worthy husband after all.

"My dear Mr. Robinson," came the high-level reply, "or should I call you Doctor? I am a gentleman. I was educated at Eton and went to Oxford to take First in Politics, Philosophy and Economics, at Baliol. My word is my bond. And I don't mean James Bond! I undertake, quite solemnly, to use this machine to destroy all weapons of war in this conflict, not just my side, but the other side too. I will not use it for other purposes. I undertake to return it to you as soon as hostilities have ceased and we have a peace treaty. Are you prepared to trust me?"

Larry stared him in the eye. He was clearly impressed with this gentleman from Oogie-googie Land. "How do you manage to speak English so well, Sir?" he asked, "and how did you manage to get to Eton and Oxford? I mean, that must have cost you a pretty penny."

"It did indeed," replied Baba, "but then, my father is the King of Oogie-googie land and he can afford it. I am now the Crown Prince. I expect to be the chief negotiator in the peace conference. Please help us!"

"He's offering you a million quid, Larry," Sally intimated.

"Cheap at the price," murmured Jimmy, "and that's only the rental. I think we'd better say it's not for outright purchase. I mean, there's no telling where it might land up…"

"I will not let it out of my sight," insisted Baba, "and I will return it to you as soon as is reasonably possible. That is an absolute promise, Dr. Robinson."

"I think we'd better send someone along with you," Jimmy scowled, "and what's more, two million might be a bit more interesting for us."

As the others came down from the lab, Larry proclaimed that he was going to rent out his invention, just one example, a pocket version, to Prince Baba, and that it needed one of the team to accompany him to Africa. After all, it would need some basic training in how to use it effectively. Then the gadget would come back to Venture Street.

"Any volunteers?" teased Sally. "Or nominations?" Silence fell on the room.

"You 'aven't told us how yer goin' ter pay for it," scowled Jimmy.

"Oh that's quite easy," breezed Baba, "I can ship in gold bullion to the value of two million. Doesn't that tempt you?"

"Not much point in giving us gold," retorted Kevin,

"since we can make…" Someone kicked his foot under the table, aggressively. "I mean, you make it sound like the end of the rainbow, Baba. You sure you've got that kind of lolly?"

"Perhaps Kevin would like to come with me?" Baba asked, as he began to take a fancy to the Irish lad. "We've got an interesting kind of poteen in our country. You interested?"

That had Kevin motivated to pay a visit to Oogie-googie Land. The assurance that he could take Betty Marston along as well clinched it for him. The couple were determined not to be parted.

CHAPTER 12
THE KING OF OOGIE

As the plane touched down in a remote part of Africa, Kevin spotted a welcoming party out on the tarmac. Baba grinned eagerly, knowing the kind of reception they were to be regaled with. Betty was the first out of the executive jet, and was met with cheers of adulation. The locals had never seen such an exquisite young lady from England before. Kevin's welcome was rather more muted, but when Baba appeared, high-powered adulation swept across the runway. Clearly, the Crown Prince was popular. They were soon to discover that the King himself was held in high esteem.

A superb Rolls Royce swept them away to the Royal Palace. This was a modest building but was clearly a modern structure with all up-to-date appurtenances. The King himself appeared at the front door, with his hands outstretched to greet them.

"Welcome to my humble abode," he cried, "let me introduce myself. I am King Jaja the 29th of Oogie-googie Land. I am so glad you have come. I hear you have brought a mysterious machine…"

Baba cut him short. "Shshshshs!!" he waved his hands, "hush Dad, this is all highly top secret. Mr. Kerry has something special in his suitcase, and no one but you and me ought to know about it."

Jaja showed them to their rooms and the Queen, Mrs. Jaja, helped them to settle in. Apart from the wonderful tribal costumes they were wearing, everything else was quite contemporary, with bathrooms, showers, toilets, every modern convenience. Then they were invited into Jaja's own sitting room, for afternoon tea. It was all so very English, with cucumber sandwiches and Earl Grey.

"You know," began Kevin, "I had expected it would be all grass huts and pretty basic."

"My son, Baba, came back from England with so many good ideas," Jaja explained, "so we have moved into the modern world. I must say, that my poor old Dad, the old king, learnt his lesson the hard way, fifty years ago." It was perfect English, with not a trace of accent.

"You mean, they sent him to a missionary school?" asked Betty.

The King burst out laughing. "No, no, my dear Betty. You see, he had a big grass hut, large enough to hold himself, three or four wives and his throne. But it was so crowded in there that he had to make some space."

"So did he do a bit of divorcing?" teased Kevin.

The King rolled about with laughter, nearly dropping his cup and saucer. "No, no, Kevin, he decided that if he fixed up a hoist and pulley in the ceiling, he could lift the throne up out of the way when they felt like doing some dancing..." he watched their faces for a reaction... "this worked for some time, but no one noticed that the grass hut was wobbling a bit. Well one day, when the throne was right up out of the way, the whole lot came tumbling down with an almighty crash. Poor Dad, he got his head bashed in." There was a fatalistic shrug of the royal shoulders, "but never mind, that's how I got to be King."

"Don't make that mistake again, Dad," warned Baba, "I'm in no hurry to get to be the King."

"Hardly likely," the King chuckled, "since my throne is ensconced in my throne-room and there is no need to hoist it up."

"I suppose the lesson from that," grinned Kevin, "is that those who live in grass houses shouldn't stow thrones." His fiancée kicked his foot in dismay at the plagiarism of a well known proverb. The three royals split their sides with laughter and were incapable of further coherent comment for about a quarter of an hour.

"My word, Mr. Kerry," King Jaja slapped him on the back, "you have got a sharp wit."

"More like a sharp twit," rejoindered Betty, "he never stops joking, your Majesty."

"There's no need to be so formal, dear," the King laughed, "would you like me to play something on the piano for you? Do you like jazzy music?"

"I certainly do," Kevin's eyes widened with amazement as Jaja took his seat at a massive Bechstein and began to play the Blues. "Fancy dancing, dears?" he teased, "or is it too hot for you?"

"They need to acclimatize, Dad," suggested Baba.

"So I'll give you a quick dollop of the Boogie-woogie,"

as the left hand began to pour out the bumpy bass line. Mrs. Jaja did feel like dancing, and girated all round the sitting room. "So you see, I'm the King of the Oogie-woogies, doing the Boogie-woogie, and I can go faster…" he upped the tempo, "and even faster still." Mrs. Jaja collapsed into a chair and became overwhelmed with side-splitting laughter.

"Oh my dear husband," she chuckled, "he is a comic."

Just then, the revelries were tempered by the sound of gunfire in the distance. Baba went to the window and watched as a squad of Oogie soldiers fetched in a couple of prisoners.

"This is your first sight of the Widgey-widgeys," he proclaimed, "they did a surprise attack and it all went wrong. Shall we fetch them in, Dad?"

"Why not?" cheered Jaja, "I shall give them my kindest regards."

The two Widgeys looked exactly like the Oogies. Except for their different Army uniforms, it would have been impossible to tell them apart.

"Oh my dear fellows," began Jaja, "why are we at war? Come sit down and have a cup of tea. Would you like to ring up home and tell them you are safe? We can release you after 24 hours."

The Widgeys seemed to take this hospitality all as a matter of routine. They sat there, chatting to their captors, as if nothing unpleasant had ever occurred. Kevin was totally astonished. "Anyone would think these guys were your favourite cousins," he murmured, expecting another outburst of violence.

"You know what it says in the Bible," Jaja picked up

his King James Bible, "love your enemies. Jesus said this himself. So we do. It's so ridiculous that we are shooting at each other. If my boys got captured, they would get the same treatment from the King of the Widgeys. It's a very decent war, except that people keep getting killed. The whole thing is ridiculous."

One of the Widgeys, Kuku by name, spoke up. "We have the greatest respect for King Jaja and the Oogies the same for our King. The whole thing is completely mad, but we can't stop it. It's a habit of life. Perhaps you could give us a reason to stop it, Mr. Kerry?"

Kevin was impressed by Kuku's perfect English, even better than his own. "But what is the difference between your two people?" he asked, totally baffled.

"None whatsoever, " stated Kuku, "we have the same DNA, the same tribal origins and our two royal houses are distantly related. We are all Methodists; the Oogies are Catholic Wesleyans and the Widgeys are Catholic Primitive Methodists, but since that is practically the same thing, we are not fighting over that. We don't want any of their land, and they don't want any of our land. It's just a stupid habit we've got into. Surely you can help us, Mr. Kerry, coming from Ireland, can see the nonsense of it all. Have you got a solution for us?"

Kevin looked at his fiancée and then at the royal trio. "As it happens," he stated carefully, "I have got a solution. King Jaja knows about it. Do you think Betty and myself could pay a visit to your King and explain it? The war could be over and done with by tomorrow if you would just listen to what I have to say."

Kuku beamed across his coffee-coloured face, which was hardly any different from that of Baba. "If you release us, we could go and tell the King right away," he offered, "flag of truce and no filthy tricks."

"We are not given to filthy tricks, dear boy," stated Jaja, "we are all gentlemen here of the highest principle, and so is your King, Chuchu. In fact, we were at Eton together as boys and were the best of friends. That just goes to show how ridiculous the whole thing is."

•

That evening, as bedtime approached, Kevin and Betty sat in their room, trying to cool off from the heat of the day. The room contained a massive double bed, which the couple kept eyeing thoughtfully for some time.

"I suppose you expect me to sleep with you, Kevin?" she yawned.

"How do you feel about that, my darling?" the Hibernian lad wondered, "I know for one thing, my old mother back in Kerry, she said to my sister, as she left home, 'don't you dare come back home pregnant, do you hear?' She was very strict and so am I. What about you, dear?"

"My mother would say the same thing, Kev," she agreed, "but we can share the same bed without going in for…"

"Just what I was thinking, my love," he smiled, "anyway, it's far too hot for anything like…"

"That does raise the question of when we could get married, Kev," she teased, "I can't wait. I wonder if we could get married in this country. Would it count back in England?"

"I don't see why not," he frowned, "but there is one thing I really should raise with you before we go the whole hog. I should really have told you this from the start, but I was terrified of losing you. You are just the thing I need in my life. I don't care if you're a Proddy. I suppose my old mother will have a fit, but then I'd better not go back to Ireland, ever again."

"Kevin, if you have something to tell me, let's get it out into the open," she held his hand.

"My past in Ireland... " he began to confess, "has not always been of the best, Betty. To be blunt, I was in the IRA at one time..." He went on to describe the incident that had changed his thinking. He stared at her face and waited for an explosion. But none came.

Betty squeezed his hand and then administered a kiss. "You don't have to worry about it, dear," she soothed. "I've known about it for some time. I made a decision. If you were genuinely repentant, I would stick with you."

"I am really, truly sorry I ever got involved with them," he insisted, "and I can't get that little girl out of my mind, her losing a leg, and she was a distant relative of mine." He wept. "How did you find out about me?"

"Sally told me. She things you're really sorry and she is prepared to give you a safe house."

"I'll make it up," he stated with great conviction, "I will be the peacemaker tomorrow. When I meet that king of the Widgeys, I will get it through to him, the nonsense of it all. Why is it that innocent people have to be caught in the crossfire? How cruel! Little children damaged for life."

"How true!" she sighed. "This situation reminds me of

the standoff between Britain and Germany in two world wars. The same people, racially, the same religion, sharing kings and queens for many years, and yet it all descended into barbarity never seen before. How many people were caught in the crossfire, as well as the Jews? The whole thing could have been avoided if they had just stopped and taken a look at the Bible that they both have. Then we look at Ireland."

Kevin's early indoctrination began to stir his hackles. "Proddies..." he sneered.

"Ah come on now, Kevin, this is where it all goes wrong. If you can care about that little girl, what about caring for all people? What about me? I'm a Proddy myself, rip roaring Evangelical."

"What I'd like to know?" he was half-teasing, "these Methodists? The Weslayans, are they the Catholic Methodists, and the Primitives, are they the Proddy Methodists."

"Are you serious, or is this another of your quirky jokes?" she demanded.

But what it did was to underline a basic platform of prejudice borne of centuries of distrust, hate and conflict. Kevin's knowledge of religious divisions was sketchy to say the least, but also there was a nasty jarring of confusion in it. This is something that dogs many people. They like to categorise and stereotype people. But life is seldom as simple as that.

"Kevin. Can't you just accept people for what they are, human? These people are happy, loving, trusting. They need help just as much as the Irish do... And anybody with a deep seated prejudice. Just learn to love them all, can't you?" He nodded, in total agreement.

CHAPTER 13
THE KING OF THE WIDGEYS

The King of the Widgeys, Chuchu, sat on his throne and stared thoughtfully as his two European guests strode up to the Palace. Kevin could almost have mistaken him for King Jaja, except that this king was wearing a slightly different set of robes. He rose to greet them, smiling and welcoming.

"My dear friends," he enthused, with not a trace of accent in his English, "I hear you have something to help us all. You are the peacemakers. Jesus said such people are blessed. Can you bless us with peace?"

Betty squeezed Kevin's hand in an encouragement to do his best. Kevin had a straw basket in his hand; this concealed the Robinsonian gadget from public gaze. The King was intrigued by that engaging Irish accent.

"To come to the point, Your Majesty," Kevin cleared his throat, "we have a gadget that can neutralize all weapons of war. This would mean that all your armaments would become useless."

"Just a minute," cut in a soldier, who turned out to be the chief general, "what about the other chaps? They will quickly overrun us…"

"No they won't," cut in Betty. "They have agreed to have the same thing done. If all your weapons on both sides are rendered useless, you won't be able to fight any more. You might as well have a peace conference and decide to be friends."

"That would be wonderful," enthused the King, "but is it a reality? This isn't some sort of cheap trick to let the other side steal a victory, I hope?"

The general frowned, since he realized he would be out of a job. But King Chuchu gave no indication of disbelief. He was prepared to take Kevin at his word. The general, however, wanted a demonstration. This was quickly organized as a squad of soldiers came in with their rifles and stood to attention.

"Now watch carefully," Kevin wagged a cautionary finger. He aimed the straw basket in the right direction, pressed the switch inside and the gadget made a funny noise, not as raucous as in times gone by, but enough to have the general inquisitive. All the rifles disintegrated, leaving the wooden stocks and piles of bullets on the floor. The bullets, being made of lead, did not react in the same way.

Astonishment swept round the room. Mouths dropped wide open and the soldiers fidgeted curiously with the wooden remains of their rifles. Kevin switched off, in the hope that the battery would not be exhausted too soon.

"A miracle!" gasped King Chuchu," can you do that with field guns and tanks?"

"Let's try," Kevin offered.

•

An hour or so later, the Widgey army was left with rather a strange collection of knackered armaments. There was a field gun with its barrel curled round not unlike a piggy-wig's curly tail. There was a tank with its turret turned into a curious form of toffee. There was a pile of shells which had just collapsed, leaving the explosive charge in a messy heap.

"And what about the other side? They will come charging in and win the war," nattered the general, "this is hardly fair."

"Oh yes it is," insisted Betty, "earlier this morning we gave the same demonstration to King Jaja and his men, and they know that all these weapons of war are now useless."

"So you might as well get round the table and decide to be friends," Kevin stated with great conviction.

"How do we know this is the truth?" worried the general.

"Come and do an inspection," invited Kevin. "Their armaments are all jiggered as well."

•

It was later that morning when the two Kings met on the parade ground of the Oogies. For a moment, Betty could not decide which king was which, since they looked so alike. They advanced on each other, embraced and wept with joy.

"My brother!" exclaimed Jaja, "such a long time since we were together at Eton. And now the war is over. Thank God!"

"I know you as my brother," cried Chuchu, "at last this

nonsense is over. Our peoples can work together in peace. No more killings or cruelty. All our weapons have been neutralized."

"Our generals must shake hands too," invited Jaja, as the two top military strategists advanced on each other. Again, they looked exactly the same except for the different uniform. "Come on, you two. You are both Christians, and Methodists at that. Smile, please, and make friends. Jesus wants peace on earth, not conflict." They both followed orders, but there was that lurking feeling in both their minds that burying the hatchet after so many years of distrust, would not be an easy matter. The troops, however, formed up in two detachments on the parade ground, threw their berets in the air and gave three resounding cheers. The ordinary squaddies realized that there was no longer any danger of killings, widowing, orphaning, or serious injury, and all the other horrible results of war.

The peace conference was quickly convened with Kevin Kerry in the chair. Betty kept a wary eye on that straw basket, as she had noticed that the two generals had been particularly curious about its mysterious abilities. As the treaty came to be signed, a mother came running up to the table. She was in a panic.

"My little girl has fallen in the river," she screamed, "can anyone help me? I think the crocodiles will get her."

Kevin jumped to his feet, tore off down to the river bank and plunged into the muddy water. After a struggle with the panicking girl and a gallant assault on the crocodile, the situation was saved. The mother was overjoyed but also collapsed with laughter when she saw that Kevin's trousers had fallen down. He had used his leather belt to secure the crocodile's jaws, as a measure of desperation.

"That poor crocodile will starve to death now, Kevin," remarked Betty, as she caught up with him.

"No he won't," he snatched the straw basket from her hands and aimed it at the dangerous jaws. The metal clip on the belt came apart and the crocodile was able to rejoice in his new gob-freedom. The other watchers on the bank stared in amazement. Some of them began to wonder if this Hibernian lad was actually Jesus?!

•

Saturated with mud and mess from the river, Betty dragged the hero back to the palace. She got him into the shower and began to clean him up. His suit was ruined, but Baba appeared with some apparel more appropriate for the tropical climes and Kevin soon began to feel much more comfortable.

"Now you are a real hero, darling," she knelt before him, "you saved that little girl from a horrible death. That makes up for everything in the past." He knew what she meant; was no need to go into details.

Baba reappeared shortly afterwards and made an important announcement. "My dear friends," he enthused, "this is a wonderful day. Our two kingdoms are at peace and there will be a big ceremony this evening, with cultic dancing and sports. Also there will be an important wedding."

"Who's getting married?" asked Betty.

"Me," he announced grandly, flourishing his arms, "to cement the treaty, I am to marry Chuchu's favourite daughter."

"I had the idea that you had a wife already," puzzled Kevin.

"Two, actually," the prince let drop, "but now it will be three, and this one will take precedence over the others. Oh, I know you English guys only have one wife…or at least, you're supposed to," he teased, "but here it is perfectly legal as long as you treat your wives fairly and equally."

"I thought you guys were strict Methodists?" frowned Betty.

"We are, but you who know the Bible, will remember that lots of chaps in the Bible had more than one wife. Jesus never said you could not have more than one. It is part of our culture. There is no shame in it as long as you play fair over it. Anyway, the wedding will be this evening. Do you fancy having your wedding as well? We could make it a double occasion. Just think, Kevin, you could take two or three lovely Oogie maidens home with you, along with Betty." He was partly teasing, but not entirely.

King Jaja appeared, with that lovely smile on his face. "Is he tempting you into naughty ways, Kevin?" he jibed. "If you care to stay on with us, it would be perfectly legal in this country. But I know perfectly well that back in England it would hardly be seen as decent. Would you fancy one of my daughters?"

Kevin stared at Betty, as if to say, 'help!' She wagged an admonitory finger to quash the idea. "All the same," Kevin resumed, "if we could get married today that would be fine by me, and I know Betty is dead keen."

"Consider it all fixed up," stated King Jaja with great conviction and confidence.

Amidst all the jollifications, Betty kept tight hold of that important straw basket. She was not slow to notice those two generals eyeing the thing with looks on their faces which betokened envy combined with curiosity.

•

As the jollifications came to a close, Kevin, being the bridegroom, was asked to give a speech. It had not occurred to him that he would be expected to harangue the multitude, and he had no idea of what to say. He shrugged his shoulders and pleaded stupidity.

"Come on, " egged Baba, "I know you've got a fund of silly stories. Why don't you tell us one about the little folk? The little green guys that live in Ireland."

"You mean the wee folk?" he grinned. "The pixies and the leprechauns? I can tell you one. Would you listen now?" he tried to calm the multitude. "You see, it was like this. There was a leprechaun who lived dangerously. He was always doing risky things."

"Or was it whisky things?" interrupted Chuchu.

"It could have been on St. Patrick's day," Kevin giggled. "Anyway, he took his friend's advice and bought himself a helmet. At least that would keep his head safe."

"Not much good if he fell in the bog," remarked Baba.

"No, no, no," corrected Kevin, "he was not that careless. Instead of that he walked into a tree and banged his head."

"And knocked himself out?" Bitty sniggered.

"Not a bit of it," grinned Kevin, "for being a wise old leprechaun, he was now aware of 'Elf and Safety.'" He waited for a response, and waited and waited.

It was Betty who burst out laughing; the rest of them just stared, waiting for the punch line. The reason was, that in that kingdom, no one had ever heard of Health and Safety. They just used common sense instead.

CHAPTER 14
THE HOMECOMING

The gentle hum of the executive jet lulled the honeymoon couple into a doze. They were now somewhere over Spain and their arrival in Britain was imminent. Betty Kerry held the straw basket on her knee, in spite of the stewardess' attempts at locating it in a locker.

"Must be careful not to activate this thing," she whispered in his ear. "The whole plane might disintegrate, and none of us have got a parachute."

"Won't work now," murmured Kevin, as he proudly twiddled his wedding ring, "I took the batteries out, just as a precaution."

"Very thoughtful of you, darling," she congratulated, "typical of you. I never thought I'd get a husband as thoughtful and considerate as you. I am a lucky girl."

Their visit to the two African kingdoms had been a swingeing success. Peace had been established, and even the two generals had decided to chum up and become best mates. Baba had been concerned that since there was now no conflict, the two tribes would be bored out of their minds. It was Kevin who had managed to fix them up with plenty of shellalahs so that they could play sports all day long and take it in turns to win. For those who were not quite so muscular, there were plenty of board games such as chess and draughts to occupy their minds. But in general terms, they were all mightily relieved that warfare had become impossible, and even if someone did make an attempt at fabricating weapons, Kevin would return with his miraculous straw basket and quash the whole thing all over again.

As the jet landed not far from the Robinson home town, they began to wonder what fresh challenges might occupy their minds. Everything seemed perfectly normal as the taxi swept up to the outskirts of the small market town, but then a curious thing hove in sight. It was a thirty limit sign canted over at about 60 degrees. It was just one of them, but not both.

"Oooops!" remarked Kevin, "that one's been down the pub, by the looks of it."

"And that one's been to a Welsh pub," sniggered Betty, as she pointed out a lamppost with a curious kink in it.

"Hey! What's happened there?" marvelled the taxi driver, as they drove past a building site with metal fencing all buckled, twisted and a complete shambles. "Looks as though the navies have had a freakout."

"What do you expect from the Irish?" teased Betty.

"Must have come all the way from County Kerry," hick-upped Kevin in a souped-up accent. "All hooligans and dooligans, swinging their shellalahs around. Probably a touch of the poteen." This was rounded off with an aggressive HICK.

"My word, what's happened there?" gasped Betty, as she pointed to the fancy iron work that at one time had decorated the tower on the town hall. It was all twisted and wobbly, and there were firemen clambering up ladders in an attempt at rendering it safe.

They pulled up by the house in Venture Street, to find that the front door had been reinstated, but not with the normal metal fittings. The knocker was enswathed in plastic, and when operated, made a rather dull sound as it clonked against a lump of oak. It was Jimmy the Whizz who opened up to give them admission.

"Well-well!" came the Cockney accent, "back 'ome to blighty! 'Ad a good time?"

"Splendid!" chirped Betty. She charged through to the kitchen, to find Sally and Larry sitting hand in hand and eyeing each other in a most sentimental and apprehensive mode. Kevin came in right behind her.

"What's that I see on your finger, Betty Marston?" demanded Sally.

Larry was miles away as ever, but Jimmy, who had managed to filch it off Betty's finger, held it up and proclaimed, "she's reverted to being a spinster, by the looks of it."

"Give that back to me at once," blasted Betty, "you're supposed to be a reformed character, young Jim. No more nicking!"

"My gosh, that looks like a wedding ring!" gawped Larry, coming a little into present realities. "Did that gadget fiddle it for you? I say, that was clever."

Betty replaced the ring on her finger and proclaimed,

"you are now looking at Elizabeth Kerry, newly espoused in Oogie Land, and ceremony performed by King Jaja himself."

"And he offered me a selection of concubines to come home with us," cheesed Kevin, "but Mrs. Kerry had the notion that that might place rather a strain on a poor wee country lad like myself, all innocent and inexperienced, like the rest of us from the Hibernian hills."

"Did 'e offer you the money?" demanded Jimmy, the financial whiz-kid.

"Oh blimey!" expostulated Kevin, "I never gave it a thought, but never mind, me treasure is sure to be in heaven, as that Catholic Methodist king assured me."

While they were all laughing at that deliberate confusion of thought, Betty the Bride pulled out two pieces of paper from the straw basket. She waved her marriage certificate round as if it were a flag of truce. Everybody clapped. Then she produced a cheque for an amazing sum of money. This had them all stunned and totally gratified.

"And now? What about the gadget?" Sally demanded. "You have brought it back?"

Betty fumbled with the straw basket and pulled it out. Kevin fished out the batteries from his pocket. "Want to test it out, to see if it's in good shape?" he teased.

"No, no, no!" came a chorus from several throats. "Give it back at once," demanded Sally.

"We've had enough of that blessed thing," yelled Jimmy, "I could smash the lot of them."

Larry looked quite disconsolate. The mood in the room was intense in a negative way. Clearly something had gone wrong while the Kerries had been away in Africa.

"What's the matter?" demanded Kevin testily. "Somebody bust the Lord Mayor's lavatory chain… I mean, his chain of office." He tried to snigger but thought better of it.

"Mrs. Kerry stared at them questioningly. "You've had big troubles down town, I see. Who's been fooling about with one of those gadgets? Come on, own up, Jimmy. Have you pinched one from upstairs and gone on a spree?"

"All my eye and Peggy Martin," he disclaimed, "would I do a stupid trick like that? I'm a reformed character, Mrs. Kerry. They call me Honest Jim now. Even the coppers are pleased with me."

"I was a fool to invent a thing like that," moaned Larry, as he clutched Sally's hand, "I should have listened to what you said, Darling. It could ruin the entire world. I just wasn't thinking of the consequences. I need you, Sally, to knock some sense into me."

"All right, Darling," Sally reassured him, "it was a very clever idea, but we must keep your stock of gadgets away from idiots. You see," she gave the information, "somebody… we don't know who, has pinched one of them from upstairs and is causing mayhem in the town."

"At least we've made a few quid out of it," came the spondulick-minded Jimmy, as he waved a piece of paper about the room. "And there's more to come if we go about it the right way."

"What is that?" demanded Betty, as the thought occurred to her that it was the cheque she had received from King Jaja.

"Want your cheque back?" Jimmy teased, waving it in

front of her nose. "Best keep your 'and on yer wallet, Misses Kerry."

"Jimmy, you blighter!" she snapped as she snatched it back. "I thought you were a reformed character. Don't you dare play tricks like that. I shall tell Muldoon of you…" She wagged an admonitory finger.

"Mind you, he's just the guy we need to solve this problem," Kevin frowned.

"What? Muldoon?" chirped Sally, "he's got no idea."

"No, I mean Jim here. Why don't you ooze around the town, find out who's got the gadget and nick it back. That's a little project for you, Jim. Failing that you can always nick the batteries out of it…" Kevin showed him what they looked like and how to remove them from the gadget.

At that point, Derek Normbrain rattled down the stairs and advertised himself in the kitchen doorway. "I think we've done it," he chirped cheerfully. "We've got it to focus on just the thing we want to bust. No more incidental mishaps."

Sally, who now felt rather more confident about the integrity of her bra, issued a sigh of relief. "And does that mean we can have a decent knocker on the front door again?" It was slightly sarcastic but very much to the point.

"Wish to God I'd never even thought of the idea," moaned Larry.

"Now, now, Dr. Robinson," came a soothing comment from Kevin, "you should have seen how those chaps in Africa made peace. They were so delighted and grateful. If we handle this thing carefully, it will be a great boon to all of mankind…" Betty nudged him… "and all of womankind," he added hastily. Betty's eyes gleamed.

"But in the hands of an idiot, there will be nothing but trouble," warned Derek Normbrain, "and I wouldn't be surprised if I didn't know who that idiot might be. Do we need to guess?"

"That thieving b...d that came from the Ministry," grinned Jimmy, "bent as a corkscrew. Makes me look like a saint." Everybody sniggered. "What was his name, Wally-something?"

"Wallet-less, " Sally wagged a finger at Jimmy.

"Wallibrain," sighed Larry, whose grey matter was just beginning to display a little touch of rationality. "I should never have let him into the house."

"Wallitude," corrected Betty. "Fred Wallitude. Complete cuckoo if you ask me, and very sly."

"At least he suggested I should work on how to dematerialize plastics," ruminated Larry, "That would be something useful."

"Just a minute," Sally warned him, "if you do that, all the insulation on the wiring will slurp off and then we shall have the one hell of a bang. You, my love, have done enough. Now just think of something else to do in life. Just look at that lovely garden out there. You could spend all day working on that and it would keep you out of mischief."

"By the way, have you got that thing patented yet?" Betty challenged, "what would there be to stop Wallitude patenting it himself and claiming the credit?"

"We got that done while you were away," Sally reassured them, "mind you, if it had been left to Dream-boat here," she pointed at Larry, "it would never have got done. Derek was a great help."

Just then, the telephone shrilled and Sally picked it up… "yes? The republic of Whipplitude?…Where the dickens is that?… You are at war with the republic of Chiploddy?… Why don't you just stop it?… " A fatalistic air settled on that kitchen. The message was getting round. The whole world was beginning to realize that a compulsory peace was now available. That would we a great advance for civilization, except to say, what would come as a substitute for warfare? The receiver went down. "More trouble," sighed Sally, "you ready for another trip, as an extension to your honeymoon?" She grinned at Kevin and Betty.

CHAPTER 15
THE REPUBLIC OF WHIPPLITUDE

As the executive jet touched down in a remote part of the world, Kevin squeezed Betty's hand and stared out of the window. There was a reception party on the tarmac; red flags were fluttering in the breeze. Kevin wondered what they were in for; it might be completely different from the Oogies and the Widgeys.

Indeed it was. They were shown into the presidential palace to meet the supremo, a Mr. Chom. He sat there in an elaborate and imaginative military uniform, with a chest loaded up with medals and a superior look about his face.

"Welcome to the People's Republic of Whipplitude," he extended a hand. "Mr.Kerry, I believe, and this is your wife? Do take a seat. We have much to discuss. We have heard about what happened in the Oogie Kingdom. Not that we have any time for kings, of course. We go in for democracy."

"So do we," remarked Betty.

"No, no, no, all that about monarchy. Old fashioned nonsense. Contrary to the spirit of Socialism." Mr. Chom was quite dogmatic. "Anyway, to the point. I understand you have some kind of method for neutralizing weapons of war. This sounds a bit fantastic, but it seems to have worked in Oogie Land. We have a problem here. The country next to us cannot accept that we have the right political solution. Essentially, they are Fascists, and as such, ought to be defeated and turned into good Communists as we are."

Kevin nearly said, "I didn't know there were any good Communists," but managed to think of something less provocative. "What sort of system do they have, Mr. Chom?"

"They have a nasty dictator called Mr. Flam. He's got a little black moustache and makes them all dress up in military uniforms and do the goose-step. Rather comical really until you realize he's telling them all what to think. He tells them he's always right on every issue and they must just follow orders. Anyone who disobeys is packed off to a special re-education camp. He's a complete control freak and mentally unstable. The sooner someone shoots him, the better."

"So what do you want us to do?" asked Betty cautiously.

"I want you two to infiltrate his country, bust his weapons of war and then his regime will collapse."

"And you'll come storming in and rescue all those poor goose-stepping souls," suggested Kevin with a touch of sarcasm in his voice.

"Of course. They all need to be rescued and given a new start with sound democratic Socialist basics," came the self-assured, but eager response.

"We do not wish," stated Kevin slowly, "to make judgments on either of your two systems. What we do insist on is that the situation is fair on both sides. If we bust one lot of weapons, we must bust the other lot as well. If the balance of power is unbalanced, it will lead to all kinds of trouble. Both sides need to disarm. That way you can have a peace conference and decide to live and let live."

"But we don't want a peace conference," snapped the chest full of medals, "surely you must see that Fascism is wrong. It has to be defeated," he slapped the desk like a spoilt child. "Don't tell me you're a Fascist, Mr. Kerry?"

"No. I'm not, neither am I a Communist, Mr. Chom," stated Kevin, "I'll tell you something. I am totally against violence or any kind of cruelty. I want world peace."

Mr. Chom was getting annoyed. "But surely you must agree with the ideas of Karl Marx? Have you read his book, Das Kapital? He explains the whole thing very convincingly. How can you disagree with him?"

"I have read his book," muttered Kevin, "and I couldn't make head not tail of it. Have you actually read it yourself?"

"It's a brilliant analysis of the wickedness of capitalism," came the dogmatic response.

"You haven't answered the question," cut in Betty.

"The question is, what are we to do with Mr. Flam?" came the sidetrack.

"No. The question is, have you actually read the book?" Betty insisted. "For instance, what does it say about religion?"

"Oh! That superstitious rubbish," Mr. Chom wafted his hands dismissively. "Let's get rid of it and come down to realities."

"Well actually, Marx hardly says anything about religion, and he certainly doesn't say anything about persecuting people for their faith. So I want to know why these Communist states have gone to great lengths to wipe out religion. Can you tell me?"

"Because the religionists have been backing up the reactionaries," came the doctrinaire response.

"So you think my husband and I would be in favour of Mr. Flam?" Betty teased.

"Why? Are you a religionist?" Mr. Chom frowned.

"Kevin's a full-blown Roman Catholic and I'm a rip-roaring Evangelical," Betty claimed proudly, "so does that mean you're going to pack us off to some kind of prison camp to be indoctrinated with atheism?"

"No, no, nothing like that," came the fib.

"So we can go to church in this country, just like any other country?" inquired Kevin.

"Better than that," came the evasion, "I will give you a guided tour of the Republic of Whipplitude and you can see for yourselves what a wonderful system we have. You will be so pleased that you will wish to come and join us and help us with our developments."

•

Next morning, Mr. and Mrs. Kerry found themselves being chauffeured around the Republic of Whipplitude in an exceedingly expensive Cadillac. The chauffeur wore a smart military uniform with a peaked cap, and everywhere they went they could see people in the same regimental attire. All the housing was exactly the same style, a tawdry ultra efficient architecture which allowed of no variation whatsoever. They saw shops, outside of which were queues, the length of which varied according to the goods on sale. Food shops, especially, had by far the longest queues, and the patient housewives with their empty baskets were yawning and frowning with frustration. The car pulled up outside a school and they were invited to sample the educational system.

The head teacher, who wore the same uniform as everyone else, gave them cause for thought. Was this person male or female? But the voice gave it away; she was a woman. All the teachers wore the same uniform. The children stared in amazement at the Kerries. The girls were clearly astonished at Betty's smart but cheerful dress and high heeled shoes, and a whiff of expensive perfume. The boys' eyes popped out on stalks at the sight of Kevin's smart, tailor-made suit.

"Where have they come from?" whispered a boy with a stunned look on his face.

"Ah! They come from Britain, which as you know, is a corrupt, degenerate Capitalist society with all sorts of social problems and a government that is quite obviously on the brink of coming to its senses, in other words, embracing the truths of Communism," emphasized the head. "It is quite amazing that they still persist with that idea of having a monarchy... Tut!"

There was not a ripple of emotion as Kevin and Betty eyed the whole class.

"And today, they are studying how the gallant Red Army stormed in to rescue the enslaved peoples of Western Europe. Sadly, they only managed to free off half of Germany. The rest of Western Europe was messed up by the

British and the Americans, but we shall get there one day, and let all of Europe come to understand democracy and freedom." It sounded so self-convincing. Kevin and Betty grinned at each other as they noted the little red tie under every little chin.

Out in the corridor, Kevin decided to dare ask a naughty question. "Excuse me, what if one of those children says he disagrees with your version of the Second World War?"

"My version? May dear fellow, that's everyone's version. The truth. If a child wants to be difficult over it, he is taken out of class and we take steps to correct him. This seldom happens but it usually indicates that the parents have got some false information from abroad. This means we have to interrogate the parents and put them right. If they persist in failing to accept the truth then we have to take further steps."

"What further steps would those be?" persisted Betty.

The woman came over all vague. "I… erm… believe…" She coughed diplomatically, "that certain gentlemen from the… Erm… Ministry of Truth…" she applied her handkerchief to her nose," relocate them, so that they can't spread their mistaken ideas around the community."

"Thought police," whispered Betty; Kevin nodded. "And where are they relocated to?" Betty spoke up, deciding to dare a little.

"Oh I'm not sure," came the prevarication, "I think there's a special settlement for such people that are trying to undermine our magnificent Socialist state."

"Can we visit this settlement?" asked Kevin.

"I have no idea," the Head passed it off as if it were a

tea-bag trodden into the ground. "I don't even know where that would be. Anyway, it might be a restricted area." Then, trying to change the subject, "as you see, all our children are miles ahead of yours back in Britain. Nearly all of them go to University."

"And what do they study there?" asked Betty.

"Politics, of course," came the self-assured answer.

On the way out, one of the teachers bumped into them. The look on his face was one they had never seen before. He looked round furtively to assure himself that no one else was listening. "You had the usual spiel?" he whispered, "Bollocks! No more Socialist than flying. Mr. Chom is the dictator and everyone jumps to it. Equality be blowed! Democracy; that's just a joke. It's only democracy if there's a healthy opposition, and that's illegal in this country." He shut up abruptly as the Head reappeared. "Oh yes, you must be impressed by our superb system here," the teacher raised his voice, "Wonderful leadership. Everyone thinks the world of President Chom…" he looked round, "Oh hello, Head, I think our visitors are really impressed."

"Of course, how could they fail to be?" It was like a mother hen coaxing her chicks.

•

The Cadillac swept past a quaint building that was clearly in poor repair.

"I bet you that's a church," whispered Kevin. It was.

The chauffeur turned to them and explained. "It was a building used for strange goings on, but now it's used as a warehouse. I think it's going to be demolished when they get a decent storage facility built." That confirmed their worst fears.

As they drove out into the country, Kevin spotted some sort of settlement down a muddy track. "Let's have a look down there," he supplicated the chauffeur.

"I wouldn't like to get the car messed up," came the excuse.

"We'll walk it then," offered Betty.

"Oh madam, in those funny shoes you're wearing?" the chauffeur kept trying it, but in the end he gave in. "I can only take you to the entrance," he waffled, "and they won't let you in. There are some funny people down there. Mentally deranged, I believe."

As they pulled up at the gates, an armed soldier advanced and tried to make them turn around and depart. But Kevin was determined to find out what was really happening. They stepped out of the car and explained that they were visitors from Britain, with permission to tour around and see what a magnificent Republic this was. The guard shrugged his shoulders and made a collection of excuses, which amounted to 'clear off or I will arrest you.'

Kevin put his hand inside the straw basket and made the gadget swing into action. "I don't like being threatened with a gun," he murmured, and the guard's weapon collapsed into nothing, leaving the wooden stock dangling in his astonished fingers. "Now let us in," Kevin asked politely.

"How did you do that?" the soldier quavered.

"Never mind. Just let us in, would you?" As the soldier was clearly not going to co-operate, Kevin tweaked his gadget and the barbed wire fencing disintegrated, and the gates collapsed asunder. "Just a quick look. Come on, Betty. My driver here might like to take a peek," and he encouraged the chauffeur to accompany them.

The circumstances that met their eyes was not at all a pleasant one. There were people who were clearly malnourished, and that included children. They were shuffling about in rags and the housing that could be seen was a nasty example of shanty-town. In the distance they could hear some sort of chanting which set Kevin thinking.

"It's the Mass," he whispered in Betty's ear. "They've got a priest, be-jabers. Come on, Betty. Let's join in."

It would seem that half the camp was gathered round, kneeling in the mud, and there was a priest behind a makeshift altar, conducting a service.

"I told you there would be some strange people in here," cautioned the chauffeur.

"Well that makes me a strange person," Kevin riposted, as he worked his way to the front and knelt in the mud. Betty decided not to kneel down but did feel she could join in.

"I really would ask you not to mention this episode when we get back to government house," begged the chauffeur.

"Why? Isn't this sort of thing supposed to exist in our wonderful Socialist republic?" challenged Betty. "Is this what happens when you dare to object to what Mr. Chom tells you what to think?" The chauffeur went white with fear. "I want to join in with Kevin. I don't care if it's Roman Catholic. I'm all in favour of religious freedom." The chauffeur was trembling, in fear of his exalted position.

After the service, the priest came up to Kevin and Betty. "I'm so glad you came to join us," he shook their hands. "This is what happens if you dare to argue with the regime. We've got lots of Roman Catholics here and Protestants, and people with other ideas."

"It's a concentration camp, isn't it?" stated Kevin, "what a disgrace!"

"We aren't supposed to call it that," cautioned the priest. "The proper label is 'a centre for re-education and correction'. That is just a joke. The truth is that hardly anybody ever gets released. I have estimated that there are about a dozen camps like this in this country, but the rest of the world is not supposed to know about them. Can you get the information out, please?"

Kevin assured him that news of these dreadful circumstances would become known in the free world. The United Nations would be informed, as well as the world press. Perhaps that would shame this government into behaving more reasonably towards those who would criticize the regime.

CHAPTER 16
THE REPUBLIC OF CHIPLODDY

It was a Rolls Royce that conveyed Kevin and Betty up to the Presidential Palace of Chiploddy. All along the road they had noticed banner posters with Mr. Flam's face grinning hopefully at the general public; this was in contrast to the exposition of Mr. Chom in the neighbouring territory. Mr. Chom had a purposeful frown on his face. They were conducted into the presence of the august Mr. Flam, who was seated behind a massive mahogany desk which was piled high with important papers.

The president shook hands with both of them and settled them into chairs. "Welcome to our republic," squawked Mr. Flam, as his little black moustache vibrated. "I understand you are here on a peace mission. We, in Chiploddy, certainly do want peace. All this warfare is such a waste of resources. We could spend all that money on schools, hospitals, farms and a dozen other things. But Mr. Chom is determined to wipe us out and turn us all into Communists. What a wonderful system," he sneered bitterly. "Solves all their problems; ha-ha!" He was at his most sarcastic.

"We were quite impressed with some of the things we saw," offered Betty.

"Oh, I'm sure you would be," came the pseudo-cheerful reply, "but you would only be seeing the success-story stuff. By the way, that has been achieved by borrowing vast amounts of money from abroad, mostly Capitalist countries," he sneered. "I doubt very much whether he ever intends to repay those loans."

"We also saw one of their concentration camps," stated Kevin sadly, "the sin-bin for anyone who objects to the regime."

"Ah well, they aren't supposed to exist," came the hushed reply, "everyone is supposed to be equal."

"What about religion in this country?" asked Betty.

"No problem," Mr. Flam smiled, "you can be anything you like… As long as you are loyal to this country. We have all sorts of different beliefs going on, and they relate to the various clans we have. One of my sociological experts is devising a kind of common ground religion, one that will unify us despite our differences. There is only one God, and we can all be one family…"

"With you as his Messiah…" Kevin nearly blurted out, but managed to modify it, "and with you as the guarantor of freedom."

"What's all this about clans?" asked Betty.

"Ah now there lies our chief problem," Mr. Flam explained, "we are accused of not having a democracy, free elections and so forth. But we can't, or at least, if we did, it would achieve nothing. We have five racial groups here and each one thinks it ought to be the leading element. If we had an election, there would be five parties, one for each clan, and since they are more or less equal in numbers, no one party would manage to gain a majority, and if one ever did, the others would go mad and cause a riot. But the one thing that binds them all together is the fact that none of them want Mr. Chom to come and mess things up with his version of Socialism."

"So which clan do you belong to, Mr. Flam?" asked Kevin.

"None of them," he stated dogmatically, "I am strictly neutral. They invited me in from Nonkey land to be a sort of referee, and that seems to work. I admit that I carry on like a dictator, but that's the only thing that will work. But in fairness, I have five representatives coming, one from each clan, to explain their needs to me, and try to do something about it. I do my best to be impartial," he coughed, thoughtfully.

"So what about this war?" asked Betty.

"It's getting nastier and nastier," growled the dictator, "there's an arms race going on, and I am very much afraid that Mr. Chom is working towards nuclear weaponry. I understand you have a method for messing up weapons of war. That would be a great help, but only if both sides have their weapons ruined. If one side gains the advantage, we shall have a mess on our hands."

"Ideally, both sides could just live in peace and leave each other alone," suggested Kevin. "Can we have the guided tour of your country and see for ourselves what's happening?"

"Of course," Mr. Flam cried enthusiastically, "my personal car is waiting outside."

As they emerged from the front door, there was a full-blown inspection parade, with four ranks of Chiploddy soldiers on their best presentation. These guys wore a more impressive uniform than the ones seen in the streets and on the tarmac. They all snapped to attention and presented arms. Kevin had the distinct urge to apply his gadget then and there, but Betty hissed at him to desist. The Rolls swept them away to town and out into the villages.

What struck them immediately was the variation in housing. While some were quite opulent, there were others that were just hovels and even garden sheds. The shops did not appear to have queues, although a glance in the windows suggested that the supply of consumer goods was somewhat meagre. They passed several churches which had the distinct appearance of thriving quite well. Then the chauffeur swept into a school yard as it was morning break.

"Mr. and Mrs. Kerry," warmed the head teacher, as they found his study. "You are a guest of Mr. Flam. How are things in Britain these days? You lucky people! Do feel free to inspect the school and have a chat with the teachers."

The atmosphere gave the distinct impression that there was nothing to hide and things were quite open. They slipped into a classroom and observed a teacher conducting a Maths lesson. It was an old fashioned approach with all the pupils facing the front and paying attention. There was a cane lying across the teacher's desk. All the children were wearing grey shirts and purple ties.

They got chatting to a teacher in the staffroom. "I have the greatest respect for Mr. Flam," she remarked, "it is a most difficult situation, holding five clans together, and if he ever got shot, Heaven forbid, there would be absolute chaos. I don't like him, actually, but I think it's the best solution the way things are."

"And what if someone objects to the system?" asked Betty.

"I think most of us do," sighed the teacher, "we would all like to see a unified country. There are a few that are clearly communist inspired and likely to betray our country to Mr. Chom."

"What happens to them?" tested Kevin.

"There are special centres for them, where they can rant and rave at each other all day long and not rock the boat, so to speak," the teacher explained, "I'm sure you can visit one of them and see how it's arranged. I have the impression it's the life of riley in there, but I wouldn't want to finish off with no job…" she tailed off, diplomatically.

•

The Rolls pulled up outside a building which was clearly an old country house with a security fence around it. The guard on the gate was unarmed, but insisted on seeing their credentials. The governor conducted them round from one sitting room to another and explained what was happening.

"These are all the people that want to disrupt our republic," he explained, "communist inspired."

"If they're communists, why not send them off to join Mr. Chom?" asked Betty.

"I wish we could, except that Mr. Chom does not want them. He thinks they would all be spies. None of these chaps need to be here, except that they sneer about our dictatorship and want Mr. Flam to be turned out. We do our best to explain why our system is the best we can do, but they just won't listen." The governor shrugged his shoulders, sadly.

Kevin peered into one of the sitting rooms. It was quite comfortable in there, with armchairs and a drinks cabinet, but he noticed that all the occupants had earplugs in their luggies. An attendant quickly flicked a switch, but rather too late to stop Kevin hearing the tail end of an indoctrination which went… 'Mr. Flam is our only hope; you must beli…" and it stopped.

"Rubbish!" shouted a young man sitting in an armchair. Two men in smart uniforms darted in and heaved the chap out and away down the corridor. "Another session with your truncheons!" he shouted, hoping that Kevin would hear. "Ouch!" could heard in the distance. "You coward! Just because I come from Nimby land."

"What's Nimby Land?" asked Betty. She was now trembling.

The governor hedged a bit but admitted, "the Nimbies are a sort of tribe that has a funny sort of ancestry, and weird customs, " came the vague reply, "I think they came from another part of the continent, but they have never integrated with the rest of us."

A scream was heard from a distant room. Another inmate wandered back, swaying somewhat and with a few nasty bruises about his person. "You again, Finkelstein," snapped the governor, "have you learnt your lesson?"

"Go fart in your smelly pants," came the defiant

response, "and if the United Nations found out what you're up to... " but this was cut short as Finkelstein was abruptly yanked off in another direction.

"Torture chamber," hinted Betty to Kevin. "Dear me!"

Back in the President's study, Kevin decided to start the peace process.

"Did you learn anything from your tour?" asked Mr. Flam, as he offered them drinks.

"We learnt a lot," stated Betty. "We think that the sooner you find a peace solution, the better. We have the means to destroy all your weapons, which means that the war will have to end. I offer you a challenge; why don't you and Mr. Chom have a summit meeting and decide to work together for the good of all your peoples?"

"I couldn't possibly do that," came the categorical retort, "and I'm sure he'd say the same. We are Fascists and he is a Communist. Totally opposite political thinking."

"Well my impression is," Kevin sipped his whisky and soda, "that the only difference between you is the labelling system. After that, you both have the same methods of repression, indoctrination and discrimination. You might as well do an amalgamation for all the differences you've got. Had you thought of that?"

"If you didn't have this absurd war going on, you wouldn't have to persecute people for their religion or racial background," Betty put her glass down and clutched her straw basket.

"I'm not a racist!" snapped Mr. Flam, like a caught thief.

Betty and Kevin decided that discretion was the better part of blurting contradictions. They quickly assured Mr.

Flam that they would have another meeting with Mr. Chom and arrange a summit meeting. That would be just a glimmer of hope that peace could be arranged. They could see that neutral territory ought to be found, but that would not be too difficult, since the neighbouring country which was solidly Buddhist, was totally espoused to world peace and appalled at the loss of life and cruelty involved in this crazy conflict.

As Mr. Flam waved them off at the airport, Betty felt sure that the summit would make some progress. The reason for this was that with both presidents, they had left a slight innuendo that they knew about the concentration camps and re-education centres. That information would not sound too pleasing to the rest of the world. The United Nations would almost certainly decide to intervene in some way, and neither side wanted that.

CHAPTER 17
PRECIPITOUS SUMMIT

Kevin Kerry was in the chair and Betty was the secretary, taking the minutes. On one side sat Mr. Chom, backed up with an array of uniformed officials, their chests all covered with an array of medals. On the other side sat Mr. Flam, in a smart suit, but supported by a collection of officials, some of which sported elaborate uniforms. The two chiefs frowned at each other in a threatening manner. In the background sat a miscellany of observers, some from the Buddhist government of that country, but others from the United Nations, the Vatican and Nato. All of them had an interest in establishing peace in that area, albeit for various reasons.

"Thank you for coming to this meeting," began Kevin, putting on his poshest voice. "Both Mr. Chom and Mr. Flam have invited us to broker a peace deal which will end the war between those two countries. I want an undertaking from you both that no one leaves this meeting until we have the deal sown up. Do I have your word, gentlemen?"

"You have my word," stated Mr. Flam steadily, "as a gentleman," he emphasized slowly, "but I wonder if the other guy is a gentleman."

Mr. Chom winced a little at the implied insult, but hurled it back with his doctrinaire retort, "gentleman! Huh! Bourgeois reactionary fascist claptrap."

The exchange of provocations was cut short by Kevin tapping his gavel on the desk. "that's enough. We will never achieve anything if we go on like that. I know that both sides are in urgent need of a peace settlement. That in effect means give and take on both sides. If the war escalates and the weaponry gets increasingly devastating, that will ruin both countries and there will be no winners."

"What makes you think it will escalate?" demanded Mr. Chom.

"It always does," replied Kevin, "and if it comes to nuclear weapons the whole area will be saturated with radio-active fallout."

"We haven't got any nukes," lied Mr. Chom.

"Don't pull my leg," replied Kevin, "one of your lads let drop inadvertently."

"Well he's got chemical weapons," pointed Mr. Chom at Mr. Flam.

"I have not," lied Mr. Flam, "what a nasty accusation."

"True though," countered Kevin, "why don't you just admit it?"

"You're bluffing," snapped the little black moustache.

"No I'm not. Tell me then, why did Betty and I see blokes wearing chemical suits?"

That shut him up, and Mr. Chom.

"Now you see the urgency for settling this matter up," emphasized Kevin. "We have had a tour of both your countries, and to be quite candid, you both have the same problem and the same sort of dictatorship, the same repressive measures to cope with your dissidents. The only difference between you is the labelling and swanking. You might as well shake hands and decide to work together for one big improved country.

"There can only be one president," nattered Mr. Chom, "so one of us will have to go."

"How about you, you Marxist idiot?" jeered Mr. Flam.

Mr. Chom stuck his hand in his pocket and pulled out a revolver, aiming it at Mr. Flam. This was only matched by Mr. Flam dragging out his revolver. But something strange happened to both weapons. To the amazement and consternation of all present (except Betty) both weapons sagged down into soggy plasticine and deposited a wad of bullets on the carpet. One of the Buddhist observers at the back burst out laughing. Betty hastily slid her straw basket out of sight again before they could work out what had happened. A ripple of laughter gradually seeped through the entire assemblage of dignitaries.

"What's happened?" juddered Mr. Flam.

"Here!" snapped Mr. Chom, grabbing at one of his Field Marshals, "lend me your rifle."

But this was to no avail for when he aimed it at Mr. Flam, the rifle did a curious wibbly-wobbly, leaving itself doing a creditable imitation of a piggy-wig's curly tail. The whole room descended into tumultuous hilarity, except for Mr. Chom who was flabbergasted.

"Now can you get this into your heads?" shouted Kervin, "stop this infantile nonsense, this cowboy pop-gun mentality. We have the means to bust all your weapons of war and we will do it unless you grow up and renounce warfare. NOW!"

"How did you do that?" demanded Mr. Chom, totally amazed.

"Can you show me that again?" stared Mr. Flam, totally intrigued.

Two soldiers, one from each side, stepped out and held out their assault rifles. Everyone watched in anticipation. There came a sort of burping sound from below the table as Betty kept the basket out of sight. Both guns collapsed into wibbly-wobbly jelly, leaving a pile of bullets on the carpet. After three or four demonstrations, everybody dissolved into hysterical giggles and belly-laughs. The war was as good as over; there was no more point in threatening each other with weapons.

"Now!" demanded Kevin, "I want all your armaments dragged out and assembled at a given spot on the frontier… all of them…and no cheating, and we shall jigger the lot of them."

This was met with a massive cheer from the observers at the back, and gradually the diplomatic corps on both sides began to join in. There was no way the war could continue given this mysterious method that was at work, wrecking all their weapons. The two presidents converged on each other, hands outstretched to shake hands and sink their differences.

It was a pity that both of them chanced to walk into the residual beam emitting from that straw basket, for both of them did a slight trip up, caused by the descent of two pairs of trousers! But the net effect was, that they banged their heads together; but this was a tactic which ought to have been administered to them years ago. But the head banging had the effect of clouting their egos down to some extent and advising them to have just a smidgeon of humility and co-operation. The whole room erupted in hilarity and congratulation.

•

Home was not very far away now, as the executive jet pulled to a halt on the tarmac. Betty was still clutching that all-important straw basket and Kevin kept fingering the battery in his pocket. It had been quite a tour de force to extricate themselves from the Republic of Chiploddy. Both dictators had decided that the romantic couple were the best idea since the advent of sliced bread. There had been many inducements to stay on and help with the bright future that both countries could welcome, now that warfare was a thing of the past. The chauffeur, who was still terrified out of his wits, and wanted to disappear off to Britain with them, had to be assured that he would not be victimized. But a new atmosphere of freedom, acceptance and democracy was now emanating from both presidential palaces. They had even reached an arrangement whereby each president took a turn at being head of state of the two combined countries, the swap over being effected on January 1st each year. Everyone was totally relieved and thankful.

The other important item being fetched back from Chiploddy was a cheque for a rather large sum of money. This was carefully lodged in Betty's handbag. As the taxi conveyed them through the town, they gained the impression that there was no further damage caused to the metal fittings on view. Whoever it was that had vandalized the town last time, must have thought better of it.

As they approached the house in Venture Street, they were enraptured by the sound of a violin being played in ecstasies. Sally was clearly at her best and the men of the house were hovering about the corridor to give their ears the full benefit. A tap on the front door (newly installed) at first failed to grab their attention, until at last, Jimmy the Wiser, gave them admittance.

"What's this we've been hearing about you two?" he rejoiced, "the great peacemakers."

They all gravitated to the kitchen for that vital cup of tea that Sally always had ready. Kevin and Betty gave a full account of their exploits, much to the delight of Larry, who at last could see that his ground-breaking idea was now actually breaking something. That something might not be ground, but it certainly was prejudices, penal compounds, and arbitrary labelling systems.

"We've been following you on the news," jazzed Sally, "those observers at the peace conference have told the entire world about you two. Everybody is excited. Already we have had a dozen invitations from as many countries to go and settle their disputes. Where would you like to go next? America, or Russia?"

"I wouldn't like to go anywhere," Kevin shook his head wearily, "I could just do to have a few quiet weeks with my wife," as he embraced Betty, "and keep out of sight."

"So who can we send now?" Sally quizzed, "how about Jimmy and Derek?"

"I don't know about Jimmy," Betty shook her head, "there might not be any wallets left in that country when he comes back." Everyone laughed.

"I'm on the level now," came the protest from the Cockney expert, "and anyway, I haven't managed to find that con-artist that's pinched one of your machines."

"Have you made any progress with that?" asked Kevin.

"We don't think it's Fred Wallitude," sighed Sally, "I rang his office every two days and he was actually there, making a fool of himself as usual. He thinks K stands for cretin, nine means nearly ten, and P is something you have on your lunch plate." She pulled a face, and everyone laughed.

•

As the firm wandered off, leaving Sally and Larry on their own, a strange quiet descended on the house.

"Larry," she confided, "where is all this leading?"

"Down to the vicarage to put up the Banns," he remarked, goofily.

"My word, you've actually thought about that, Larry," she congratulated, "and when will that auspicious occasion come to pass?" It was a fact that Dr. Lawrence Robinson was not quite so fixated on cloud-cuckoo land as he had been. The thought of marrying Sally had gradually wrought a change in his psyche. He was now hook-line-and-sinker in love with her. "What about tomorrow?" he gurgled into his cup of tea, omitting to take the legalities realistically.

"That sounds a bit precipitate," she teased, "but seriously

though, Larry, can you honestly say you are in love with me?"

"Yes!" he slammed his cup down, "I'm crazy about you."

"And are you going to let me just keep tabs on some of the daft ideas you get?"

"Yes darling," he admitted, "I need you like Pooh Bear needs his honey pot. You keep me sweet and focused on life, you know, realities. You can be the boss, Boss," he proclaimed.

"The first reality to face, Doc, " she warned, "is that money that keeps rolling in. I think we are probably worth about two million now... And it will get to be more as more countries come seeking our help. Clearly we need to have some sort of plan..."

"Have a snorting good honeymoon," he exploded, slapping the table. "You are a lovely young lady."

Sally's mouth dropped wide open. She had no idea how much Larry had changed over the last few days. He was clearly losing interest in gadgets and fiddling in his laboratory. The romantic bug had caught him. He was turning into a high-powered Casanova. It occurred to her that this might not last forever. Never mind; make hay while the sun shines, went through her head, or to put it another way, make love while the Robbo is smiling.

CHAPTER 18
GOVERNMENT INTERVENTION

One find morning, just as breakfast was coming to a conclusion, the telephone rang. It was Frederick Wallitude at the Ministry, wanting to pay a visit. It sounded urgent.

"You don't seriously want to come again," teased Sally, "after that unseemly scene with your trousers falling down."

"Ah well," he prevaricated, "the precipitousness of the nether garments has been corretituded with extra reinforciments of a non-metallic naturaltude."

"In other words, you've got a piece of string to hold your bags up?" she sneered. "No, I really think you ought to think better of coming here. After all, you aren't very popular, after the way you tried to pinch one of our gadgets."

Derek Normbrain was shaking his head solemnly. "Not that fathead again," he sighed into the toast and marmalade. "Can't they send someone with a smidgeon of grey matter?"

Fred probably heard that, but it made no impression. "I have to stratify," he coughed, "the top gentlemen from Downworthy Streak are compulsifying me."

"In other words," Sally sniffed, "the PM says you've got to. Is that right?"

"The responsitude would tend to be on the affirmitatiousness. It's an order."

"What makes you think we will allow you on the premises, Fred?" she threatened.

"I'm sure that blokey Chobinson will see a little reationalisatitude. He likes me, I think," he added with a touch of uncertainty in his usual self-assured tone of voice.

"That bloke Chobinson, I assume you mean Dr. Lawrence Robinson, will do as I tell him," she snapped archily, "I am his keeper, his moral controller and his wife," she bluffed.

Fred ignored that and tossed out the threat. "I'll be along in about an hourfulness, and I shall have policeperson with a warrant-document in attendance with my very good self."

"Bad self," muttered Sally as the receiver went down. "Now chaps, that idiot is coming with a warrant. I assume it's a search warrant."

"What if it's a warrant for Larry's arrest?" speculated Jimmy. "Mind you, he 'aint done noffink. He's too stupid to commit a crime."

"We have an hour to get ready," shouted Sally, "and we need a plan. Shut up and listen."

•

The looming crisis of forty nine and a half minutes expectation turned out to be more of a crisis than any of them had imagined. Mind you, they could have expected something like this, given the significance of Larry's invention for the whole world. The message had got round, not just Africa, but everywhere else. Warfare and armaments were a thing of the past. At least, everybody else thought so, even if Fred Wallitude was in denial of it.

A car pulled up outside the front door, but it was not the only one. There were two others. Fred Wallitude found himself confronted by a beefy gentleman with a massive Havana cigar in his mouth and a self-introduction which went like, "Well, wadyer know, pardner?" The other gentleman, immaculately smart, emitted a heavily accented greeting, which was suggestive of the highest level of KGB-it is. As they tapped on the front door, each eyed the other with suspicion.

"I have an appointment at this house," Fred tried to sound super-important, "I suggest you wait outside in your cars."

"The Hell we will," snapped the American, "we wanna know about this invention."

The door opened on a chain, mind you, it was a new one from the DIY. "Not today, thank you," called Sally. "Jehovah's Witnesses, by the looks of it. Or is it the Mormons? We've got religion already, so go away, please."

At that moment, Sergeant Muldoon appeared with Julie Mayfair. He held out a warrant to search the house. "Now Sally, let's have no nonsense. Mr. Wallitude is from the Ministry and we urgently need to find out what's going on here."

"Coppers?" spat the big cigar, "why? Is this guy a crook?"

"We've been through all this before," sighed Sally, "and

who the dickens are these other blokes pestering us? Why don't you all clear off?"

After some more altercation, the visitors oozed down to the back yard in another attempt at contacting Dr. Robinson. Kevin and Jimmy decided to keep the foreign visitors talking in the yard while the Police and Wallitude invaded the kitchen. Sally held Larry's hand and advertised the gold ring that he had hastily planted on her fourth left. "So what's this all about?" she demanded aggressively.

"It's something of a crisicus," began Fred, as he poured himself out a cup of tea.

"Look!" stormed Sally, "just use plain language will you? You don't impress anyone, Fred, in fact, you just make a complete idiot of yourself."

"I think we are in deep waters this morning," warned Derek Normbrain, "you see those two gentlemen outside in the yard? The one with the cigar is Charles Nonkwhistle, one of the leading scientists from America, and the other is a top scientific adviser from the Soviet Union and he's in the KGB."

It was as if the sun had come out to shine; Fred Wallitude's face lit up with one of those 'ah-ha' realizations. "K_9P!" he enthused, "obviously a mistake for KGB. A shame that Irish bloke didn't speak clearly. Of course! And I thought it was meant to be a chemical formula, well, well!" It was so self-congratulatory that Sally and Larry split out laughing.

Normbrain stared at him in derision. "You clot, Fred! Now just what are you up to today? Stop messing us about."

"For starters," Fred looked around furtively, "I want my secretary back. That Miss Marston has gone missing for too long. If she doesn't come back pronto, I shall have to sack her."

"I don't think she'd mind at all if you did that, Fred," grinned Larry, "you see she's changed her name. She's entered into a new phase of life, a thing called Holy Matrimony."

"And the other person I want back is you, Derek," he nattered, "what on earth are you doing here? You can't just walk out on us. You're a vital part of our team."

"I'm very happy here," replied the senior scientist, "much valued and most welcome. Doc Robinson and I make a splendid team. We have achieved so much, that I wouldn't dream of coming back to your bonkers Ministry."

"You can't just walk out on us," yapped Fred, "you know too much. Official secrets and all that. Anyway, this business going on here. That ought to be under official secrets, instead of which, it's in the newspapers all over the world. We are faced with a jumbo-sized crisis."

"Well so far, we've managed to bring two pairs of warring countries to the peace conference and stop them shooting at each other," Larry sounded so pleased with himself, "aren't you pleased about that?"

"That sounds all very well," nattered Fred, "but we've got to consider the bigger picture. The Yanks and Reds are yelling to have this gadget that they think will disarm the other side." He pointed out into the yard, "you see, they've found you and they won't go away until they've got a gadget. Heaven knows what the long term consequences will be."

"Peace and security for the whole world," stated Derek with some conviction.

"Back to blowpipes and catapults," muttered Muldoon,

cynically.

"But according to you," smiled Sally, "it's impossible to de-materialize metal, so that gadget is a con, isn't it?"

"Of course it's a con," snapped Fred, "I don't know how your friend Kerry managed it, but he got those stupid countries to disarm. Clever lad! But how long will that last? It won't take them long to realize it was a conjuring trick, and then they'll be back where they started, knocking the stuffing out of each other." It was about as cynical as it was self-assured.

"Well actually, it isn't," stated Derek solemnly, "Fred; for Pete's sake face realities. That gadget can de-materialize metal and you're losing the plot... In fact, you never actually had the plot."

"OK!" the clotworthy expert sighed, "in which case you won't mind if we take one away to London and have it analysed. Sergeant Muldoon, why don't you go ahead and search the house and see if you can recover a gadget?"

"Just a minute," demanded Sally, "you may have the right to search this house, but you haven't any reason to remove anything which is not illegal or stolen property. I would point out that my husband," she gave him a surreptitious grin, "has patented this machine and he has all the rights on it. If you try to pinch his idea, he can sue you."

The confused expert gestured to Muldoon to commence his search, but Julie Mayfair remained at Sally's side. "Fancy marrying a genius like that," she whispered in Sally's ear, "you could make a fortune with an idea like that. What are you going to invent next, Doc?" she enticed.

"I erm..." Larry winked, "what about a machine that will fix charming young police ladies up with suitable boyfriends," he teased. "I know what it's like to be in love," he jigged up and down. "It's absolutely wizard, don't you agree, Miss Wil… Erm, I mean, Mrs. Robinson?"

"That's a wonderful idea," giggled constable Mayfair, "but seriously, you need a machine to get rid of people like that in the yard…" she pointed through the window, "would you like me to move them on… You know, charge them with obstruction?"

At that, Jimmy tapped on the window. "They want to talk to you. At least give them a chance, Mate."

Muldoon reappeared, holding a small metal box in his hand. "Is this what you're looking for, Mr. Wallitude?"

"Careful!" gasped Larry, "you could do a lot of damage with that."

Fred yanked it out of the hands of the Law and beamed all over his self-assured face. "Terrific!" he ranted, "my colleagues in London will soon have this analysed and assessed," and he started for the door without so much as a thank you or a by-your-leave.

"Oi! Come back with that," shouted Sally, "you idiot. At least you can give me a receipt for it."

But the expert was in no mood for courtesies and decencies. He was off to his car. They could hear his door slam and the engine rev up, and he was off with screeching tyres and disregard for speed limits.

"Sorry about that," murmured Muldoon, "that is your property, I assume, Dr. Robinson. I will fix you up with a receipt, though I doubt whether you will ever get it back."

"Can't you nobble him for speeding?" demanded Sally, "anyway, I think we might be having a stormy session in a minute, with these two foreign gentlemen. Are you any good at keeping the peace, Sarge?"

The scientific visitors infiltrated the kitchen and sat meekly awaiting a conference.

"All right!" Sally dominated the scene, "I'm in charge here. No nonsense! No insults! You can have your chance if you are polite, reasonable and have peaceful intentions. You first, Charlie."

The American looked a little surprised, but then he recognized Derek Normbrain. "Is this Dactor Robinson?" he pointed with his cigar, "well wadda guy! You invented a machine to bust all the armaments? You need a Purple Heart, Buster."

"I'm quite happy with this red one," Larry slapped his chest, "and I've given it to my true love," and he squeezed Sally's hand. "She's the nicest lady I could wish for, as my wife."

"A red one?" interrupted the Russian, "we've got loads of red medals. Just name the one you want, Mister." The accent was so heavy, they could hardly decipher it.

"Thing is, we gadda have peace…and away with this nook-threat," Charlie recommenced. "My pal Ivanov agrees with me. It's such a waste of dough and nobody's safe. How d'we get this idea off the ground?"

"We can ask that nice Irishman to come and broker a peace deal?" begged Ivanov, "is he here? That gentleman we saw on the newsreels. He was absolutely charming, and managed to convince those idiots to stop it. And that charming lady, his wife."

"They've managed to nip off on their honeymoon," explained Sally. "But they'll be back and they are keen to broker all kinds of peace deals to a dozen countries." She picked up a fistful of papers, all of which were appeals to pay a visit to troubled parts of the world.

"I think the first thing is to ask you two gentlemen, have you got authority from your governments, to enter into negotiations?" Derek was the usual sane brain with basic common sense.

"I can assure you, you guys," Charlie fished out a piece of paper, "that I have full permission from the White House, to find out what's going on, from Dac Robinson himself, and report back so that a proper summit conference can be arranged. As a leading scientist in the States, they will listen to what I say."

"I can say the same for my government," the Russian gentleman insisted, "they are very keen to find out the truth in this matter. If you can assure us that this new idea really works, then it is obvious, we need a summit conference and tell the world there is no point in hoarding masses of weapons. We could decommission them all, and spend the money on something worthwhile."

There was so much good will and atmosphere of co-operation, that Sally was quite impressed. The gentlemen were conveyed upstairs to view a demonstration of the gadget, while Sally and Julie Mayfair stayed behind to have a woman to woman chat.

"But that Fred's removed the gadget," Julie realized, "they can't have a demonstration."

"Between you and me," Sally wagged a finger, "and this is strictly confidential. We left out just one, the prototype for Muldoon to find. All the rest of them, about ten, are hidden somewhere else. They are the ones that work properly, and the controls are perfected."

"So what about this prototype? Can Fred pinch the idea from that?"

"I suppose he could, but knowing that idiot, he won't be able to resist having a fiddle with it, and he has not had any training in how to use it. The result might be very interesting," she sniggered. "He might get a nasty surprise."

"Serve him right if he does," Julie concurred, "he's such a pushy clever-dick."

CHAPTER 19
RIGHT SORT OF TONE

"It's got a lovely tone," sighed Julie Mayfair as she imbibed the lovely medodies coming from Sally's violin, "had you ever thought of going professional?"

"I don't think I could stand it," muttered Sally into the bridge, "these big orchestras expect you to drop everything with a few hours' notice and hurtle off to some faraway place. I'm quite happy settled here and I'm getting married, so that puts the lid on it."

"Are you sure that isn't a Strad?" frowned Julie, "it sounds absolutely sublime. Have you ever had it valued?"

"I know it's a very old one," agreed Sally, "and I once had a dealer take a look at it. He told me it definitely isn't a Strad. It's been in the family for umpteen generations."

"Do play some more," begged Julie. She stared out into the street and became aware of an assemblage of strange-looking people of many different nationalities, all pushing and shoving to make an approach to the front door. "I think I might be needed to stay on with you. It seems you've got company."

As Sally played on, making a superb rendering of one

of Handel's sonatas, Julie went out on to the pavement and began to shoo people away.

•

As the gentlemen from upstairs descended, their ears were blessed with the lovely sounds of a Mendelssohn Concerto. Mr. Nonkwhistle leant against the doorpost and flicked his cigar.

"Well waddayer know?" he murmured, "what a little honey?"

"We could do with her in the Soviet Union," added Ivanov, green with envy.

"Leave her to it," ordered Larry, "she's mine, so hands off! You said you wanted to make phone calls, gentlemen… come this way."

As the strains of Mendelssohn drifted through to the kitchen, Charlie won the toss and put in a call to his embassy in London. "No kiddin," he insisted, "the doofer sure works. What shall we offer them?…a million?" he cast a glance at Larry, who shook his head. "Gatta do better than that, Buster… No time to waste…there's a guy here from Redland… Baloney!… AW shurrup!" The receiver went down. "We need a top level conference on nootral ground, you guys."

"The doofer, as you call it, is not for sale," stated Normbrain, firmly. "There is a fee for one of our team to come and operate it, as you have already seen, but we are not letting this doofer out of our sight. In the hands of someone irresponsible, and not properly trained, it could cause all sorts of problems."

Mr. Ivanov was now calling his embassy. "Whatever they want, we will double it," he repeated, "you sure we can afford that?...no choice, if it's the real thing."

"Two million," muttered Ivanov.

"Two million what?" cut in Jimmy, "monopoly money, is it?"

"We certainly would like the monopoly on it," replied Ivanov, "but I suppose that is like wanting to own the Moon. I suppose the best way is to have a turn with that nice Mr. Kerry and his wife. We shall invite them to the Kremlin and give them the freedom of Moscow."

"We are sure impressed with your demonstration, Dac," Charlie enthused, "do yer think that thing could bust a big thing like a battleship or an aircraft carrier?"

"We haven't tried anything as big as that yet," explained Larry, "but we do know it can bust a tank and an artillery gun. We could always do some trials."

"Might not actually need to bust an entire ship," added Normbrain, "if you just jigger the controls that would be enough, or perhaps muck up the propeller or the rudder. That would render the whole thing as scrap."

"Whatever it can or can't do," cut in Sally, "it's important that we all work together. It would be a big mistake if one side should gain the advantage and upset the balance of power. We are going to keep control of this gadget. It is not for sale. There is a fee for our team to visit your several countries and effect the disarmament."

"Quite right," sniffed Nonkwhistle, "fair does and no cheating. You agree, Mr. Ivanov?"

"It is only common sense," he smiled, "we, the big

powers, must behave responsibly over this matter. We need a summit conference somewhere like Iceland and map out a process for disarmament."

Just at that moment, the kitchen door burst open and a scruffy bloke with a camera began to point it at the assembled group. It was a newspaper reporter. Jimmy was right behind him and jogged his arm every time he tried to take a picture.

"Out!" bellowed Sally, "who the dickens are you?"

"Daily Gutterscraper," the man boasted, as if he owned the place. "Must catch the evening issue. This is Dr. Robinson?" he pointed at Normbrain.

Sally pushed Larry down under the table and held a serviette over Derek's face. "I said, get out," she shrieked, "how dare you come bursting in here like the Light Brigade. Jimmy; chuck him out and send him packing."

"No problem," Jimmy replied, as he got the bloke into a half-Nelson, "this way, and don't bother to come back." As the reporter found himself in the yard, he collided with about ten more of the same ilk.

"Did you get a picture?" fussed one of them, "I'll pay you for a copy." As he reached for his wallet, he came to realize that it was somewhat difficult to locate.

All this commotion was quelled as Julie Mayfair applied the authority of the Law and made them all ooze out into the street, to merge with the foreign diplomats. Whereupon another brouhaha developed over who was to be the first to interview the famous Dr. Robinson.

Julie returned to the kitchen, flustered and annoyed. "You are going to need a security fence round these premises," she suggested, "they will be pestering you all night. Is there anywhere you can move out to, to escape from them?"

"Not really," cried Sally, as she was near to tears, "I suppose we're under siege here. Can we have police protection? Can't you arrest the lot of them for something?"

Muldoon appeared in the kitchen doorway. "In the circumstances, and seeing how important this matter is, I think we can have a police protection arrangement fixed up. I have just been on to my superiors and they have been on to Scotland Yard. These premises are to be kept under police patrol until we can decide what to do with you people. I would also suggest that Mr. Nonkwhistle and Mr. Ivanov should stay on here rather than try to go away."

"We orta stay on," the big cigar wobbled, "and let our guys from the embassy fill us in with the next step. The whole thing is a matter of tight security now and we can't just have any idiot bursting in here trying to harass the Dac and his missus."

"I am right with you," concurred Ivanov, "and since we are in complete agreement, I think this calls for a celebration, don't you?" Whereupon, he pulled out a bottle of vodka. Sally produced some glasses. The first round of drinks had the wonderful effect of easing off the tension. Ivanov wanted to know about the resolution between the Communists and the Fascists in Chiploddy Land.

"Quite simple really," Derek sipped, "Kevin and Betty did a tour of both countries, found out what was going on behind the scenes, you know, the concentration camps and what-have-you, and threatened to expose both of them to the world. Even the citizens of those countries were largely unaware of what was going on. Anyway, the threat of that, and the promise of cessation of hostilities was enough to make them see sense."

"I take my fur hat off to them," Ivanov elevated his hat, "down with all the political prison business, gulags and the like. We all knew this Stalinist method would come unstuck in the end. You may win battles and defeat the enemy, but you can't defeat the people. In the end, freedom will assert itself, and now we can have our opinion and whatever religious faith we want without the police poking their noses in. Bravo for Kevin and Betty.

The second round loosened them up even more. "I think your noo bloke, what's-his-name, Nokker-moff, is it?" Charlie slurped.

"Mr. Nockermov," Ivanov double-slurped.

"Will he knock 'em off like old Jo Stalin did?" Charlie was becoming increasingly loquacious.

"Thank God we've got away from that era," sighed Ivanov, "he was just a criminal, and mass murderer. I don't think any of your presidents have been like that."

"Nah!" snorted Charlie, "just stoopud instead. These rich guys have no idea what it's like to be poor. Why they can't bring themselves to have a National Health Service like this country, Heaven only knows. They think it's Camyernism. Phaw!"

The third round, at which Derek Normbrain began to show a modicum of restraint, had the two foreign visitors joking, teasing and belly-laughing. Sally began to feel most uncomfortable and Larry just stared in amazement. At that moment the kitchen door began to open yet again, as Jimmy infiltrated the house.

"I fink we'd better let this one in," he besought, "'e's not a reporter or a foreign diplomat, but 'e is from the British Government."

Sergeant Muldoon eased a certain bedraggled spectacle into the house and sat him down in between Charlie and Ivanov. The specimen in question was indeed a sight to be seen. His suit was rumpled and torn, his face was blackened with soot and he exuded a perfume which was a cross between sulphur dioxide and essence of petroleum. He was speechless, but two little tears began to form in the corners of his eyes, and then trickle down his cheeks, making artistic streaks down his collar which might have been white some time ago. Do we need to guess who this was?"

"Fred Wallitude!" gasped Normbrain, "what on earth…?"

Muldoon produced his notebook and spake forth the oracle. "This gentleman," there was a sneer in his voice," on leaving these premises, in possession of a certain stolen item, went through a speed trap at the rate of 90 MPH. The police car decided to give chase. When it caught up with him, he was found to have parked in a layby, but strangely, his car had just disintegrated and the gentleman," the sneer slightly increased, "was sprawled over a pile of dirty plastic bits and sitting in a puddle of petrol. My colleague had the presence of mind too pull him out of the wreckage just as the petrol caught light from someone throwing a cigarette butt from a passing car."

"The question will be, Sir and Madam, do you wish to press charges?" Julie quizzed, hopefully.

"See you in court," coughed Fred indistinctly. "What a filthy trick, handing me a nasty thing like that, and why is it that I smell of bad eggs?"

Jimmy winked at the assemblage. "I slipped a couple of stink bombs in his car," he whispered.

"Well, Mr. Wallitude," the Sergeant resumed, "I am a witness to your removing that so-called nasty thing against the wishes of Mrs. Robinson, who ordered you to hand it back. But you ignored that and drove off."

"You asked for that, Fred," snapped Sally, "and are you going to hand it back to us, our rightful property?"

There was an awkward silence which was an indication that the gadget was in no shape to be handed back to anyone. Charlie and Ivanov, who were both rather tanked up, dissolved into giggles and chortles, uncontrollably. They thought that was just poetic justice; and indeed it was.

CHAPTER 20
THE NEGOTIATIONS

After some discussion and a sobering up session, it was decided that Professor Derek Normbrain was the best gentleman to conduct negotiations on neutral territory. Everyone agreed that he had a generous slice of common sense and was quite well experienced in coping with idiots. Mr. and Mrs. Kerry, who were the main target of appeals, were still not back from their honeymoon and no one had the heart to drag them back prematurely. Fred Wallitude, now totally discredited, was regarded as a numbskull even by the other numbskulls at the research establishment. The gentlemen in Downing Street had decided that no more frantic mistakes like that could afford to be perpetrated, and resolved to take matters into their own hands and impose their own version of crackpot strategies on the situation.

So it was that the next morning, no less, a smart political gentleman from the Ministry of Defence was ushered into Sally's kitchen. He was now not quite as smooth and self-assured as he had been when he had set out from London. This was because it had taken half an hour for him to battle his way into the back yard and impress the urgency of his having an interview with the great inventor. Jimmy opened the kitchen door and inserted the gentleman rather abruptly.

"And who the dickens are you?" demanded Sally.

"Let me introduce myself," came the posh voice, "I am Arthur Richardson-Maudsley, the under minister for defence. I urgently need to confer with this Dr. Robinson. We have a full-scale diplomatic brouhaha on our hands."

"It's no good trying to arrange anything with Robbo," she riposted, "he's a complete nit-wit. I am his spokesman…"

"Don't you mean 'spokesperson'?" came politically correct tut-tut from under the bowler hat.

"I think you'd better chat to Professor Normbrain. He is Robbo's development partner…"

That cheered Arthur up a little, that bit of sociological phrasing. "Oh wonderful! Yes, I've heard of him at the research establishment. Very sound man. Can be relied upon to offer reliable advice. Is he here?"

Derek shuffled his way into the kitchen. "Oh, it's you, Arthur, " he exclaimed, as he finished chewing his toast and marmalade. "Yes, we need someone in authority to sort things out. You realize that we had Charlie Nonkwhistle and Mr. Ivanov here, both wanting a top level deal."

"Well I don't think," came the elevated comment, "that that was quite politically correct, old chap. I mean, before inviting in people like that, you could have consulted with us, for goodness sake. I mean, there are procedures," he wobbled his eyebrows in a threatening manner.

"You mistake the situation, Arthur," came the steady reply, "no one invited them. They just turned up on the doorstep, demanding to discuss things with Larry... I mean, Dr. Robinson."

While this was going on, Larry was staring from one gentleman to the other, with that goofy look smeared all over his face, that is, apart from the recent application of marmalade to the end of his nose. His mouth steadily dropped wide open with admiration at Derek and Arthur's elevated discussion. Arthur stared at Larry and rapidly came to the conclusion that he was faced with a complete cuckoo. "Is this Lawrence Robinson?" he stared, "did he really invent that funny machine?" It was loaded with disbelief.

"Yes of course he did," snapped Sally, "he's brilliant but on the other hand, he's a complete nooney-brain, aren't you, Larry?"

"Yes darling," he gawped, empty-headedly.

"I am in charge of him. I am his keeper. His housekeeper, zookeeper, gamekeeper, and anything else keeper, such as the utility bills. If it weren't for me, he'd be in piles of trouble. As it is, we're all in piles of trouble together, unless of course, Mr. Maudsley, you with your political skills can fix things up between the nations."

"I'm not sure I've got the clout to do that," coughed Arthur, "I mean, the Yanks and the Ruskies are tussling over this new development, and if one of them gets it and the other doesn't, we could be in for massive trouble."

"I can correct you on that, " interposed Normbrain. "Those two are not tussling. They are in full agreement with each other. They both want disarmament as long as it applies to both sides equally. The only thing they're not agreed on is the money that should be paid to rent this gadget."

"What if one of them buys it outright?" snapped Arthur.

"It's not for sale," retorted Derek, "it is kept firmly in the hands of our trained representatives, and they do all the negotiating with the heads of state."

"Would that be Mr. and Mrs. Kerry?" came the suspicious retort. "They can't do that! That's outrageous! Neither of them represent this government or any other as far as I know. This task must be taken on by properly appointed persons in discussion with the top level. I mean, that Mr. Kerry," it came down his nose, "is Irish, isn't he, and a Roman Catholic," the voice registered disgust.

"So what?" exploded Sally, "what difference does that make? If he can do the job, so be it. He's a lovely chap, and has an engaging way with everyone, and so does Betty. They have just managed to charm two warring states into coming to their senses. Why not let them carry on?"

"Because he has no mandate," yapped Arthur.

"And Betty hasn't got a womandate, you're going to say," chimed Sally, "come on. All these years, with the Cold War, and you chaps in London haven't managed to sort it out. All you lot have done is bunk up the arms race. Now is your chance to chuck it completely and have world peace."

"I don't know what I'm going to say to the minister," muttered Arthur. "Anyway I am empowered to make you an offer. Her Majesty's Government is prepared to buy this invention off you, complete with all the rights."

"Not for sale," Derek shook his head, firmly. "In any case, you'd probably blow yourselves up, like that idiot Wallitude. " That caused sniggers all round.

"How about £500?" suggested Arthur.

That caused hilarity all round the room.

"Why don't you start at twenty million?" jeered Jimmy.

"Twenty million," choked Arthur, "it's more than my job's worth to offer that sort of money."

"Keep trying. We can already get twenty five from the Yanks and even more from the Reds," boasted Sally.

"My dear young lady, haven't you got any sense of loyalty to your country?" Arthur tried the patriotism-glug.

"I might, but Kevin won't. Remember, he's from Southern Ireland and he doesn't like you guys in London.

Arthur tried the threat-glug. "We could of course confiscate the thing and charge you with inventing a dangerous gadget," came the penciled threat.

"It's not a dangerous gadget if you know how to handle it," insisted Derek, "of course, if you're an idiot like your friend Wallitude, then you will cause all sorts of problems."

"All these new ideas are potentially dangerous until we learn how to handle them," cut in Larry. "Take for instance electricity, and nuclear power. In the wrong hands or being messed about with by an idiot, what do you expect?"

Arthur stared at Larry for a moment and nearly said, "he's not completely goo-goo after all, that Robinson." Then he coughed a little and began again. "I've had an idea," he ameliorated his tone a lot and came over all helpful. "Supposing… Just supposing, we fix you up with a decent laboratory of your own, Robinson? A secure research establishment so that people can't invade you and mess you about… like it is here…" and waved a paw at the hubble-bubble outside. "We look after you and you look after us? Does that sound fair?"

"Will the government swallow an idea like that?" Derek gawped.

"What about us?" Sally objected, "I'm his wife to be, and there's Jimmy to consider and the Kerries. And there's some blighter out there that's stolen one and pranking about with it. We have no idea who that would be."

"What sort of thing would you expect us to research?" asked Larry, "I mean, would you have some sort of expectation, such as…erm…?" he scratched his head.

"A gadget that could neutralize nuclear radiation," murmured Derek. "If we could devise something like that, it would solve all sorts of problems. All those atomic weapons stored up somewhere, could be neutralized and rendered safe. How does that grab you?"

"Now that sounds like a really worthwhile project," Arthur's face lit up. "I will now go and discuss these matters with the Minister and his advisers. We need a solution to this as soon as possible. In the meantime, I would ask you to keep the lid on this matter as much as possible. If I manage to arrange something, ideally we would move you out of here to somewhere secure and out of the public gaze. In addition, I would like to meet Mr. and Mrs. Kerry and resolve that problem. When are they due back from honeymoon? Have you any idea where they are?"

"I have no idea," stated Sally, "and if they do reappear, they will be in demand in America and in Russia. Both sides have taken a fancy to them."

Arthur Richardson Maudsley arose from his chair and raised his bowler hat. "I bid you good morning," he coughed, "and I will do what I can with the powers that be."

"How long will that be?" asked Jimmy as he slipped in from the yard.

"Same length as a piece of string," sighed Arthur with a tone of resignation.

"I'll ring yer up every day, Mate," came the generous offer, "and chivvy yer along, like."

"I would ask you to desist from such a course," came Arthur's snuffy official response. "In any case, you haven't got my number."

"Oh yes I 'ave, Cock," Jimmy waved a little card in his face. "good idea keeping it in yer wallet. I suppose yer want yer wallet back?" And he waved the object in front of Arthur's nose.

"Jimmy!!!" exploded Sally, "you blighter."

•

A few moments after Arthur's departure, the telephone rang. It was the Kerries.

"Sally!" Betty moaned, "we're back, but we can't even get into Venture Street. There's mobs of people and police everywhere. What can we do?"

Sally described how they could sneak in through the back garden and into the kitchen. A few minutes later, the slightly less happy couple managed to fight their way through the back yard and into the kitchen. Totally exhausted, they related how they had fared on honeymoon.

"Everywhere we went, people kept recognizing us," moaned Betty, "our faces have been in just about every newspaper in the world. It was that peace conference at

Chiploddy Republic. We just had to keep moving on. I think we've toured just about every part of Britain."

"But not Ireland," cut in Kevin. "How long will it be before certain people decide to track me down? I wish I'd never got involved in this business."

"Well you're in it up to your neck," sighed Derek, "the Yanks and the Ruskies both want you."

"What? To shoot me?"

"No, you nitwit, to broker a disarmament deal," cheered Derek.

"That sounds like progress," smiled Betty into her teacup.

"It would be if the British government would keep their big noses out of it," Sally sniffed.

"Anyway, we are going to be relocated," explained Jimmy, "to somewhere away from the public. It's going to be pretty soon."

"Why?" asked Kevin.

"Because a certain big-boy from Westminster is getting fed up with me ringing 'im up at the most embarrassing times of the day, like when 'e's chatting up his mistress."

CHAPTER 21
NEW QUARTERS

The poor old house in Venture Street looked particularly forlorn. All its occupants and contents had departed under police escort, and the place was sealed up in the face of any intrusions. All the luggage had been packaged up and taken off to the new venue.

A large Georgian Mansion stood imposingly a few yards from the beach. It was a beautiful cove on the south coast, but the whole area was sealed off by security fencing and armed guards. Jimmy had arrived with the furniture van as the first installment. He had an idea of how to furnish the house and set up the laboratory according to Larry's wishes. The guards on the gate eyed Jimmy with some suspicion until they saw his pass and identification. Jimmy was dubbed as essential personel for the research work. He thought that was quite a joke, but had every intention of staying with the action, since there had to be plenty of spondulicks chucking around.

The next vehicle was Mr. and Mrs. Kerry's car. With all that money coming from abroad, they had splashed out on a really posh automobile. The guards hardly needed to question their identities. Their faces were now world famous. Kevin was mightily relieved to enter a secure area, since that would mean his 'friends' from the Emerald Isle would have problems if they decided to nobble him. The expensive car was flanked by police motorcyclists and the barrier went up more or less automatically on their approach.

The next car was driven by Professor Derek Normbrain. He too was accompanied by police outriders. He had a stack of mysterious gadgets in the boot, and was glad to enter a secure area with them, for there was always the risk that someone like Wallitude would attempt to purloin one of them.

Sally had been persuaded to tootle along somewhat more slowly than the others, which would give the early birds a chance to set the house and laboratory up, so that they would not have to tire themselves out. Larry, who had failed his driving test about four times, sat beside his true love and was in total admiration of her driving skills. Sally had shooed the police away, for she found it most annoying to have two motorcyclists buzzing about in her wake. Since nobody knew who she or Larry were, it was reasonably safe to proceed on their own together. They had never appeared in the media so they were never recognized.

As they pulled up at the gate, the guards motioned her to stop.

"No entry here, Madam, this is a restricted area," the guard stated firmly.

"This is our new home," moaned Sally, "aren't you expecting us?"

The guard inspected his paperwork and coughed. "I

am expecting a Miss Sarah Wilkins and a Dr. Lawrence Robinson, a research expert."

"That's us," smiled Sally. "Go on, lift the barrier."

"I must ask you to identify yourselves," came the reply, "we can't have any old riff-raff interfering with the research. Have you got your passports, for instance?"

"No," Sally fumbled about, "but I've got my driving license. That should be enough for you."

The guard scrutinized the license and decided that was enough. "And what about the other feller?"

"I'm Larry Robinson," came the goofy remark from the passenger seat.

The guard scrutinized the imbecilic face for a moment or two. "Yes, I can see you're a right larry, young man, but can you identify yourself?"

"Why would I want to identify myself?" came the idiotic gurgle, "I know who I am, you clot."

But I need to know who you are, dummy-brain," the guard snorted, "it's true you know; there's one born every minute. Miss Wilkins, I must ask you to leave this specimen outside the enclosure. You can come in."

"But he's my boyfriend," she protested, "and we're getting married in a few days' time."

"What do you want to marry him for, Miss?" came the obvious question.

"I often wonder," sighed Sally, "but if I don't marry him, and get him under control, Lord knows what the consequences will be. Believe me, he's about the most brilliant scientist in the country and yet he's a complete nincompoop, aren't you, Larry?"

"She's even cleverer than me," came the batty response, "you should hear her playing the violin. It's enough to charm a rhinoceros in mid-charge."

"I'm sorry folks," the guard came over all firm, "unless I can see the gentleman's particulars, he will have to turn back and go away."

"He certainly will turn his back if he has to show his particulars," Sally was outraged, "how dare you speak to me like that? I would have you know, this is the famous Dr. Robinson, who invented the peace machine."

"What him?" the guard snorted, "blooming idiot. How could a clot like that invent anything apart from a botched up booze-up in a brewery?"

"I insist on speaking to your superiors," blasted Sally, "how dare you!"

The guard handed her a telephone receiver. It was a Captain MacDonald in his office at the nearest military base. "Who is that and what's the problem?"

"I'm Sally Wilkins and I've got Doc. Robinson with me. Your guard won't let him in, and he's being quite insulting."

"If Robinson has been insulting my staff, it's no wonder they won't let him in," came the stiff reprimand. "I knew there was something wrong with that bloke. Completely potty, if you ask me."

"He may indeed be completely potty," snapped Sally, "but you've got all his possessions, research equipment and his personal staff set up in that house, but you won't let him in, himself."

"Doolarly!" muttered the guard, "like something out of a Whitehall Fart, I mean Farce."

After about thirty minutes of wrangling, during which insults of many and varied qualities were exchanged over the telephone and with guard on the gate, permission was at last given for Larry to enter, on condition that he made a serious attempt at looking just a little more intelligent.

•

"I can't help looking completely bonkers," sighed Larry as he tucked into their first meal at their new premises.

"Never mind, Doc," sympathized Kevin, "as long as you keep that heart of gold, you've got, you'll do for me and Betty. That right, Betty?"

"Never mind that 'eart of gold," sniggered Jimmy, "what about our crock of gold with the help of that gadget you dreamt up, Doc?"

The Robinsons did not wish to draw attention to the fact that the back of their car had been somewhat heavily weighted down on their trip to their new quarters. They sat listening to the strains of Bach as Sally started up in her very own special music room, overlooking the sea. It was a beautiful setting, a vast improvement on Venture Street and far more private and secure. But the privacy was not to persist for much longer. The telephone shrilled. It was Captain MacDonald on the private line. He had the task of only allowing calls from prescribed persons to reach Kevin or Sally. The Captain wanted to know whether they were inclined to speak to a Mr. Charles Nonkwhistle who was representing the United States Government. Kevin was in agreement.

"Mr. Kerry," came the American accent, "at last I can talk to you. You must have heard about my visit to the Dac. What about us meeting and pushing on with this summit conference on disarmament? My friend Ivanov is equally keen. What's been the hold up?"

Kevin explained. "The Ministry of Defence decided to relocate us to somewhere secure and private. It's taken three weeks to get it fixed up and now we are here. I don't know where this is, but you must fix it up with Captain MacDonald. I'm very keen to talk to you and have you come over."

Sally breezed in and took the receiver. "Hi Charlie!" she chirped, "sooner we get things in motion the better."

"Hi, little Miss Paganini," the bluff feller from Wyoming teased, "time for another round of drinks."

"We do have a slight problem, Charlie," Sally warned, "the silly asses from the ministry are not too keen on Kevin being a negotiator. They think it's politically wrong, or something."

"Wadda load of baloney!" the cigar exploded, "that Kevin is a Natural and his wife. We confidently expect him to be in the chair at the conference, and he will sure charm them all, even the hawks. Would yet like me to get the President to insist?"

Kevin nodded vigorously; Sally went on. "If we get this conference off the ground, surely we should invite other countries with armaments and make a thorough job of it?"

"Well honey, yer fink of everfing," Charlie chuckled, "but don't get strung up, heh!"

Kevin took the receiver. "The thing that really convinced

them, was to give them a demonstration of how it works. You should have seen the looks on their faces, when we made their guns just collapse into a pile of mess, and their tanks go like soggy ice cream. See you soon."

•

A very expensive car pulled up outside the house and out stepped Mr. Arthur Richardson Maudsley, looking even more superior and pushy than ever.

"So you must be Mr. Kerry," came the snorty remark, "I don't think this is quite on, actually."

"I don't know what you're on, Mate," sneered Jimmy, "but I'm not on anything at all, stripe me pink. Never touch the junk."

"Can you explain to me," came the snuffish question, "if you are an Irish citizen, how can you handle these negotiations on behalf of the British Government? I think we are within our rights to send you back to Ireland where you belong." It was snooted down his nose.

"Am I a British citizen, Mr. Maudesley?" chimed in Betty.

"And who the dickens are you, Madam?" came the tonking put-down.

"I am Mrs. Elizabeth Kerry, Mr. Kerry's wife. I understand that since he married me, he could become a British citizen, so you can't send him back to Ireland." It had raised all kinds of fears in her mind. The smart, purposeful insistent young lady made quite an impression on Arthur. "You can see my passport if you like." That whiff of expensive perfume and confident manner made him stop and think.

"How do you like your new billet?" demanded Arthur, "to your liking, I assume?"

"This is fantastic," enthused Sally.

"I was hoping to have a word with Dr. Robinson," came the thinly-veiled demand.

"He's already upstairs in his new laboratory with Derek Normbrain, and he's got started on the project you suggested," Sally pointed upwards. They listened for a moment and could hear various funny noises from above.

"Project?" came the puzzled reply, "what was that?" He had totally forgotten about it.

As Arthur infiltrated the lab, he could see Derek and Larry fiddling about with wires and control knobs. They were totally absorbed in their experimentation.

"Let's try a quick slurp of this," nattered Larry, and he picked up a bottle of purple liquid and applied a few drops to another strange potion. "And maybe a twinkling of this," and he picked up another bottle with a bright pink nozzle.

"Oooops! Steady," gasped Derek, "it might do something precipitate."

"This is precipitate," sniggered Larry, holding up a test tube, "by gum, that's funny colour. I say, this might do for a new kind of toothpaste!"

"You mean they could all go in for pink teeth," teased Derek, "oh hello, Arthur, come for a quick science lesson?"

Larry, miles away as ever, remarked, "thanks Sally, just put it down there."

Arthur coughed politely, like the patient butler, and ventured to comment. "Dr.Robinson," he began, "we need to discuss the forthcoming conference. You know, the disarmament talks."

"Armaments?" stared Larry, clearly in a little world of his own, "arms," he held up his arms, nearly spilling the liquid all down Arthur's smart suit, "it's not arms that talk; it's cake-holes."

"Take no notice of him," sighed Derek, "he's got a tonking new idea. That project you set him has really got him going. We shan't get any sense out of him until he's managed to perfect it."

"The peace talks," insisted Arthur.

"Peas?" Larry frowned, miles away, "they don't talk any more than beans. Have a word with Sally. She's the great horticulturalist here. Marvelous produce from the garden. Marvelous girl altogether."

"Marvelous in the altogether," muttered Derek, "and that Betty Kerry. No, I really must insist you do not interrupt Dr. Robinson's very important work, Arthur. He needs to concentrate."

"Concentrate! Concentrate!" Larry expelled a tone of triumph, "that's it! We need to concentrate the mixture. Well done, Derek. Why didn't I think of that before? Sally's right you know, I am a complete nooney. Anyway, why don't you sort out the politics with Sally and Kevin? They've got the matter in hand. I'm hopeless at that side of things. Give my regards to Nonky-tonky and Ivan-cough, or is it Ivan-asticoff?" he puzzled. "Funny guys, these Russians. Always rushin' about! Do yer get it?" he jazzed, teasefully.

A funny smell now pervaded the laboratory, followed by a pippington-poppington sound from somewhere. "My word!" Larry expostulated, "we need to follow that up and augment the process."

That was enough for his Maudsley-ship. He returned to the sitting room, relieved to be out of range of all funny reactions, both chemical and humanoid, and hopeful of gaining clarity over the next step in the international peace process.

CHAPTER 22
THE PEACE TALKS

It was a bright sunny morning as a large assemblage of dignitaries from many countries gathered on the beach outside Larry's new research establishment. It was to be noted that hardly anybody had come from the top echelons of government in London; the exception to this was our friend Arthur Richardson Maudsley, trying to look as important as ever, but beneath it all, was feeling a little unstable, since everyone in Whitehall was not taking the matter seriously.

"I say," he coughed in Kevin's ear, "do you think this is somewhat unwise? I mean, this gathering hasn't had official approval."

"Probably never will," Betty pulled a face, "after all, most of your colleagues have got interests in arms manufacture; isn't that true?"

"My dear young lady," came the expostulation, "what must you think of us?"

This was cut short by the arrival of King Jaja, having just arrived from Oogie-googie Land. That winning smile and easy manner wowed them all. He stood up on a rock and cleared his throat.

"Friends from many countries," he entreated, "I am so glad so many of you could come. This is an important encounter in the interests of world peace. Mr. and Mrs. Kerry came to our country with a certain gadget and showed us how weapons of war can all be abolished in the twinkling of an eye. I believe a demonstration has been arranged. I want you to take this very seriously. The implications in it are vast, and can offer us a bright future, for all of mankind." There was the sound of applause and cheering.

As they gazed out to sea, an ancient seaplane, a Shagbat (to use the naval slang word) came in to land and pulled up about twenty yards from the beach. They watched as the pilot hopped out of his cockpit and paddled away in a rubber dinghy. That all-important straw basket, looking somewhat larger than usual, appeared in the hands of Mrs. Kerry. Mr. Kerry advised them to pay particular attention, since there were not many Shagbats abailable with which to repeat the experiment. There came a tweaky-weaky sound from the basket, and the seaplane just evaporated, with tiny bits floating on the water and sinking down, leaving a slick of petroleum products floating about.

The assembled dignitaries were absolutely flabbergasted. When the pilot reached the shore, he assured them that it was a real aeroplane and certainly not a papier-mache mock-up!

A few minutes later, a massive tank lumbered out from among the trees and pulled up on the shore. The driver jumped out, beseeching them to let him get clear before the axe fell. That funny noise was heard again and the tank at first appeared to be the same, with its six inch armour plating. But Jimmy sauntered up to it and swiped it with a garden spade. To everyone's amazement, the spade sank right in and the whole structure wobbled like a birthday party jelly. Then, with a bit of a push, it all squattered down into blobs of something harmless on the sand.

"What about intercontinental missiles?" demanded someone.

The response to this was a large lorry making an appearance, with a rocket mounted on the back. It stopped on the shore and the rocket swung upwards, pointing to the sky. The driver scrambled out of his cab, unnecessarily, as was soon to be seen.

Again there came that intriguing noise from a certain basket, and the rocket just disintegrated before their eyes. Fortunately it had no fuel or payload on board, but the message was the same; it was now a waste of time storing up hundreds of missiles as some kind of deterrent. But the lorry was intact; Larry had now reached a level of perfection which made it possible to wreck only the bits one wished to wreck.

The fourth example was a massive artillery piece, which could be spared since that sort of thing was miles out of date. They all watched as the enormous barrel curled round and did that imitation of a piggy-wig's curly tail. Everyone laughed and applauded. The gun was rendered useless, but the steel was still fit for scrapping, in the hands of a tattyman.

After a lot of hand shaking and congratulations, most of the dignitaries climbed into their cars and set off for home, in the knowledge that weapons of war were now a waste of time. It only needed someone like Kevin to infiltrate their countries and fiddle with a certain gadget, and whatever war was being waged would be over in about five minutes. The two dignitaries who did not depart were Mr. Nonkwhistle and Mr. Ivanov. They trailed Sally, Betty and Kevin back to the house and planted themselves in the drawing room, determined to come to some sort of deal. Arthur Richardson Maudsley arrived a little later at the front door but managed to inveigle his way into the discussion.

"My offer still stands," the big cigar wobbled, "thirty million for the sole rights on the thing."

"Not for sale," snapped Sally.

"I'll make it forty million," added Mr. Ivanov.

"No deal, " she insisted. "We are keeping control of it."

"Can't we have Dac Rabinson make that decision?" carped Charlie, "after all, it's his bright idea. Come to think of it, I haven't seen him yet today."

"I'm speaking for him," Sally emphasized, "he's such a twit, he'd probably hand them all out to anyone who looked slightly honest. He's very busy upstairs with Derek Normbrain. Leave him alone."

"I have a question for you," Mr. Ivanov interjected, "if those missiles have nuclear warheads, what will happen about the radio-activity? We shall all be faced with that problem."

"That's precisely the point," Kevin explained, "that is the next project…"

"How do you come into this?" demanded Arthur indignantly.

"Why don't you just shut up and listen?" snapped Kevin, "it was your idea in the first place to have this new project, and now you can't even remember putting it to us. The next phase is a method for deconstituting radio activity. Mr. Ivanov is right. We shall have piles of radio active material, spilling out from all those rockets that have been wrecked. Dr. Robinson is working on it right now."

"Is that what he was plonking about with when I went up?" puzzled Arthur.

"Yes, and you nearly put him off his stroke," objected Betty.

"I like the cheek of this," carped Arthur. "Here we are, we've set you up with your own research establishment in a secure area and you're about to develop another world-shattering gadget, and what do we get out of it? Nothing! I will make you an offer; the last one, by the way. I will offer you fifty million for the sole rights on anything that you invent."

"Sixty!" snapped Charlie.

"Seventy!" blasted Ivanov.

"Don't be silly," sneered Sally, "we're not letting that thing out of our sight. It can be rented out on condition that our highly trained personnel are at all times in charge of the thing and no one else is allowed to interfere with it."

"How are you going to disarm both of us at the same time?" nattered Charlie. "You need two teams with a gadget each to disarm us both at the same moment, otherwise it isn't fair."

"Give us a chance to sort something out," promised Sally, "it can be done where there is goodwill on both sides.

No filthy tricks and no concealing weapons just in case things turn nasty."

"We solemnly promise," chanted Charlie, as he held hands with Ivonov.

"In any case, it would be a waste of time concealing weapons," Ivanov shook his head, "as soon as they come out of concealment, you could still bust them. This is our main chance for world peace and security," he rejoiced, "all thanks to you."

•

Arthur Richardson Maudsley sat there frowning as the representatives from the super powers took their leave. "All sounds so wonderful," he remarked sarcastically, "Who knows what will be the end result?"

"Aren't you going to toddle off to your masters in Whitehall?" suggested Sally, "and report on these matters? Surely the PM will want to issue instructions?"

"Between you and me," Arthur came over all conspiratorial, "it wouldn't surprise me if the government decided to nationalize the lot."

"The lot of what?" demanded Kevin.

"The whole caboodle," came the solemn reply, "all those gadgets you've got in various sizes and capabilities."

"In other words you want to confiscate the lot," nodded Kevin, "I wonder if I'm at all surprised. Is that really the best you can do? Why don't you join in the peace process like all those other countries that sent representatives today? They were all stunned and all in agreement that warfare is now a thing of the past."

"Unless you're talking about boxing and wrestling," put in Jimmy.

"That's precisely the point," emphasized Arthur, with a slightly optimistic regard for Jimmy's wisdom, "it will be back to fists and clubs again. Do you really expect the human race to stop being aggressive and the major powers to stop bullying the minor ones?"

"Come on Arthur, you aren't going to manage to put the clock back," teased Betty.

"Now listen," he appealed, "personally, and you must not quote me on this, I am full of admiration for Dr. Robinson's invention. As long as it's in responsible hands, that's fine. But how long will that last? When some idiot gets hold of it, we shall have no cars, no electric wiring, no gas pipes, nothing metallic at all. I think there will be a clampdown on this gadget."

"Which means you'll stick it in a cupboard, lock it up and throw the key away," cheeked Jimmy, "typical of you lot. Can't see beyond the end of your noses."

"I suppose you're right," sighed Arthur, "but if that happens, you should be adequately compensated… Not just for the machine, but to keep your mouths firmly shut. I am going to suggest 60 million. That means ten million for each of you, since there are six in this team."

"And now we shall enter into temptation," sighed Betty, "some hope."

"A bit like closing the cowshed door after the Aberdeen Angus has trotted off," Kevin sneered. Everyone laughed.

Arthur parted from them with a certain dollop of foreboding as to how things were going to materialize, or rather de-materialize. As his car joggled up the track to the security gate, the friends continued their deliberations in the lounge.

"The Aberdeen Angus toddling off from the cowshed is putting it mildly," Betty chortled. "The secret is well and truly out and no one will now take no for an answer, even if the British government tries to smother it."

"You're forgetting one thing," warned Sally, as they heard more funny noises from upstairs, in conjunction with certain ronky odours from sundry chemical reactions. "We have nearly all the stock of those machines, one has been destroyed, or so we think, and one is still at large with someone who seems to have pinched one. So where does that leave us? In the piggy, I suppose."

"It means that if we can find the thief, we can carry on regardless, whatever the government tries to impose on us," concluded Betty. "Jimmy; I suppose you have no idea who nicked that machine?"

There was an awkward silence as all eyes focused on Jimmy who might even yet be the Wiser. He shilly-shallied a little, but decided that he was going straight, according to the dictats of his pal Kevin. "All right," he sighed, resignedly, "it was me that pinched it, but it's not here. I've got it hidden away, just in case." Everyone felt a sense of relief for Jimmy's purloining skills.

CHAPTER 23
DISARMAMENT

It had come to the big occasion on which weapons of war were to be wiped out. Betty and Kevin had gone off to America with an example of a big and a small gadget; Sally and Jimmy had gone to Russia with the same equipment. All during these actions, the media were following the whole process so that each side could see that the other side was doing the same thing. The nuclear element in the weaponry was now being placed in repositories against the day when they too could be rendered safe. That pointed up the urgency of inventing a gadget that could 'defuse' radio activity.

•

Dr. Lawrence Robinson and his development collaborator, Prof. Derek Normbrain were spending hours working in their laboratory overlooking the sea. To Derek's dismay, he observed a certain car pull up by the beach and a certain Arthur Richardson Maudsley advance to the front door.

"Oh no, not that one again," growled Derek, "I suppose

we shall have a bit more bureaucratic flap-doodle thrown at us."

"Flap?" murmured Larry, "no need to flap. I think we've got the basics of it sorted out." He was miles away again, probably on planet 23, but that was how his brilliant mind worked, even when doors were falling off their hinges and government officials were bearing down on one, to jam the works up.

Derek showed Arthur into the lab and put his finger up to his mouth. "Sh!" he intimated, "there's a genius at work."

"I'm glad to hear that," Larry muttered, "we could do with one of those right now."

Derek flexed his eyebrows, something that had become quite a habit with him, as he was attuning himself to Larry's zany mind.

"The Minister of Defence wants to know how much progress you've made," demanded Arthur, imperiously. "Can you really devise a method for making radio active…" he was cut short by a most peculiar noise coming from a half-developed gadget on the bench.

"It's quite easy to make the radio active," Larry yawned, "all you do is switch it on. But not now, please, unless it's the Archers. Even you could exert a little grey matter and operate simple switch, Arthur," he remarked, vaguely.

"Take no notice," sighed Derek, "the main problem is that we still need something radio active to work on. I mean, we have managed so far with something that's naturally radio active, like granite, but that's not quite the same."

Just then, there was a most frightening gurgle-gurgle sound coming from a vessel full of a curious mixture and a ronky smell filled the room. Derek opened a window, as calm as a cucumber but Larry seemed completely oblivious to it.

"Phaw! What is that?" spluttered Arthur, yanking out his hanky, "anyone would think this was a gas attack on the Western Front."

Larry sniggered into his experiment. "Can't be a gas attack; both ladies have gone away to foreign parts."

"I thought you were fond of your lady-love, Dr. Robinson!" protested Arthur.

"I am," came the abstracted reply, "I love Sally very much, but with all this going on, that wedding we had planned has had to be postponed yet again. And now we haven't even got a vicar or a church handy. I suppose we might have to be very naughty indeed and just live in sin."

"Anyway," Derek tried to get back on track, "we need something radio active to practice on. Can you arrange that for us, Mr. Maudsley?"

"You have to be joking," came the snorty reply, "I mean, that sort of stuff is highly dangerous. You would both get radiation…"

This was drowned out by another quirky noise coming from another flask full of something with a lurid colour. "My word!" expostulated Larry, "look, Derek, it's done it! I think we are on our way."

"I think I'd better be on my way," Arthur tried to edge his way off. Derek decided to corner the bloke. "Look! How do you expect us to crack this problem unless we have a sample to work on?" he blazed.

"It's against all the rules and regulations," nattered

Arthur, "you are asking me to do something completely illegal and unethical. What do you think I am? I would be sacked without any compensation."

"We've worked out what you are," retorted Derek, "a proper jobsworth, Jack in the Office."

"What was that you said?" frowned Larry, in a rare moment of paying attention to something else.

"Jobsworth," despaired Derek.

"No…no.before that; com…compen…" Larry stared, thunderstruck at Arthur, "was it compensation, you said? He began to grin, then smile, then jig up and down with excitement.

"He's had an idea," murmured Derek, "just keep still and shut up. This could be it."

"Not 'pen', and not 'penny'. POUND!!!" he shouted like a desperate mummy on the phone to a wayward daughter, "compound-ation." Larry grabbed a piece of paper and began to scribble away, "got it! GOT IT!!! All we have to do is compound the process and it should work. We just need a sample. How about it, Arthur?"

The bureaucrat shook his head solemnly, "I can't provide a sample," he prevaricated.

"Go on, you can manage it when the doctor wants you to provide a sample down at the surgery," teased Derek.

"Don't be disgusting," snapped Arthur, "you two are clearly completely demented."

"That's just a fancy way of saying bonkers," nodded Derek.

"Ah well, I know I'm bonkers," giggled Larry, "Sally keeps telling me. But that's how I get new ideas. It's no use going over the same old ground and getting nowhere. You have to think out of the box; try something completely way-out. But I think I've got it!"

•

At that very same moment, Betty and Kevin were staring triumphantly at a row of intercontinental missiles, about twenty of them, all busted up, bent, botched and bibbly-bobbly. Thank Gad for that," sighed an American general, "I think we've come to the end of stock-piling junk like that."

•

"Like this," gurgled Larry, "eeny-meeny-miney-mo," and he poked his finger along a shelf loaded with chemicals. "Let's try this one; oooooh! Nasty! Try a spoonful. Now something else…" And it went on like this until he had a crucible with funny coloured mixture sloshing around. "Now we warm it up and bingo, we have a new idea."

The new idea, so-called, was not quite a new idea. As Derek Normbrain tried to stir it with a plastic spoon, he discovered, to his annoyance, that the spoon was no longer inclined to be a spoon. Larry stared in amazement. Derek picked up another plastic spoon and tried again, but with the same result. Arthur began to smile.

"Now that's a really useful invention," he crowed, "I hope you've written down the recipe?"

"Damned nuisance," nattered Larry, "we shall soon run out of spoons."

"Well of course, if you can't see the potential in that," sniffed Arthur, "you really must be a complete cuckoo." He picked up the mixture and taking a paintbrush, applied it to the window frame. "Let's see what happens now," he came over all curious.

For a few minutes, they resumed their conversation about obtaining a sample of radio active material for testing. Arthur at last was persuaded to tackle the right people and have something fetched in to solve the problem.

All at once there was an enormous crash, as the plastic window frame fell out of its ensconcement in the wall, and made short work of the cucumber frames directly beneath.

"We've certainly discovered something today," gawped Derek, as he leaned over the gap, "your girlfriend will be furious."

Larry leaned over and sighed, "a bit of practice in keeping as cool as a cucumber," he pondered, "I wonder how that came about? Anyway, we shall discover just how forgiving a person she is. I think she's very patient."

•

Jimmy and Sally stared with great glee at a row of rockets in a Russian repository. All of them had gone wiggly-woggly, soggy and like melted toffee. Mr. Ivanov, who was conducting them round, gave them a round of applause as an accompaniment to his massive grin.

"This is a day to remember," he rejoiced, "we shall arrange for you to be awarded the rank of Heroes of the Soviet Union."

"I just want to get home and get married," murmured Sally.

"And I want to get 'ome before they discover what's missing," whispered Jimmy.

•

From the gap in the wall, caused by the unscheduled descent of the window frame, the three gentlemen spotted a van pull up in the company of a police escort.

"What's all this?" Arthur stared in amazement.

"Oh! It's our friend Wallibrain," rejoiced Larry, "he's managed to get us a sample."

"What's that?" demanded Arthur, filled with suspicion.

A secure flask was fetched in by Fred Wallitude, and deposited in the correct spot on the bench. "Sorry about the delayitude," he fussed, "there was a bit of an argumentitation over the realismus of chunky-wunky of uranitation."

"Do you mean 'urination'?" protested Arthur as his nose went up. "How disgusting!"

"No; he means Uranium," corrected Derek. "Well done, Fred, that makes up for being a stupid blighter. You can stay to lunch now."

"Just a minute," exploded the bureaucrat, "you can't have uranium. Why, that's downright dangerous, radio active. How did you get that? There'll be hell to pay over this. Against all the rules and regulations. And anyway, you need special protective overalls. I forbid you to go any further with this; highly dangerous!"

Fred reappeared with various safety garments and

Larry was delighted. "All is forgiven, Fred," he crowed, "and we may have another surprise for you later on. Now let's try my new machine on this sample."

Fred reappeared with a Geiger counter and they ascertained that the 'sample' was indeed radio active. That had the effect of encouraging Arthur Richardson Maudsley to do a quick skidaddle off out to his car. Derek called from the window that was no longer there, "don't you want to see the results, Arthur? You might have some positive news for your line managers." There was no response, but the car did not race off anywhere.

"Now let's see!" jazzed Larry, as he prepared his new invention for the moment of truth. He twiddled with various controls and then came the climactic moment as he commanded the attention of Derek and Fred, the scientific boffins. "Ping!" he proddled a switch.

For a moment, nothing seemed to happen. They waited with baited breath. Then a curious booping sound warbled forth from the gadget, and the sample of uranium had a slight change of mind about its colour. The goldy colour dipped a little to silvery and then back again. The machine decided that it had done its best and would like a tea break. Larry advanced the Geiger counter and cried out in triumph, "whooopeee! Done it!" The Geiger counter was registering an almost complete wipe-out of the radio activity.

"A triumph for us all," eulogized Derek Normbrain, "I knew you could do it, Larry."

The clever lads were sitting round the kitchen table, sipping coffee and listening to the lunch which was sizzling in the oven.

"I shall have to report this," nattered Arthur, "highly dangerous and highly irregular. The minister will be most displeased."

"I wish I could whistle up a minister," breezed Larry, "a minister of religion, to solemnize our marriage. Sally ought to be back today, in theory."

"And in any case, that uranium sample is still radio active. That machine doesn't work properly," came the carping criticism from Whitehall.

"It's less dangerous than that sample of granite we've got," Larry explained, "Can't you see the importance of this breakthrough?"

"It is very important," insisted Derek, sipping his coffee, "it means that when we have this process set up properly, all the nuclear power stations can be rendered safe. That means cheap electricity without having to use fossil fuels. Just think of the advantages in that!"

"And all the nuclificatious warfare nobblies can be multi-wobblified," Fred chimed in.

"What is he talking about? Why can't he speak proper English?" complained Arthur.

"Because he's such a clever chap that he has to devise his own vocabulary as he wobbles his way through various wonderful wishful thinkings," teased Derek. "I bet you can't talk all clever like that?"

Within moments of lunch being ready, two cars pulled up behind the police car. It was the emissaries returning from their tasks in the USA and the USSR. Sally stalked up to her cucumber frame and failed to keep her cool.

"What the dickens has happened here?" she screeched.

Larry came out to her and administered a kiss. "Sorry Darling," he hugged her, "but we have had a double breakthrough today."

"You don't say," she expostulated in dismay.

CHAPTER 24
WEDDING DAY

At last, the big day had arrived. Sally was insistent that she should have a proper church wedding, and Larry was very much in agreement with that policy. It had taken quite a lot of negotiation to fix things up with the local church and the nearest vicar. The nearness was about ten miles away, since the military secure area was quite extensive. It had also been arranged that the wedding was to be a low key affair so as not to attract any attention from the media. Although Larry was almost completely unknown to the general public, Sally, Jimmy, Betty and Kevin were firmly in the public eye as international peace celebrities, and anything they did would attract undue attention. It was like being royalty; you just had to wipe your nose with a hanky and everyone was gasping at the thought that you might have a nasty bout of flu.

The ceremony was planned for eleven o'clock, but it was thought advisable to have the cars process to the church with plenty of time to spare. So it was, that Kevin Kerry ascended to the laboratory only to find that Larry was fiddling about with yet another bright idea. He was in his wedding suit, but the button hole had had a collision with a flask of something that had as yet not received a civilized label.

"Here; you'd better borrow mine," the Irishman pulled out Larry's rose.

"Borrow what?" came the dopey, abstracted voice, miles away as ever.

"Your button hole is messed up, Larry. Have mine."

"What for? What would I need a button hole for?" he was in a dream-world.

"It's your wedding day, you clot. Your bride is setting off for the church now. So come along." Kevin tugged at his sleeve. "You're not going to disappoint that lovely Sally of yours."

"Oh Sally!" Larry gasped, "wonderful girl. Just the one for me. But just a minute, I'd better just check on this experiment." He proddled the mixture in a test tube and gurgled goofily, "my word, that's a good-un… can't we hang on a minute and see what happens?"

"NO!" shouted Kevin, "you have an appointment with your Proddy vicar. Yes, I know Proddies are always messing their vicars about, but I won't let you today. Come on."

"OH! I like that vicar," grinned Larry inanely, "and he likes me, strange as it may seem."

It became even stranger just then, for as they were just departing through the door, there came an enormous BANG from that funny mixture and clouds of black smoke belched out in all directions. It caught Larry full in the face, but Kevin managed to dodge into the next room, just in time.

Betty and Derek Normbrain were just ahead in their car, closely followed by the bridegroom and his Irish best man. They reached the gate in the security fence and the guard began to check their passes.

"So appropriate I've got one of my cousins to be the best man," Larry sounded so self-confident. Kevin kept his mouth shut. He did not wish to disillusion the brainstorm lad on his wedding day. "I hope you've got our passes ready."

Kevin pulled up by the gate and handed two passes out to the guard. He watched Betty's car pull away, and assumed he could easily catch up with her, since he was not quite sure of the route.

The guard scrutinized the passes. "Very good, Mr. Kerry," he saluted, "you can proceed, but what about the other fellow? His face does not match this photograph."

"Don't be silly," jibbed Larry, "how can I be anybody else but me?"

"Like something out of darkest Africa, Sir. Mind you, the face looks right, but the colour is all wrong. I think I will have to say you cannot proceed. Please step out of the car."

"Just a minute, I can vouch for him," shouted Kevin, "he's on his way to his wedding. Don't go and mess things up now, have a heart!"

"Sorry Sir, but this face does not match the photograph," came the tedious repetition.

Kevin sighed with annoyance. He took hold of Larry's chin and turned it round. "Oh Be-jabers and the blessed Virgin," he panicked, "just look at your face, all black!" He made Larry look in the mirror, and he too was astounded to realize that that was one experiment that had shot him in the foot, or rather, in the face. "Let's see if we can get it off."

Kevin took out a hanky and wiped the brainstorm brow. The smuts were coming off to some extent, but not completely. Still Larry was a funny sort of dingy, grubby colour, not unlike a chimney sweep after a particularly busy day. Eventually the guard managed to be convinced that Larry was really Larry, in spite of being a trifle mucky.

Kevin set off at an augmented rate, in the hopes of pulling up with Betty and Derek. For a long time, he could follow the tyre tracks in the road, but eventually they came to a crossroads and it became a trifle less clear.

"What did you say the church was called?" demanded Kevin, now getting slightly steamed up. "Was it Saint Mary's?"

Larry studied the signpost. One way pointed to the village of St. Mary's; the other one said to St. Twit's. Straight ahead said to Dorchester.

Kevin felt sure that it was St. Mary's, since that was his favourite saint, so he turned left. It was a mile or so along, but he felt he had not been this way before. He felt sure he would have recognized the way, since he had been to visit the vicar and the church during the preparations. So he turned the car round and went back to the signpost.

"Let's try St. Twit's," he foamed, glancing at his watch.

"That sounds like me," sniggered Larry, "a complete nitwit."

They encountered someone standing by the roadside.

Kevin pulled up and enquired, "is there a wedding going on at St. Twit's?"

"Saint Ooooo?" gawped the villager.

"Sent Twit."

"Well I don't know," came a gawmless reply, "last Christmas they sent Santa, and he was a twit and no mistake."

"Is there a wedding going on?" fumed Kevin.

"There might 'ave been," the old villager shrugged his shoulders, "they wuz saying they wuz short of some sort of a bridegroom, so I think they were all off down the pub to console themselves. Somebody said the bride was fit to shoot somebody, as long as it wasn't herself."

"And did she shoot anybody?" Kevin was now frantic; Larry was gawping in the mirror in the hopes that a European countenance might yet be achieved. He seemed blissfully unaware of the developing crisis.

"Naw, naw," came the reply, "I managed to cheer her up. I offered to be the surrogate bridegroom, you know. She was a proper little cracker. I'm amazed some bloke couldn't be bothered to turn up on time." And he began to sing that song, *'Oh get me to the church on time...'*

The car shuddered to a halt behind Betty's car and they raced up the path to the porch. The Vicar appeared, somewhat annoyed since they were half an hour late.

"Most of your guests have given up and gone off," remarked the vicar, "but fortunately, your bride is still here, even if she is inconsolable."

But there was one guest who had not nipped off down to the pub. A Methodist gentleman from African climes, and wearing a lovely tribal costume.

"For I know this gentleman," enthused Kevin, "it's my friend Baba from Oogie-googie Land."

Baba was delighted to renew acquaintances with Kevin. "I'm afraid your wife has gone off for a quick drink," he offered an apology, "and taken two of my wives with her. Hey, what's this?" he cried in exultation, "is this the great inventor?"

"Yes," stated Kevin, stolidly.

"I never knew he was one of us," exulted Baba, "well my word, it just goes to show, our lads are cleverer than you guys. You ought to come and naturalize with us in Oogie Land."

The bride, now consoled at the thought that her bridegroom had arrived after all, issued forth from the vestry in the hopes that the ceremony could begin. The guests, now suitably lubricated from the local hostelry across the road, took their places and Kevin fidgeted with two gold rings. Larry felt rather pleased with himself, since his funny machine had obligingly produced them for him and Sally, but free of charge. Sally's eyes were so swollen with tears that she hardly dared look at Larry. The thought had occurred to her to pack it in then and there and remain a spinster to her dying day. But that thought seemed even more depressing than proceeding with the ritual. Derek Normbrain processed her up the aisle, since he was giving her away, not that he wanted to, since he thought she was a fantastic girl, and would have been even more so if she had actually been his daughter.

The ceremony proceeded normally, except to say that when it got to 'for richer for poorer', Larry almost burst out 'for richer and even richer still', but Kevin poked him one.

The reason for that near-blunder was because in his pocket were two cheques from foreign parts, both of which made the team an exceedingly wealthy combination indeed.

Towards the end, Jimmy was seen to be fiddling about with something in the near distance. Larry was fascinated to notice that the vicar's white clerical collar seemed to do something very strange. It went all wibbley-wobbley and crenulated and then disintegrated altogether.

"That's a funny do," he remarked as his eyes went goo-goo at the sight.

"You may feel that way, Lawrence," the vicar eyed him curiously, "but Holy Matrimony is a serious matter, a commitment for life. You may now kiss the bride."

Larry scooped her into his arms and administered an almighty kiss on her cherry lips, and then on each cheek and then on her forehead. "My lovely girl," he pronounced, "how I love you."

No one dared to comment on it; but everyone could see the alteration on Sally's beautiful countenance. She stared at Larry and expostulated, "what have you done to your face, Robinson? Hey, vicar, I think I've married the wrong bloke. Can we have an annulment?"

Kevin took a few minutes to explain that there had been a slight mishap on leaving the laboratory. At last, Sally managed to see the incongruity of it all, and smiled benignly and pronounced that she understood all too well the blunderings of the scientific world. As she and Larry processed down the aisle, everyone managed to withhold comment on Sally's altered countenance. It was Baba that spilled the beans, as they processed down the churchyard.

"My word, you two," he teased, "both of you could qualify to emigrate to Oogie Land now."

"What?!" gasped Sally, as she stared at Larry's darkened face.

Baba held up a mirror to her own face and she got the shock of her life. There were grimy black lip marks all over her physiognomy, and her dress as well as her veil. It took a minute for her to realize what had happened. Larry still stared at her goofily, expecting another indication of endearment.

But this dream was shattered, as Sally's bouquet sloshed with angry intent on his head. "Robinson!" she stormed, "I'll kill you, you stupid blighter! No more scientific fiddle-faddle from you, mate," she shouted, as she chased him down the path, lamming him with the remnants of her bouquet.

Everyone roared with laughter, especially the ones that had got themselves well oiled down at the pub beforehand. Baba's wives were particularly tickled by the whole episode.

CHAPTER 25
REPRODUCTION

We can now fast forward about nine months and review the effects of the stunning developments in world politics and also at home in the Georgian Mansion. Betty and Sally were sitting together in a drawing room, both of them knitting away like fury in anticipation of what was to arrive in a few days' time. Guesswork is hardly needed to explain the necessity of waggling the knitting needles so ferociously. Both of them were about eight and a half months pregnant. It had been a difficult time, not for the fact that they were pregnant, but for the awkward matter of the doctor having them down to visit the surgery in the village of St. Twit's, and also the visits of the midwife to check their progress at home. Two enormous tummies bulged out as the knitting needles waggled purposefully. Larry and Kevin were full of expectation and excitement.

The world scene was a transformation of its former self. Kevin and Jimmy had been off on peace missions to many countries and it was calculated that hardly any weapons of war were now surviving, except perhaps in military museums. Since they were all out of date and minus any ammunition, they were a complete irrelevance now. There was some suggestion that far away, there was just one rogue state that was concealing its weapons and trying to deceive everyone that it had peaceful intentions. Kevin decided that a wee postcard, explaining that this new gadget could marmalise all weapons of war at the flick of a switch, and that stockpiling rockets was a complete waste of time. The president of that aforesaid country could not even be bothered to send a reply, but then, that is now the fashion all round the world. Why bother to answer a letter?

With regard to the neutralization of nuclear fallout, this too had been a total success. Larry and Derek had managed to perfect a machine that could cancel out radio activity. This meant that all those nuclear warheads, stored away, could be cancelled out and rendered safe. It also meant that all the nuclear waste from power stations could be dealt with. The result from this was cheaper electricity and less use of fossil fuels.

"I am so happy," sighed Elizabeth Kerry, "Kevin is a wonderful husband. I can't believe my luck. He is so considerate."

"And somewhat weighed down," remarked Sally. She was talking about the dozens of medals awarded by a whole list of countries, in recognition of his peace-brokering. "You notice us girls never seem to get a medal."

"I'm not too bothered about that," Betty sniggered, "if they send me a bunch of flowers, I'm quite satisfied." She glanced around the room and rejoiced in the beauty of floral congratulation which kept appearing via the good offices of the security guards.

"Jimmy's doing quite well out of it," remarked Sally, "but we have to watch him. On his last trip he came back with twenty wallets. I stuck my hand out and demanded, 'come on, Jim, hand them over,' and he did. Then I managed to post them off back to their owners. You know what he said? 'It's a habit of mind, Sally. I can't help it. I don't mean to diddle anyone, but I just can't stop it. You can help me.'"

"All the same," replied Betty, "oooh blimey, he's kicking again, Jimmy's talents keep coming in useful, so I wouldn't be too hard on him."

The scene in the laboratory was much the same as before. There were the half-consumed mugs of coffee ranged along the windowsill. Not that there was any danger of them falling out into the garden, since a new window had been installed, this time made of hardwood as opposed to plastic. Larry, as usual, was miles away fiddling with his latest brainchild. Derek Normbrain, now accustomed to Larry's mentality, kept a close eye on him, for the sake of potential problems on the world scene.

"I say, Derek, just look at that," came the inane remark, as a test tube full of something vile decided to pass its aroma around the room.

"Larry, I hope that's nothing completely daft, like that stuff that wrecked the window frame." Derek frowned as Larry decided to poke it with a glass rod. The self-same glass rod decided that it did not appreciate being dunked in a funny sort of mixture, and did the best it could to reverse the process.

"I should pour that down the sink before you dissolve all the window panes in the world," worried Derek.

"Fortunately we managed to talk you out of that stuff that wreaked havoc with the plastic. What did you do with it, Larry?"

"It's up there on the shelf somewhere," he coughed vaguely, "I wonder where it is."

A clock downstairs struck eleven o'clock. ""Larry; it's time for bed. How about a bit of shut-eye?"

A massive yawn oozed out of the idiotic face. "Just a bit more," he gurgled stupidly.

"Kevin and Betty have settled down. How about you and Sally? Don't neglect that lovely wife of yours. She needs all the support you can give her at this time."

"Does she?" the saggy jaw indicated a complete failure to recall his wife's condition.

"Larry; we are expecting a new little Robinson any day now? How does that strike you?"

"Jack Robinson, Heath Robinson, Robinson Crusoe?" he went all vague, "or is it Red Robbo?"

"Your son, Lawrence!" emphasized Derek, "doesn't that mean anything to you? I grant you you had a completely successful honeymoon…"

"I grant you that. She was such a wonderful girl. She forgave me completely, after I'd spoilt her nice dress. It shows how much in love she was with me. And I with her," he went all romantic, "she's one of the few people who can really understand me and make allowances for my stupidity."

"You can say that again," murmured Derek, "and I would claim to be another in that league."

"Why? You in love with me, Prof?" he teased, not very tactfully.

"The very idea!" protested Derek, "I'm not one of those. I have to say, I like you very much, Larry, and I have the greatest respect for your inventive genius, but I despair of the loopy ideas you get. Don't you think you've done enough to transform the world already?"

"And still they don't know who I am," he giggled, like a child hiding in a wardrobe.

"That's another thing," sighed Derek, "Kevin Kerry and Jimmy Whitlock get medals from every country in the world, but you get nothing."

"Same applies to you, Derek," he shrugged his shoulders. "But you're right. Time for bed."

They shuffled their way towards the door, but something strange was happening to the door. All the paint was going peculiar and starting to peel off.

"How odd!" remarked Larry, "I know I generally peel off to go to bed, but this door, I assume, doesn't have to go to bed, indeed, it probably doesn't have a wife."

"What have you been up to again?" demanded Derek, "another daft idea! Now we shall find that all the painters and decorators in the world will be shrieking blue murder."

"Oh I don't know," came the crass rejoinder, "it'll keep them in work, so they needn't complain too much."

•

There was one thing very much in Larry's favour, even if he was a complete wozzlebrain; he was a born romantic and lover boy. In addition to that he was heavily committed to his lovely new wife and there was never any thought of another woman. He cuddled up in bed with Sally and kissed her frantically.

"You are the most wonderful thing in my life," he crooned in her left ear, "how could I ever manage without you, Mrs. Robinson?"

"Larry darling," she intoned lovingly, "I know you're a complete cuckoo, but I've come to terms with that. You're also a steaming genius and there's so much potential in you. It just needs Derek and myself to stop you dreaming up a really mad idea. I forgive you all the daft mistakes you've made, but please, please, just be a bit more careful."

"The next excitement will be the arrival of Robinson junior," he sounded so pleased.

"Will he be as daft as his father or as brilliant?" she pondered.

"Or a brilliant violinist like his mother?" he speculated, "incidentally, did we ever get that violin seen by an expert? It must be worth something."

"I did have an expert take a look, and he said it definitely was not a Stradivarius. He offered me fifty quid for it. Haha! Cheeky blighter. I love my violin, and I'm certainly not parting with it," she stated firmly. "Anyway, what crazy invention have you perpetrated on us today, Doc Robinson?"

"Oh I made a funny concoction with a murky colour, and guess what? The paint is peeling off the bedroom door. I wonder if the two things are connected."

Sally sniggered into the pillow. "So you've devised a fancy stripper," she put on a funny voice, "all the woodwork will be naked now. How embarrassing for it! But what in tarnation would be the use of that, Robbo?"

"We could use it on people like Wallitude and Maudsley," he speculated, "and induce them to do their very own strip show in Whitehall. In fact, next time one of them comes, I'll try it on with them and see how they scarper off in their cars."

"Now Larry," she impressed on him, "you really will have us back to the Stone Age and running round all starko. There has to be a limit. Why can't you think of something positive, like making something instead of busting everything? There's a challenge for you, Mr. Expert."

He sat up in bed. Astonishment shot all over his face. "You know, that's a brilliant idea," he trumpeted. "Why didn't I think of that before? Yes! I'll invent something tomorrow, that will fix the world up with something really helpful and worth having. Any ideas?"

"How about food and drink for everyone, especially in the poorer countries?" she slipped in, almost as an afterthought. But the thought stuck with the funny workings of the Robinson grey matter.

•

The expostulation of 'brilliant idea' was clearly heard two doors down in the Kerry's bedroom. They both woke up and sat up in a panic, on the assumption that there had been a thunderclap. Then it dawned on Kevin that another brainstorm had invaded the Robinson bonce.

"Heaven help us; Blessed Virgin protect us," sighed Kevin, "he's had another mad idea."

"I think we've had enough of his barmy ideas," yawned

Betty, "I hope Derek will calm him down a little. We don't want all the plastics ruined, or we shall be in a mess."

"No; we managed to talk him out of that idea," Kevin sounded somewhat confident. "Anyway, we shall doubtless find out in the morning. Now darling, let me cuddle you once again."

Mrs. Kerry never refused an offer like that. She was crazy about Kevin, his accent which was not quite English but nearly, and his jokes which were mildly amusing but not all that funny.

"Send me off to sleep with one of your jokes," she teased.

"Right you are, Mrs. Kerry. This is all about religion. In a street there lived a Rabbi and a Roman Catholic priest and an evangelical minister."

"Did they get on well?" she whispered hopefully.

"It was a bit like keeping up with the Jones. The evangelical went out and bought a new car and parked it outside. Then he took out his prayer book and said a blessing over it, for the sake of safe motoring. The Roman priest saw this and decided to up the anti. He bought a car and then took out the incense and holy water, waved them about in the road and gave the car a holy blessing."

"And what did the Rabbi do? Splash it with kosher wine?"

"He did not wish to lay out on a new car, so he bought a cronky old Ford Popular."

` "So how did he bless his old antique?"

"He waited until the other two were peeping out of the windows, and then took a hacksaw and chopped a couple of inches off the end of the exhaust pipe."

Betty lay there pondering for a minute or so, trying to figure it out. "I don't get that," she piped, innocently.

"No, you won't get that if you're a girl. There's no risk of you being circumcised, I hope."

At that, Betty split out laughing, so loudly that Derek (next door) and the Robinsons found themselves perplexed at this hilarity at midnight.

"That reminds me, darling," she giggled, "when junior arrives, what are we going to do about his baptism?"

"He's got to be baptized," stated Kevin firmly, "I, his father, will insist."

"And his mother will also insist," she snapped dogmatically, "but which church shall we have it done at? Is it Rome or evangelical?"

"You mean, we've got to have the Proddy water?" objected Kevin, "oh heck, my old mother would turn in her grave."

It could have escalated into a full scale row, but neither of them wanted that. They were so much in love and prepared to consider each other's sensitivities on this matter that they shelved the disagreement and went in for an elongated snogging session. It was Betty that had a stroke of genius that would settle the matter.

"Kevin," she cosied, "neither of us has been near a church for ages, at least not since the Robinsons got married. Why are we arguing over this? Neither of us jibbed at being married by King Jaja, the chief Methodist in Oogie-googie Land. Why don't we get Jaja to baptize our little Kerry?"

"Now that's a brilliant idea," Kevin rejoiced, "he's a lovely man, and one I could really respect. He's the finest Catholic Methodist of them all. We've solved the problem."

Betty sniggered into the duvet. "You and your labelling system," she teased, "it reminds me of the troubles in Belfast, when a motorist lost his way and found himself in the middle of a street riot. A bloke came up, brandishing a petrol bomb, and demanded, "are ye a Catholic or a Protestant? The bloke thought carefully and replied, 'neither; I'm an atheist." To which the Irish bloke demanded, 'are ye a Catholic Atheist or a Protestant Atheist?' Certain amount of confusion there, I think."

"Not at all," Kevin sounded so ameliorative, "we're all God's children, and I'm sure the Blessed Virgin cares for us all." With that, Mrs. Kerry felt reassured that progress had been made.

CHAPTER 26
ANOTHER OFFICIAL VISIT

A day or so later, Derek was gazing out to sea, only to spot two cars and a van appear in front of the house. He wondered if this spelt more trouble. This apprehension was confirmed as he descried Arthur Richardson Maudsley and Frederick Wallitude alighting, in company with a coterie of gentlemen in white coats. They stalked into the house without so much as a knock on the door and ascended to the laboratory. Larry, as ever, was completely absorbed in fiddling with some kind of hare-brained experiment, which left Normbrain somewhat perplexed and apprehensive.

"Morning, Dr. Robinson," came the official bossy voice from Arthur.

Larry did not even bother to look up. "Oh just leave it over there," he remarked casually, "what is it this time? Coffee or tea?"

"It's us from the Ministry," stated Wallibrain, "I'm afraid we must curtail your researches forthwith and commandeer all your materials."

"What?" exploded Derek, "you have no right…"

"Yes we do," insisted Arthur, "the Government has

made a decision. No more clever ideas from you, Sir. We agree, you've achieved an awful lot so far, and world peace is a great boon to us all, but any more ground-breaking ideas… we tremble to think of what you might dream up next. We are going to confiscate all your equipment. Carry on, gentlemen," he ordered, as a squad of chaps in white coats began removing all the contents of the laboratory.

Larry, as oblivious as ever, remarked, "careful, you might blow yourselves up like Fred did last time he pinched some of my gear."

"This is preposterous," ranted Derek, "here we have a genius at work, who has done so much for progress in this world, and you just want to stop him from developing any more ideas. This is disgraceful. I shall protest to the PM."

"You can if you like," sneered Arthur, "it was his idea in the first place."

The clanking and bumping of men removing the contents of the laboratory alerted Kevin Kerry to peer round the door. When he realized what was happening, he was outraged.

"You can't do this," he blazed, "fancy treating a genius like this! Where's your authorization?"

Arthur produced a document, signed by the PM, and it clearly stated that all of Dr. Robinson's scientific equipment had to be impounded and removed from his quarters.

"This is just a waste of time," objected Kevin, "this won't stop him. All he has to do is nip off to America and start all over again. You may as well be realistic."

"Robinson is not going anywhere," came the clamp-down, "you and your team are now confined to this military area and you are not going anywhere. It's for your own good. There are nasty people out there that are not too pleased with this world peace idea. My advice to you is to keep your head down and stay out of sight. No more of this high-profile peace conference business. You are attracting the wrong sort of attention." Arthur frowned threateningly.

Larry, still oblivious to the emptying of shelves and cupboards, went on prodding with his latest bright idea. "I say," he chirped innocently, "mind out, you nearly tipped that flask over."

"Now what crazy idea are you working on this time, Robinson?" demanded Fred.

"Not a crazy idea at all," came the abstracted remark, "my wife approves of it, so it has to be common sense."

"If you tell me what it is, I might see my way to letting you carry on with it, otherwise, I must remove everything." Arthur was at his most dominating.

"Remove everything?" breezed Larry, miles away, "What? Are you going to strip off?"

"Don't be disgusting," snapped Arthur, "a man in my position can't indulge in such disgraceful behavior. Now what is that experiment? Let's have the truth."

"If it's a method for de-materialising plastic," began Fred, "I'm afraid that idea will have to be shelved."

"Just a minute," objected Kevin, "that was your suggestion in the first place."

"Oh never mind that now," snorted Fred.

Larry glanced up at his shelves and sighed, with a slight touch of regret, "someone's already unshelved it, Fred. If it's you again, pinching, do be careful with it. You might get a nasty surprise. By the way, what are you going to do with all my stuff?"

"That is uncertain at the moment," came the ponderous response from the bureaucracy, "the decision will have to go through various channels and then be implemented by our top scientists."

"But this is our top scientist," riposted Derek. "He's cleverer than the lot of them."

"Come on, Robinson, what scheme are you working on?" nosed Fred.

"What about a scheme for producing enough food for the starving millions?" he teased.

"Starving millions?" stared Fred, "no one's starving in this country. Waste of time, that idea."

Derek Normbrain was incensed by that remark, as indeed was Kevin Kerry.

"You may have noticed that in the Third World, there are people starving to death on the streets," Kevin stated, "there is no need for that. It's a disgrace. Dr. Robinson is trying to rectify that problem. Don't you have any smattering of humanity about you, Wallibrain…?"

After a bit of huffing and puffing, the ministerial visitors decided that it would be a political disaster if they were seen to be inhuman about human starvation. The notion that the press would play havoc with them over this, introduced a smidgeon of caution.

"All right," conceded Arthur, "let him carry on with that experiment, but we want to know how it turns out, the results and how it may be implemented. Is that clear, Robinson?"

They left him with enough material to carry on that

piece of research. On the way down stairs, Sally appeared. She had caught the drift of what was going on. She was mightily relieved to discover that the ministry had done some sort of clamp-down on Larry with his bright ideas. Betty was less thrilled. The idea that they were confined to this area for good, with no freedom of movement, evoked deep concern in her beautiful head. She followed the two experts out to the car. The van, containing most of Larry's material, chugged away to the guard post.

"If we're stuck here for good, how will we manage?" she demanded.

"You will be well supplied," came the snooty reply, "nothing to worry about."

"I think there is," came the retort from the extremely beautiful young lady with her tummy sticking out, "you may have noticed that there are two babies on the way…"

"No problem," wafted Arthur, "we have the matter in hand."

Derek and Larry were watching from the laboratory window, which was now disinclined to collapse into the cucumber frame below. Fred was seen to be holding the very bottle that contained the plastic destroyer.

"Be careful with that," shouted Larry.

"What is it?" snapped Fred, unscrewing the top and shaking it slightly. A few drops landed on both their suits. Betty did a quick skidaddle indoors, since she had an idea of what might happen. And it did. That funny, smelly mixture got to grips with Fred's clothing, which incidentally was 70% man-made fibres, ie. Plastic. The suit simply disintegrated, followed by his underwear, and even his shoes.

"You disgusting blighter," snapped Arthur, "no sense of decency at all. I shall report this misdemeanor to the minister. There are ladies present, you know?"

A moment later, the same result came over Maudsley's apparel. Seconds later, he was stark naked as well. Words fail to express his consternation, intermingled with accusations levelled at all and sundry who might conceivably be implicated in the outrage. No one seemed to notice that there was a sort of flash coming from somewhere behind the cucumber frames.

"Well it was you that claimed he wanted to remove everything," sneered Larry, as the two streaked into their cars and drove off at a rapid rate. Providentially, that suspicious bottle of something nasty was left standing on the grass in front of the house.

The two charming reproductive young ladies were peering through the lounge window. They thought the whole episode was hilarious. A few minutes later, they were admiring two photographs of the ministerial gentlemen, in the altogether, as they scrambled into their cars. Larry and Derek descended, not exactly pleased with how things had been managed. Jimmy the Whizz (possibly the Wiser) also appeared with a Polaroid camera in his hands.

"Where shall we send the pictures?" he cheeked, "the Daily Mirror or the Prime Minister?"

"Jimmy, you are the limit!!" shouted Sally, "fancy pulling a trick like that?"

"Serve 'em right," Jimmy waved his fist, "cheeky blighters. But they haven't got all your stuff, Doc."

"I know," Larry showed them the bottle of something

nasty, "they were a bit reluctant to take that away."

"Don't hold that stuff near me," snapped Betty, "I'm not a nudist."

"Nor am I," cut in Sally.

"All you have to do is wear something like wool or cotton, and it won't work," Larry assured them, "it's only plastic and artificial fibres that it attacks."

"And what about all the rest of your stuff?" stormed Derek, "it's a diabolical liberty."

Jimmy the Whizz grinned and made a self-congratulatory noise. "Never fear, Jimmo is 'ere," he chuckled, "you may be interested to hear that I found out from the guards that this was going to happen, so last night, while you lot were not quite asleep, I did a lot of swapping. Most of those bottles they took away are loaded up with something even nastier than K_9P."

"You little blighter, Jim," exploded Derek.

"And all your important stuff is tucked away in the shed over there," he pointed, "including your metal busting gadgets."

"But I saw them taking them away," cut in Derek, "they've got the whole stock."

"They may think they have," grinned Jimmy, "but I took all the insides out and put something else in instead; something far nastier."

"What was that that was far nastier?" came the goofy question from Larry.

"Mouse traps," proclaimed Jimmy, "if they interfere with the insides, they're going to get some nasty surprises."

"Jimmy; you are a genius," crowed Sally, "all is forgiven. You will have to be called 'the honest thief," and they all laughed at that.

They spent the next hour or so speculating on what would happen when the experts at Whitehall decided to mess with Larry's material. Then their thoughts moved on to what was to become of them, if they were stuck in this security area for the rest of their lives.

"I think we need to get a message out to Charlie Nonkwhistle," suggested Derek, "I know he and his friends would be delighted to have us come. What about sending him a letter?"

"That might be problem," frowned Betty, "since we are more or less sealed off in this place. It's like being a bird in a gilded cage." They all nodded solemnly.

CHAPTER 27
ANOTHER DISCOVERY

For several days, the beleaguered six carried on as normally as possible. Since that delivery van failed to appear, and the larder in Sally's kitchen was becoming increasingly depleted, it became clear that a crisis was looming. In addition to that, none of the midwives were allowed past the guard post, and neither of the ladies were allowed out to the surgery. What the beleaguered six did not know, was that their only contacts with civilization, namely Wallitude and Maudsley, were not in any position to solve the problem.

The following is a précis of what did happen to them, as they drove off in great haste. When they arrived at the guard post, the soldier on duty refused to let them proceed. Not only were they stark naked, but their passes, being made of plastic, had disintegrated, so they could not identify themselves. No amount of ranting, raving and pulling of rank would alter the situation. Eventually, the guard became deeply suspicious of them, and summoned back-up from the local Military Police. Both of the ministerial gentlemen were arrested and taken away for confinement, on suspicion that they were some kind of enemy infiltrators.

This explains why the beleaguered six found themselves even more beleaguered than ever. This prompted them to give some kind of emergency thought for the future.

It was Sally who invaded the laboratory one morning, as the shelves in the pantry were looking even more meagre than before. "Larry!" she moaned. "What are we going to do?"

He was miles away as ever, poking inquisitively at some weird substance. "Just leave it over there," he remarked, assuming it was his morning coffee.

"Larry!" she insisted, "we are running out of food. What are we going to do about it?"

As usual, he was only half-listening, but picked up the words 'running out'. "No need to run anywhere. Anyway, there's nowhere to run to." An ever-widening grin gave the hint that the Robinsonian grey matter was on to something, yet again.

"Food!" she emphasized, "oh Larry, do listen!" she slapped the bench, "we shall all starve!"

"Just a minute, just a minute," his voice rose in climax, "do that again."

"Do what again? Shout at you?" Sally was becoming frantic, for not only was the baby kicking, but her husband was being even more obtuse than usual.

"Thump the table," he ordered. "Quick! Do it again… yes, even harder." He watched her administer a fist to the cluttered surface. "Go on, don't just tickle at it."

Sally took off her slipper and walloped the bench . He was eyeing the blob of weird substance keenly, using a magnifying glass. A really nasty smell pervaded the laboratory, suggesting that this was a lavatory instead. "Poo!" gasped Sally, holding her nose.

"I've done it! I've done it!" Larry jazzed up and down. "I say, that's a relief."

"Where?" she scrutinized the floor, "you really must develop self-control, Robinson," she snapped angrily, "what did your mummy do about your potty training?"

"Mummy?" he was miles away, "what was that about Tutankhamun? Yes, he had food tucked away in his tomb. He thought he was going to have a party while the judges in the Underworld were about to kid him on that he was going to heaven."

Sally opened a window to encourage the pong to disperse. "Larry, never mind about Toot." She was becoming frantic.

"Toot?" he went on dreamily, "why; has the van arrived at last?"

"No, Larry, we have a crisis."

"Why? Is Robinson junior about to pop out?" and he made a popping sound with his finger in his mouth.

"LARRY!!!" she blasted, "I could crown you one of these days."

"Not very likely," he mused abstractedly, "I'm not in the same league as Prince Baba."

"Larry!" she was near to tears, "we are running out of food. What can we do about it?"

"I've done it," he was triumphant.

"So I realize," she was holding her nose again, "not something to be so pleased about. We shall have enough of that sort of thing with nappy changing soon enough."

"I'm very pleased," he trumpeted, "in fact, we've solved the problem. We just need to buy a little time, while I get this idea into production."

"Heaven help us," she gasped, "we shall all be stunk out of our minds."

"No, listen, cloth brain…" he came over all cheeky.

"Cloth Brain to you, Clot-Brain," she snapped, "imbecile! Nooney-bonkers! Fathead!"

"No, listen, Woman, " he wagged an inventive finger, "I've just discovered how to fabricate FOOD. Did you hear that, Little Miss Ear-Blockage? After all, it was your bright idea in the first place. Now I've found out how to do it."

"You can say that again," she gasped, nose-holdingly, "and you can clear it up yourself."

"No, no, don't clear this lot up," he nattered, "this is a break-through with food."

"If that food smells like that, you'll have a job to persuade anyone to eat it," she wept.

"Panic not!" came the expert reassurance, "this is early days. What I now need is a patch of land dug over and cleared of weeds, and in a day or two…"

"Can we wait that long?"

"We may have no choice," he came over all reassuring. "Our problem is solved."

•

It was shortly after this encounter, that the men folk were all busily engaged in clearing a selected patch of land near the house. The two ladies, considering their condition, were not expected to do any heavy digging. Instead they came and helped to shift the weeds that had been dug out. Fortunately, the garden shed contained enough spades and forks for them all to be kept busy. Everyone was convinced of the urgency of growing their own food, on the assumption that the boys in Whitehall had forgotten all about them.

•

With the vegetable patch prepared and planted, a sense of relief spread itself amongst them. Larry assured them that if this worked, they would be eating new food in a couple of days. The other problem, that of the two babies arriving imminently, still weighed on their minds. None of them had any experience of delivering a baby, so it was an urgent matter to arrange midwifery of some description. Neither of the ladies felt inclined to entrust the task to Larry, for although he was a very clever chap, he was also a complete clot. Derek Normbrain had been present at the birth of his daughter, many years ago, but felt that only as a measure of desperation would he impersonate midwife. They decided to tackle, by telephone, the gentlemen at Whitehall, even if Fred and Arthur had not been extricated from close confinement as suspicious characters. The following conversation simply added to their apprehensions.

"Hello! Is that someone in Arthur Richardson Maudsley's department?"

"Who? Never heard of him. How did you get this number?"

"He gave it to us," sighed Sally, "in case of any problems

arising. We are marooned in this military area and two of us are about to give birth. Can you help us?"

"Oh wait a minute," came a preoccupied voice, "I think I know what this is all about. You are Mrs. Robinson and Mrs. Kerry, aren't you? Don't worry about it. We can send a doctor in to check you over. One should have seen you yesterday."

"No one came. We are getting worried. Can't you do something about it?" Sally sounded irritated. "Why don't you just transfer us to the nearest maternity unit?"

"Oh no, no, no, that's quite impossible. You must stay in the security area. I have to insist. It is very important that you are completely isolated from the rest of the world."

"So why can't a medic come in and see us? That's the least you can do for us."

"Absolutely impossible. No one is allowed into your area."

"So why did Wallitude and Maudsley manage to come in and pinch all my husband's stuff?"

"Who? Never heard of them," came the superior disclaimer. "Did they really gain admission? When we catch them, they will have to be charged under the Official Secrets Act."

"You can do what you like with that pair," blazed Sally, "but look here, my baby is due any day now, and there's no one capable of delivering him. Haven't you got the slightest bit of consideration for me and my friend? Surely you can make an exception?"

"If we did send in a doctor, he would have to be vetted and sign the Official Secrets Act. I will see what I can do…"

It went all vague. "I will set the wheels in motion to get a doctor."

"Hopefully he can come right away," Sally felt a slight relief.

"Oh no, no, no, this process will almost certainly take two or three weeks," came the official stone-walling.

"We haven't got two or three weeks to play with," Sally snapped in desperation.

"Oh I think you can," came the vague reply with the superior tone, "it's your first baby, isn't it? They are almost always late."

"This simply isn't good enough," shouted Sally in dismay.

"Now look here, young lady," came the snooty putter-downer, "you don't speak to me like that. Any more of that, and I shall leave you to your own devices. Good morning!" Click!

An atmosphere of deep annoyance and distrust of all official goings on settled on the Georgian Mansion. There seemed to be no way round this problem.

•

It was Jimmy the Whizz who had formulated a plan to solve the problem. Not only was he a highly accomplished thief, but he was also a master of sleight of person. Sleight of hand is when you can move your hand faster than the human eye; sleight of person is when you can appear not to be there, but you are, and can move faster than the human eye. So it was, that our Jim waited until dead of night, on the assumption that the guards were not exactly on top form as to observation. He sneaked up to the guard post, played a certain diversionary trick and managed to sneak out of the security area. It took him a couple of hours to reach the village of St. Twit's, but now he could set the wheels in motion for the rescue of the two ladies in an extreme situation, and also, surreptitiously send a certain telegram off to foreign parts. From this we can divine, that it is often quite useful to have someone who is downright dishonest, sneaky and well-informed, massively loyal to oneself. By the time he managed to sneak back into the compound, the ladies were even more in a panic mode.

•

"I should stop worrying," he remarked calmly, as he finished his breakfast.

"Jimmy!" gasped Betty, clutching her tummy, "what are we going to do?"

"Listen carefully," he wagged a finger, covered in marmalade.

"What are you talking about?" panicked Sally.

"Shush!" he put a finger to his mouth. He looked out to sea, went over to the window and listened carefully.

"What's going on?" Kevin frowned, "I suppose you think the leprechauns will call in and wave their magic wands."

"Better than that," Jimmy tried to shush them down, "can you hear that in the distance?"

They all poured down on to the beach and began to hear a throbbing sound way out over the sea. Then a dot appeared, whirling wings. It was a helicopter, coming in with great rapidity.

"I suggest you get your suitcases packed pronto," Jimmy ordered, "you'll be on your way to the hospital in two minutes."

The girls raced off to their bedrooms to pack up their cases and reappeared on the beach, just as the chopper came in to land on the sand. It was all a great rush, and the girls were off into the sky, leaving the boys to cope on their own and prevent the guards from firing on the helicopter.

•

Jimmy's explanation was as nothing to the realization that the vegetable patch was doing something most interesting. The gentlemen congregated around where Larry had planted the first specimen of growth. But now, after only a day, the patch was showing signs of life and productivity never evidenced before, not even with bindweed. There were little green leaves popping up out of the soil, and this betokened developments below the soil.

"It's working," proclaimed Larry, wielding a trowel, "now let's see what's going on," and he dug up a bit of the patch. "There!" he proclaimed, "we've done it! Food for the millions!" He dangled a large growth not unlike a potato, but not quite. "It's a cross between a potato and a bread loaf," he advertised, "what shall we call it? A wheatato."

"Well done!" clapped Derek, "Hey, just a minute, is that the telephone ringing?"

They raced into the house and grasped the Bell-invention.

"Yes! YES!!!" shouted Kevin. "Well done! A boy and a girl. All in good shape. HURRAH!!" he danced around the room.

It became clear that the two ladies had been airlifted to the nearest hospital just in time, since both of them had gone into labour way up in the sky. Sally had produced a girl and Betty a boy. All the men folk were over the moon. To everyone's amazement, just for once, Larry was not away in cloud cuckoo land. He was absolutely thrilled to bits to know he had a daughter. He could not wait to see Sally and the babe, but of course, that raised a certain problem; how were they going to be reunited, given the circumstances?

CHAPTER 28
THE ESCAPE

"I hope this stuff isn't poisonous," nattered Jimmy.

Larry opened the oven and pulled out a baking tin with the first sample of wheatato. It gave off a fragrant aroma which made all their mouths begin to water. Since they were now down to their last tin of baked beans, it had become a matter of no choice but to sample the new crop from the cultivated patch outside.

They sat around the table, eyeing it. Some felt suspicious; others felt on the brink of a massive new departure in feeding patterns.

"You first," egged Derek Normbrain, "it's your brainchild, Larry."

"Right!" exulted Larry, twiddling with his knife and fingering his plate. "Here goes. If I drop dead, you'll know the reason why."

Kevin Kerry watched with bated breath as the first nibble reached the Robinsonian cake-hole. Larry sniffed at it, did a cautious nibble, stopped to consider its effect, and then, scoffed a great mouthful.

"What a lovely taste!" he gurgled. "Your turn, chaps, pitch in and feel free."

The cautious Derek Normbrain kept a careful observation on his young friend. "Let's not just rush it," he murmured, "let's give it a few minutes to see the effect, if any."

Jimmy the Whizz took a chunk and chewed it up eagerly. "This is really something," he proclaimed, "I can feel it doing me good. I feel I'm a bigger, stronger, more wonderful Jim than ever before."

"What about more honest?" muttered Derek

"I 'aven't pinched your wallet for ages, mate," came the disclaimer.

"We all know why," teased Derek, "because there's nothing in it worth pinching."

"Shall we say, it's a good job we have got this rascal in with us," Kevin chided, "he's a very useful chap in his way. And what's more, we may still need his cunning in the coming days." Prophetic words!

As all four of them chewed away at the wheatato, it began to occur them that they were feeling more and more fantastic. Was this an illusion? Was there some kind of drug included in the invention? They questioned Larry as to what the ingredients were, but none of the constituents were in any way a matter of concern. There was nothing poisonous in it, nor anything that would be detrimental to one's health. All the same, Derek cautioned that they should have no more to eat until the next day, just in case any unforeseen symptoms might emerge.

"Does this mean that we will have nothing else to eat?" Kevin questioned. "Are we going to be reduced to this one diet?"

"I suppose we have no choice at the moment," shrugged Larry, "but with more research and experimentation, I ought to be able to produce variations on it and also develop fodder for animals so that we shall still have meat. It's early days, but at least we can breathe a sigh for the time being."

The next morning found the famous four standing round the wheatato patch, with every intention of providing themselves with a spot of breakfast. They felt that there was little choice, since the cornflakes had nearly run out. Larry took out his trowel and dug out enough to sustain them until lunchtime.

"Have you tried eating it raw?" pondered Kevin.

In answer to that, Larry carved a chunk off with his knife and took a nibble. His eyes lit up with excitement. "What a fantastic taste," he yuckied, "even nicer than when cooked."

As the others drifted off to the kitchen, Kevin stood observing the cultivated patch. It was now well over-grown with wheatato. It's leaves were poking out everywhere. It was clearly spreading out into the uncultivated ground. It occurred to Kevin that this was not unlike bindweed or Japanese knotweed; in other words, a weed that could run riot and go out of control. He decided to acquaint Larry with this suspicion.

This is where we must admit, with some reluctance, that for every bright new scientific idea which might be a blessing to mankind, there is also some kind of drawback. We saw that with the metal-busting gadget; it wrecked all kinds of metals (except lead) regardless of whether one intended it or not, thus producing all kinds of embarrassing situations.

It was only with time and further patience that brain-throb Robinson could find ways of controlling the gadget to do what one would wish it to do. The same was being seen with the destruction of plastic. While it was a great help to dispose of plastic bags and bottles, it was a distinct problem for anyone wearing clothing made of man-made fibres! And now, with the breakthrough in production of food, there was the indication that the whole world would be overrun by a new hybrid plant which would suffocate everyone, and one would have to eat at twice or thrice the rate to keep it under control.

"What we can do is find out what happens if it gets no water," suggested Larry. "We can divide the patch in two, isolate them and then water one patch but not the other. Will the wheatato survive with nothing to drink?"

So the experiment continued on those lines. It would take a few days to establish the results. The other thing they did was to box in the wheatato plants with sheet metal in the hopes that that would stop it spreading.

•

While all these significant experimentations were proceeding inside the security area, there were two ladies with a baby each, coming to the end of their stay in the maternity ward. The midwifery aftercare had been made thorough and extended somewhat, on the assumption that behind the barbed wire, medical care would be denied. But as they packed their cases and began to head for the door, an extraordinary thing occurred. A very tall, well-built gentleman from tropical climes appeared and flourished his exotic robes. It was Prince Baba from Oogie-googie Land.

"And where do you think you're going, ladies?" he teased.

"Baba!" Betty rejoiced, "how did you know we were here?"

"Oh! A little bird told me," he confided, "have you any idea where you're going?"

"Back to our husbands," Sally stated what she thought was the obvious.

Baba shook his head solemnly. "No entry," he stated firmly, "they won't let you back in there."

"I could go to my mum's," suggested Betty, "and Sally could come with me."

The Prince shook his head sympathetically. "No good," he affirmed gently, "the authorities will come and impound you. You know too much. Come with me, and you can meet up with the boys again and then…"

Just at that moment, a throbbing was heard in the sky. It heralded the return of the helicopter as it came in to land on the hospital landing pad. Baba hustled the two ladies and their babies out on to the grass and oiked them up into the flying machine.

"Hey! Where d'you think you're going?" came a shout from someone with an official sounding voice, "come back at once."

"Hard luck!" shouted Baba, as he tipped the pilot off to climb away.

It was not a particularly long flight. It took them over the Georgian Mansion. A quick peep over the side, reassured

Sally and Betty that their men folk were doing something interesting with spades and forks.

"We shall call for them this evening," explained Baba, "but for now, you must be airlifted out of British territory safely on to my ship. Welcome to the SS Boogie, the flagship of the fleet. King Jaja uses it as his royal yacht. You are very privileged.

A beautiful barquentine sailing ship came in view. It was no use trying to land the helicopter on it, since the masts and the rigging would catch the rotors. The ladies could see a small rowing boat waiting for them, away from the ship. The helicopter settled on the sea, since it had floats, and soon they were being rowed across to the ship.

"It's no use having a steel ship now," explained Baba, "after that clever invention of your husband's," he winked at Sally.

"How did I guess he'd mess things up," she sighed, "poor silly ass, but I love him all the same."

"Come on, Sally," coaxed Betty, "it was a brilliant invention, and just look how much good it has done already. Baba," she frowned, "I hope there's nothing important made of plastic on board."

"Why? What's wrong with plastic, dear?" the prince began to worry.

"Because my idiot of a husband has gone and invented a machine to bust anything man made, such as plastic. What about all these ropes and sails?" she tried to make out what they were made of. Then she related the sad tale of two important gentlemen who found that their birthday suits were fully advertised to all and sundry. Baba roared with laughter. He was quickly joined by the crewmen who thought that was highly appropriate. Even the two babies began to chuckle. He reassured them that the rigging and sails were all made of natural material, and also that the ship had no nuclear engines with radio active fallout.

"What we are going to do, is wait until nightfall and then sneak in and rescue your men folk from that security area," Baba explained.

"And then?" worried Betty.

"Safely aboard, we set sail for Oogie-googie Land, and you guys will be our newest addition to our population."

"What will we do all day?" enquired Sally.

"You can do just as you like, darlings," came the reassuring reply, "the Oogies are the freest people in the world. And if the British Government tries to get you back, they can whistle for it."

"What about Larry and his inventions?" asked Betty.

"He can invent away all day, to his heart's content," laughed Baba, "what's his latest bright idea, assuming he's got one…?"

Sally held her nose in a jocular gesture. "He's working on fabricating food," she sounded so dubious about it, "I don't know how far he's got with it, but it stinks to high heaven."

"Food!!!" expostulated Baba, "did you say, fabricating food??!!! Wow! If he can do that, magnificent! There are so many poor souls in Africa and they're on the brink of starvation. If he can solve that problem, that will be a major breakthrough. Don't be so dubious about that Dr. Robinson. He's a wonderful man. King Jaja… you know, my dad, he wants Robbo to be his prime minister."

The two ladies split about with laughter. The thought of Larry the loony being the chief adviser to the King was indeed a ripe thought. As the two ladies settled into their cabins and began to breast feed their babies, the gurgalatious ripples of laughter transmitted themselves to the younger generation, and gave an indication of how Miss Robinson and Master Kerry would have difficulties in avoiding being jolly, jocular persons.

It was also an indication of how a complete noony-brain can find himself invited to grasp the levers of power in the top echelons of government. There's a lesson in that for us all!

CHAPTER 29
EVACUATION

As darkness began to fall on the ocean some miles offshore from the cove, a launch set out with the intention of removing the men folk from the Georgian Mansion. The last few furlongs had to be done with the crew rowing, since they did not wish to alert the guards on duty at the gate. This is why there was no hint of the boat approaching the beach, as Kevin, Derek and Larry sat at table, devouring their latest permutation on the theme of wheatato. Suddenly there was a rap on the door. Their first impression was that it might be Wallitude and Maudsley pestering them again, so they decided to make them wait. But the rap became a thump, indicating urgency.

Kevin opened the door, and to his amazement, there were two sailors of the Oogie nationality, grinning at them in the twilight.

"Holy Saints and the Blessed Virgin," Kevin expostulated, "I didn't know the British Government employed chaps like you."

"We are not from the British Government," explained Jed-Jed, "we are here to rescue you and take you off to Oogie-Googie Land. Our king wants to save you from the British bureaucrats."

"You should pack your things at once and come with us. King Jaja's personal yacht is waiting for you out at sea. Don't waste any time," advised Mi-mo.

It only took a few minutes to explain the situation to the men, and how the ladies and the babies were waiting for them on the ocean. Derek Normbrain was delighted and threw a few things into his suitcase in readiness. Kevin Kerry, desperate to see his wife and little Master Kerry, hurtled off to his room and returned in two minutes. But Larry just sat there in a daze, motionless.

"Dr. Lawrence," coaxed Jed-Jed, "we have no time to waste. Just drop everything and come with us."

"But…but…" came a gawping groan, "how can I leave my laboratory and my latest experiment? Where would you take us?"

"Come with us to Oogie Land," they fussed, "King Jaja wants you."

Mi-mo added, "you can do all the experiments you want and you can have a super-dooper laboratory with everything laid on. But hurry; the guards will realize what's happening any minute."

That promise had Larry motivated, but he was loth to leave behind the latest idea which was a clever permutation on the wheatato project.

"I say, you chaps," he begged, "will you help me grab everything from the lab? I don't want those idiots from the ministry pinching my idea."

"But Larry," Derek objected, "what about the growing patch outside. They will find that."

"With any luck they won't know what it is," hustled

Kevin, "why don't we just grab a few roots from out there and scarper. After all, there's a limit to what we can take in the boat." He looked out at the launch and decided it would be quite a problem to get everything on board.

After a frantic fifteen minutes, cardboard boxes full of chemicals and root samples were stowed in the boat. Larry became much more motivated at the realization that he would see his beloved wife and daughter on the ship. But he was troubled at the thought of leaving various bits and pieces behind. The boat scrunched on the beach as the sailors began to push it off.

"Hey! Just a minute," gasped Kevin, "where's Jimmy?"

"He was with us half an hour ago," puzzled Derek, "and nipped out, leaving his dinner half eaten. I assume he had a call to nature."

"We can't go without Jimmy," fussed Larry, "he's been such a help, and Lord knows what they will do to him if they nobble him. He is part of our team." He began calling out Jimmy's name in the hopes of him suddenly reappearing. He did not.

Then in the gloom they spotted someone running towards them. "There he is," shouted Larry, "Jimmy, come on. Jump on board."

But the sailors shoved off and switched on the motor. They were about five hundred yards from the shore when a bullet whistled over their heads, and a voice shouted, "come back, you. You are under arrest."

Mi-mo tried to calm Larry down. "That is not your friend Jimmy, I fear, but one of the guards. Fortunately, I could see his uniform. We have just managed to escape in time."

"But what will become of Jimmy?" nattered Larry.

"I expect there won't be many wallets left in the guardroom by the time he's finished," sniggered Derek, as another bullet whistled past their luggies.

Kevin reached for a certain gadget and trained it on the marksman. They could just make out his discomfiture as the rifle disintegrated in his hands and a pile of bullets landed in the sand. In addition to that, there seemed to be some sort of a problem with his walking abilities; his trousers had fallen down.

The captain had taken the risk of bringing the yacht a lot nearer to the shore, in the hopes of recovering the launch quickly. The derricks were already swung out, as they came alongside. Two minutes later, the launch was up on the deck and the yacht under way, heading for the African coast.

•

It was the tenderest reunion imaginable as the two husbands were reunited with their wives and saw their offspring for the first time.

"Oh my darling, I've been pining for you all the time," Kevin cuddled Betty, "you are a wonderful girl. And here's Master Kerry. What are we going to call him?"

"How about Seamus?" she giggled, adoringly, "that's a good old Irish name."

And Seamus seemed pleased with the idea as his daddy took him in his arms.

•

As for the Robinsons, their reunion was not quite as full-blooded as one might have hoped. Larry hugged his wife, and Sally kissed him quite copiously. But there was a little shadow in the mind of the genius.

"I'm not quite a happy bunny," he frowned.

"Why not, Darling?"

"We had to go without Jimmy. It's very strange. He was with us a few minutes before the boat arrived and then he disappeared. No one knows where he was. We had to push off without him. The guards realized what was happening and started shooting. What will become of Jimmy? I know he was a rascal, but even so, he was a well-intentioned rascal."

The smile drained gradually from Sally's face. She liked Jimmy even if he was a rogue, and it seemed to her so unfair that the Cockney lad should have such a different fate from themselves. Then something else suddenly dawned on her, the other love in her life.

"Larry! Did you think to bring my violin?" she gasped in a panic.

He stared at her, thunderstruck. The very thought that they would never again be able to listen to that inspirational music, landed like a ten ton lead weight on his soul. He tried to think if any of the others had thought to snatch it at the last minute. But in the end, he had to admit that the instrument had not been in the boat. He emitted a gaspey expletive, which was quite unusual for the calm, politely spoken genius.

"Oh heck!" he whispered, "it must be back there. I am so sorry Darling." He held her hands, "but let's not despair over it. We are rich enough to purchase a really decent one, maybe a real Stradivarius. I know this will be a terrible blow to you, but we had to do a bunk pretty quickly when those sailors arrived on the front door step. We've had to leave quite a few things behind."

"We must turn back," she yapped in desperation, "Jimmy and my violin! How could we leave them behind? Larry; go and tell the captain at once."

The trouble was, that with it being a sailing ship, and the wind being in just the right direction to carry them along to Africa, it was going to be really difficult to return to the cove. And in any case, by now, Jimmy and the violin might not be there at all, if the authorities had come swarming in. The captain just shrugged his shoulders and explained that they were now about fifty miles off from Britain, and to go back would invite being caught by the British Navy. After a lot of pleading, the captain put his foot down and refused to turn round.

"I shouldn't worry about Jimmy," Kevin shook his head, "that lad is crafty enough to look after himself. Just remember how sly he can be."

"Yes, and he can be really cunning when it comes to the money," reminded Betty. "And that reminds me, what about all those millions we earned from those peace-brokering deals we managed? Where is that now? And how do we get our hands on it, now that we can't go back to Britain?"

"Perhaps, with any luck, we shan't need the money, at least for time being," figured Sally, "I think I get it that the Oogies are going to look after us and give us a home."

"And give us a laboratory," added Larry, who was already

beginning to feel bereft of his normal mania. "That bloke said I could have all the facilities imaginable. Just think of the ideas I could dream up."

"Larry!" the boss lady wagged a finger, "just calm down. Don't you think enough is enough?"

The only reply she got was an idiotic countenance with augmented imbecilic giggles.

•

It took about two weeks for the sailing ship to arrive at the Oogie coastline and anchor off about a mile out. The launch conveyed them into a small harbor, and as they approached they could see certain important persons waiting for them. It was King Jaja and Prince Baba, highly enthusiastic about their new recruits to Oogie-Googie Land.

"This is such a wonderful day for us," cried King Jaja, "do come in my Rolls and be my guest at the palace. All your luggage will follow on."

"Do be careful with that crate," warned Derek, "it's got a certain sort of plant in there. We must explain in detail about it. Baba knows about it."

As they approached the palace, they noticed a new building in the throes of completion. It seemed to be almost as palatial as the palace. But they swept past and were taken into Jaja's sitting room to be regaled with tea and cucumber sandwiches.

"Now, dear friends," Jaja explained, "we have been waiting for this moment for some time. While your quarters are being completed, you stay with me and Prince

Baba in this palace. I know all about your latest important development, Larry, and I am absolutely delighted. You see, in this part of the world, we have serious problems over food shortages. The great deserts are expanding and growing crops is becoming ever more difficult. This new idea of yours is just what we need. We want you to have all the facilities you need to produce what-do-you-call-it?"

"Wheatato," stated Larry. "We have been living on it for some days now, since the ministry cut off our supplies. I suppose they thought we ought to starve to death."

"How disgraceful!" chimed Baba.

"What we have noticed," cut in Kevin, "is that this new plant is inclined to spread like mad. It will almost certainly have to be kept under control or it will swamp the entire country."

"We are just testing it with watering and non-watering," added Larry, "but we got oiked out before we could see the results. We need to do careful research on how to control it. How are you fixed for water in this country?"

"We do have water shortages all the time," the King admitted, "but that is another thing you can help us with, Dr. Lawrence. If we take water from the sea, can you desalinate it for us?"

"It can be done," agreed Larry, "but the initial outlay could be expensive."

"But just think, we could be selling this product to people all over Africa, and indeed the whole world," Jaja grinned, "and that would be a great help to everyone, what with climate change."

"It would also put our country in a central position in world politics, Dad," Baba smiled.

"Anyway, did you notice that building going up as you came along?" the King pointed.

"I did," admitted Betty. Sally smiled, as she began to guess what it would be.

"That will be your headquarters, Dr. Robinson. Downstairs is your living area, with enough space for all of you, including these lovely piccanninnies. Upstairs is your laboratory."

"The only hang-up in that, is that we haven't got Jimmy with us any more," sighed Sally. "The boys lost track of him when the boat arrived, and I suppose the Brits have got him under arrest by now."

"Come with me," invited Baba, "and view your new establishment."

They followed Baba out of the palace and began to investigate the new palace. The structure was almost complete, but inside there were workmen installing the water and electricity, the gas and the decoration and carpets. As they clambered upstairs, they became aware of different kinds of noises coming from the research area. Already, the laboratory was well-stocked with materials, and gentlemen in white coats were cleaning up the benches and testing the gas taps. As they looked about, they noticed one lad in a white coat but with a lighter neck and face.

"Just a minute," Betty expostulated, "I know that face. How did you get here?"

The face turned towards them and challenged them with 'Watch-yer cock!" in that engaging Cockney accent.

It was Jimmy!

"JIMMY!!!" exploded Sally, "how did you get here?"

"Long story, mate," he chortled, "but never fear, Jimmo is 'ere."

Sally came up to him and kissed him. "We were so worried about you but you beat us to it."

"Wiv a few days to spare," he cheeked, "'ad time to pop in at Switzerland."

"What on earth for?" gawped Larry, innocent as ever.

"You might remember all that mazuma you left be'ind? Well, I never leave mazuma be'ind, as you know. I managed to get it all out of Britain and into a Swiss account, so it's all safe."

They were all staggered at the craftiness of it all.

"And 'ere's summat else yer left be'ind," he crowed, as he pulled out a certain ancient violin. "And ah fort yer might like yer music as well. He-he!"

CHAPTER 30
CITIZENS OF OOGIE

Settling in to Oogie-googie Land could only be described as a pleasure, not just for the Robinsons and the Kerries, but also for the Oogies. It was a country based on love, caring, sharing and generosity. The post of Prime Minister, which had been specially reserved for Larry, was waiting for him as promised. After due consultation, and a distinct reluctance on the part of the candidate, it was decided that a political numbskull would probably make a total mess of it. Consequently, Dr. Lawrence Robinson was glad to relegate himself to his new laboratory and continue to dream up new ideas which could potentially mess the world up even more than it was already.

One of his batty ideas, was a machine which would knacker all the elastic in the world. The ladies quickly disabused him of that idea, since they could imagine all the knicker-elastic being knackered. The gentlemen too, though not quite so fixated on the integrity of pants, were glad to support that theory. Another of his crackpot ideas was to hasten the process of evolution by making a machine which would induce the chimpanzees to turn into humans, within their own lifetime; the chimps' lifetime, I must hasten to add, not the humans'. It was Jimmy who talked him out of that notion; he pointed to himself and reminded Larry that he was a bit of a monkey already; which one? Well, both of them, but in different ways.

Another scheme, which was not a completely barmy idea, was to devise a method of halting the spread of wheatato. This innovative foodstuff was a great success in many African countries, but everyone realized that unless it was kept under control, it would swamp and smother everybody and everything. It was like Japanese Knotgrass, or Himalayan Balsam, or bindweed but only worse. In the interim, it was seen as advisable to grow the stuff in Oogie Land, process it and then sell it on to countries on the brink of starvation. The long term solution was to devise a method of restraining its eagerness to spread like wildfire.

But the most urgent need was to devise a water cleansing scheme. No one thought twice about encouraging Larry to fix that up. It was desperately needed in many sub-Saharan territories, not just for normal usage, but to reclaim areas that had turned into desert.

One day, Sally invaded the laboratory with the intention of having a microscopic conversation with her husband.

"Larry, darling," she began, as she found him proddling a funny looking substance in a test tube, "what are you up to now? Is this another caulking idea?"

"Corks!" he muttered, "yes, we've got loads of them. Not the plastic ones," he added, "but the real ones from Portugal. Just leave it over there, Sally," he gestured, on the assumption that it was coffee-break time. The other guys in the lab grinned at each other. It was going to be one of those exchanges of disconnected thought.

"Larry! Is that something that's going to make a mess of everything again?"

"Mess?" he was miles away, as usual, "is it time to come down to the Naafi? I feel like a quick dollop of tiffin."

"Larry! Before you go and devise something completely crackers."

"Crackers?" he puzzled, "it's not Christmas time yet, surely?"

"No dear," exasperation mounting, "it's you that's crackers."

"Oh well, if you pull me in two directions at once, who knows what might drop out. I'm quite used to the idea of being a bit of a joke, but it's Kevin that goes in for weak jokes."

"Larry!" she almost shouted, "will you tell me what this new invention is going to do?" She was sorely tempted to bonk him on the head with a thistle-funnel.

"Erm…well," he went all vague, "early days yet…." He puckered up his lips, "hang on, let me have that thistle-funnel," he took it off her and twiddled with it, and fiddled with it, and woggled it about with a blob of funny stuff inside. "Well my word!" he expostulated, "I think I've got it."

"What? Screaming abdabs like me?" she was red in the face. But he was miles away, again, on the brink of some strange solution to a commonplace worldly problem. "Oh I give up," she sighed.

Derek Normbrain cut in, hoping to avert a heavy

domestic. "I think he's devising a method for dealing with naughty children," the old man grinned, "so that they don't grow up to be like our Jimmy."

"You mean, a good old slap across the backside?" Sally suggested, "young Master Seamus Kerry is heading in that direction."

"And little Miss Jemima Robinson," muttered someone in the distance.

•

The post of Prime Minister, still being on offer, was still being casually debated in the halls of power in the palace. Derek Normbrain was definitely out of the running, considering his age. Mind you, with his experience of life and healthy robust wad of common sense, he might have introduced a smattering of rationality into world politics. But he stoutly refused, knowing that a younger person would make far more sense. Next on the list was a certain James Whitlock, who was certainly young and agile in his grey matter, but rather a dodgy proposition. Everyone admired his skill in bamboozling various government officials, not least the British, but the thought that a highly accomplished larcenist could occupy such an office, made them think twice.

In the end it came to Kevin Kerry as the prime candidate for the King's personal adviser. He was totally honest, fair-minded, caring and gentle. That sweet Irish lilt in his voice had them all sentimentalizing and adoring him. They all recalled how he had talked so many countries into the ways of peace. But Kevin himself was self-effacing and not inclined to push himself forward. In the end he agreed to do it as long as his beloved wife, Betty, should be the deputy Prime Minister. In other words, prime him with ideas for his prime-ministership.

So it was, that it came to his installation, with a mass gathering of the clans and even Larry was persuaded to forsake his latest potty idea and attend the ceremony. Kevin had totally forgotten that one would normally expect the newly installed candidate to make an inaugural speech. Once again he was stumped. So Betty whispered in his ear, "Why don't you tell them one of your awful jokes, Kev?"

"Nah!" he whispered, "I think I've run out of them, my darling. In any case, it will make me look an idiot."

"Well that will be no different from all these other guys that get elevated and make a complete ass of themselves," she spoke a little louder. The crowd heard that and began to cheer and wave.

"Come, Kevin, tell us a joke."

"All right, all right," he shushed them down. "Well it was like this, my dears. There was the boss in a company, and he had a whole collection of slap-happy workmen. Some were good at one thing, and some were good at others. So he spent a lot of time making sure the right bloke was on with the right job. Well one day a politician came from the government to find out what was going on. The boss gave him a guided tour, and as they went round they met some of the workmen.

"Here's Tommy," he pointed, "he's no good at painting."

"What a shame," commented the politician.

"And here's Gerry," he gestured, "and he's no good at cutting the metal."

And so it went on, so that the politician had a good idea of how incompetent the workforce was. So he asked the boss," if I came to work here, what would I be no good at?"

"Same as back in London," replied the boss, "telling lies."

"And what would you be no good at, Kevin?" called Jimmy.

"Telling jokes, of course," came the riposte from the Irish physiognomy.

"Can you tell the truth, Kevin?" came another challenge.

"I think I'll give it my best shot," he coughed, modestly.

"Then you won't last very long in politics," cheeked another. It was Jimmy.

•

Since Jimmy was slightly, but not greatly, disappointed at not being given the post of Prime Minister, they fixed him up with the post of Minister of Education. Was that a particularly wise move, one may wonder? It was based on the assumption that since most people in Oogie Land did not bother with wallets, Jim would have trouble in finding any to pinch. However, his policy of fiddling did assume two distinct aspects.

"Now, Kar-Kar, this is how you play the fiddle. You just copy Mrs. Robinson, and you'll finish off as an A-1 violinist."

"Yes, Mr. Whitlock," the little girl smiled and within minutes she was growing in proficiency.

Soon, every school in the country was blessed with a

string quartet, and some of the bigger schools had full-blown string orchestras.

The other aspect of Jimmy's expertise was the subject of much teasing and jocularity. Since there were hardly any wallets to filch, he went in for necklaces and earrings and the like. Mind you, he did not neglect to attract an elite band of little boys who were good at relieving European gentlemen of their spondulicks. One member of this coterie was a certain Master Seamus Kerry, who became known as the 'Oliver Twist' of Oogie Land. More of that later. The corrective to this was performed by Mrs. Sally Robinson, who, on Friday afternoons, as regular as clockwork, accosted Jimmy with her hand outstretched and demanded a smidgeon of honesty.

"Come on, Jim, hand over," she would demand.

"Sorry lav, can't kick the 'abit," he admitted, and produced all the stuff he had filched during the week, and that included what the boys had pinched as well.

"You blighter," she would scold, "you'll turn the whole nation into a race of fiddlers."

"Nor 'alf," he shrugged, "but then you're the chief fiddler, aren't you, mate?"

•

But the funniest thing was to come years later. There had been a communiqué from London, requesting the return of Dr. Robinson. The response from King Jaja, with the advice of the Kerries, was to give a firmly negative reply. "He's our bloke; you can't have him."

"But we are in a crisis here," came the plaintive reply, "please help us."

A few days later, an executive jet came in to land and guess who staggered uncertainly down the gangway? He was conveyed to Kevin's office and offered an interview with the Prime Minister. Kevin smiled as he noticed bits of foliage sticking out from his jacket and trousers. It was unmistakably dreary trails of wheatato.

"Top of the morning to you," Kevin chuckled, "are you in the process of becoming a leprechaun?"

"Kerry," Fred Wallitude began.

"Mr.Kerry to you," Kevin interrupted, "and what can we do for you?"

Mrs. Kerry had already guessed what the problem was. "Too much vegetation?" she grinned.

Fred Wallitude decided to eat humble pie and speak plain English. "I'm here on behalf of the government," he began. "We are absolutely overgrown with some strange new plant. It looks as though it originated in that security area you were living in…"

"Imprisoned in," cut in Betty. "You abandoned us, you rotter. We could have starved to death not to mention problems with having our babies."

"Anyway, it's spread all over the country…"

"Has it got to the dear old Emerald Isle yet?" Kevin quizzed.

"No."

"Then that's all right then," concluded Kevin, "good morning."

"Ah now just a minute," begged Wallitude, "the whole

country is clogged up with it. The roads are blocked, the drains are jammed up, even the Prime Minister's pipe has it growing out of the bowl. I had hoped that Chobinson... I mean, Robinson might have a solution to this."

"What makes you think Dr. Robinson has an answer to it? After all, you regarded him as a total quack and a loony. You stole his idea and had him locked up."

"I'm very sorry," mumbled Fred.

"Fact is, that if we hadn't developed that new strain of plant, next to the Mansion, we would have starved to death," stated Betty firmly. "You do realize that that stuff is highly nutritious? You could live off it for years and it would be no cost at all. Lots of countries in the Third World are doing very well off it. They are looking so much fitter and happier. Why don't you try it yourself?"

"Very well," sighed Kevin, "you may have an interview with Dr. Robinson, but you realize that the antidote does not come free of charge."

•

Fred Wallitude stepped into the laboratory and stared in amazement at the research facilities now well established.

"What's the first thing you're going to say?" demanded Sally. "My husband is very busy. We don't take kindly to time-wasters."

As usual, Larry was deeply engrossed in some exceedingly clever new thing in a test tube. He hardly glanced up and even less took notice of his visitor from London.

"Just leave it over there," he waved vaguely. "What time is it, Sally?"

"Time you had a break, darling," she tried to insist. "You have a visitor from London."

"London? Not bothered with that place any more," he murmured abstractedly, "after the way they treated us."

"Dr. Clobinson, I mean, Robinson," Fred coughed deferentially, "on behalf of Her Majesty's Government, I have an urgent request for you."

Larry glanced away from his experiment. "Oh for Pete's sake," he gasped, "not you again. No, you can't have my equipment. Sally; send for the security guards and chuck him out, before he pinches by latest idea."

While this was going on, young Seamus Kerry was thoughtfully pulling bits of foliage from Fred's clothing. "What a mess, Auntie Sally," he piped, "are they all as scruffy as this in London?"

"I think you'd better go," indicated Sally, pointing to the door, "young Master Kerry will report you to his father, as a tramp, and we don't have vagrants in this country."

Fred Wallitude began to head for the door, but found there was a certain impediment to his footwork. He slumped against a bench and looked round, only to spot young Seamus holding up Fred's bracers.

"You might need these," the boy grinned, "fancy showing your knickers to a lady like that."

Fred realized that his trousers had fallen down, and began to yank them up.

"And Seamus, how about the other item?" demanded Sally.

The boy shyly held up a certain wallet. "you might need this back again," he cheeked, and tossed it over.

Apart from the teasing, they decided that forgiveness is a quality appropriate to a country which was espoused to the principles of Catholic Wesleyan Methodism. Fred was sent home with a generous consignment of chemicals which had been tested and found effective in the control of wheatato. There was hope for Britain yet, in spite of all its confusion, complication and smothering of bureaucracy.

•

However the final blessing was to come a few years later, as Kevin and Betty sat in their office, issuing directives to the Oogies. They seemed to have no resentment towards their European rulers, as long as their head of state was King Jaja. A telephone rang on the desk, and Kevin answered it.

"Mr. Prime Minister," came a voice from the airport, "we have here a young lady from Ireland. She claims to be related to you… Some sort of cousin. Do you want to see her?"

"But of course," replied Kevin, "one of my own wee countrymen. Bring her in."

A few minutes later, a tall, purposeful young lady, in her mid twenties, strode in and made an instant impact. Betty was struck by her facial similarity to Kevin.

"Top of the morning to ye, young Kevin," it was a very heavy Irish brogue, but an engaging manner that charmed everybody.

"Well now," he enthused, "come on in and have a tot of the hard stuff. Are you really one of my cousins from County Kerry? Let's see now…"

After a brief discussion about the complications of family trees, it became clear that Kevin and Fiona were indeed cousins. Sadly they had never met before, but it mattered not a jot. But Kevin began to feel that strange feeling of unease at this girl. It dawned on him that this must be the child that was walking past the police station, and got blown up. He decided to play it very carefully. Betty, however, decided on the opposite course. She thought it best to get the question out into the open.

"Fiona," she began, "I'm his wife. I know all about his past and how he got involved in the IRA." This produced no reaction from Fiona; she clearly knew all about it. "He had a young cousin involved in a bomb attack outside a police station. She lost a leg, it would seem."

Kevin was thunderstruck; he wanted the ground to open up beneath him. All his life he had this chimera pressing down on his soul, and now it was all coming home to roost, so to speak. He went white and gulped a dollop of the hard stuff.

Fiona shrugged her shoulders and then proceeded to pull her skirts up. "Not quite like that," she swished her skirts, "I know I was injured in this leg, but they did a very good job in the hospital and managed to save it. I'm fine," she pirouetted about the room, like a ballerina.

Kevin, totally astonished, came over to her and took her in his arms. "I am so sorry," he came over totally contrite, "I know I was a complete fool to get involved with that madness, and I've never forgiven myself. I love you so much, Fiona, my lovely cousin."

She was absolutely charming and loving. "Well now yer mind is at rest on the subject," she kissed him, "and what a fine success story you've been yerself, me Dear."

CHAPTER 31
IN THE LONG TERM

As the years rolled by, it would be fascinating to see how things worked out, as Larry and his team became an important element in Oogie society. Some amusing anecdotes may help us to see the latter end of the Robinson mania. Sally often invaded his laboratory in the hopes of dissuading him from the latest mad idea he had dreamt up.

"Larry? What's that you're inventing now?" she would quiz him.

"I've heard a report that in Jukey-land, the silly blighters have decided that since they can't have guns and rockets, they have resorted to catapults. It's that stupid aggressive tendency in human nature," he smacked his lips.

"So what's that funny-looking brew you're making today?" she demanded.

He was miles away again, dreaming up his latest wonkey idea. "Oh, erm…" He began, "needs a bit more of this," and he reached for a bottle with a lurid coloured chemical in it. "Just a smidgeon ought to do it…" and he dumped a few crystals of the stuff in and warmed it up a bit on the Bunsen. It turned a peculiar shade of pinky-winky merging with googly-googly brown and threw off a most interesting aroma.

"Phaw! What a pong!" his wife clutched her nose. "Open the windows, chaps," she ordered. But there was no one there to carry out her demand. All the others had done a bunk, except one little experimenter who knew enough to know that if it did make an explosion, it would be a nice colourful one.

"Jemima!" called her mother, "what are you concocting today?"

The goofy look on the Robinsonian daughter's face was not far off as barmy as her father's, but as before, that look was some sort of camouflage for a genius in the making. "Mummy!" she hissed, "I think I've got it!"

"Got what, dear?" Sally came over and peered at the funny-looking liquor in the flask, "don't tell me you've got measles."

"No, mummy, " she piped, "but Daddy set me on to devise a medicine that can be prescribed to all naughty people that want a punch-up."

"That might be rather a lot of people," sighed Sally, "I mean, the intention is right, but will it be practicable?"

Larry was miles away again, fiddling with his project. He was quite confident in his daughter's abilities, even if she was only seven years old.

Sally decided to try again. "Larry!" she raised her voice, "is it practicable?"

"Oh!" he surfaced just a little, "of course it will. All we have to do is get someone to apply it to the rubber and the catapult will fall apart."

That sounded a little warning bell in Sally's cranium. "Larry! We've been here before."

"Yes, I know, I like it in this country. King Jaja hasn't tried to lock me up yet…" He sniggered, "and that lot in London have had to stew in their own juice. Serve them right."

"No dear, " she was becoming exasperated, "I seem to recall that elastic is made of rubber. True?"

"Probably…" he went all vague. Miss Jemima Robinson began to snigger. She knew the implications involved.

"I can guess why you're sniggering, young lady," her mother frowned.

"Yes. Tee-hee! It means that all our knickers will fall down," she piped, as if it were some sort of routine accomplishment. "Seamus will enjoy every minute of it.

"And how does Seamus come into this?" demanded Sally.

"Well Mummy," she stated tactfully, "Seamus has some sort of idea that he wants to be your son-in-law."

There was a highly charged silence at that point. "You mean, he wants to marry you?"

"Not half," she giggled, "cheeky blighter."

"And what did you say to that, Jemima?" the mother interrogated.

"I said I might think about it, you know, give it some thought. I explained that at the moment I was helping Daddy to devise some important new developments, so courting will have to wait a bit. Perhaps ten years or so. He looked rather disappointed at that, but if he truly loves me, he ought to be able to wait for me." It sounded like the Wisdom of Solomon in a Robinsonian mode.

Mrs. Robinson decided to take the bull by the horns. "Larry!" she demanded, "is that clever idea of yours going to ruin all our knicker elastic?"

"Oh!" he stopped for a moment with his proddling, "you know, that's quite a thought. Anything made of rubber will go kaput…" at that, Jemima burst out laughing.

"Hey! Just a minute," the mother pointed at her daughter, "I know what's going through your head, Madam!" She knew just how precocious Jemima was. "Larry!" she resumed, "you realize the implications in that, don't you?"

"Yer wot?" he breezed as he tinkered with the mixture.

"Larry! If you marmalise all the rubber, we shall have a population explosion, all over the world." She was frowning deeply; Jemima collapsed about laughing.

"Oh!" he remarked vaguely, "you know, I never thought of that. Well dear me! Mind you, with all that wheatato that we're producing, we should manage to feed the starving millions."

And so it went on, with Larry dreaming up one barmy idea after another, and his wife just managing to talk him out of it. The world had managed to settle down to a marvelous era of peace, even if there were still people using their fists and faffing about with catapults and a few remote tribes carefully conserving their blowpipes. Apart from that, weapons of war were a thing of the past, and everybody sighed a great big whopping sigh of relief.

•

The aggressive tendency in human nature was quite

epitomized with the conduct of one Master Seamus Kerry, who, as a boy of seven, simply could not restrain his itch to have a punch up. The Oogie boys found that rather strange but took it in turns to make him look a complete fool. How often did his father have to emerge from the government office and drag the boy off by the scruff of his neck and slap his backside.

But Seamus was in love. He had decided that Jemima Robinson was to be his bride one day, and nothing would dissuade him. His mother, Betty Kerry had taken him on one side and attempted to give him a certain amount of moral pep talk. But this had very little effect on the scamp.

"Hey Robbo!" he slid up to Jemima in the laboratory, "that's a funny looking concoction you've got there. Is it poisonous? What's it supposed to do?"

"It's supposed to encourage cheeky boys to call people by their proper names," she came the superior tone, "and what's more, take out that tendency to have a punch up."

"Robbo, you are a spoilsport," he sneered, "when I get older and get round to marrying you, I shall start up a boxing club in this town. Or better still, a wrestling club."

"Dream on," Jemima barked , "what makes you think I'd be barmy enough to marry you, Paddy?"

"But you are barmy, like your Dad."

"Daddy? Did you hear that? Seamus thinks you're barmy."

The Robinsonian thought machine paused for a few moments and smiled with that idiotic grin, which was more than just a winning smile. "Yer what?" he remarked vaguely.

"Seamus thinks you're barmy."

"Wise lad that," came the dismissive response, "something of an understatement. How about completely doolarly? Or moronic? Or totally bonkers?"

The two youngsters laughed themselves silly, but decided they were in complete agreement.

Seamus took her by the hands and made her a promise. "All right!" he agreed, "I promise to behave myself, but dear Jemima, I would like to give you a kiss, please," he begged.

Jemima eyed her father for a moment, but to no avail since he was miles away, wobbling his test tube. "All right," she whispered, "just a quick one. I am actually very busy."

It was more than just a quick one. Their lips met fractionally, but it meant rather a lot. Can a boy of seven be genuinely in love? Why not? What about a girl? Definitely! It was the pattern laid out for the future, even if it was going to be a long time in coming.

•

As the years rolled by, Kevin Kerry became renowned worldwide for his skills in diplomacy. He was awarded the Nobel Peace Prize about ten times. This seemed rather strange to his wife, who wondered why Doc Robinson could not be similarly rewarded. Seamus Kerry, eager to emulate his father, would sit by his side in the Cabinet Office and make increasingly sagacious suggestions.

"Dad!" he would say, "what are you going to say to that idiot in Bungle-boo-boo Land? You know, the one that thinks he can ignore the United Nations?

"Oh that inflated fathead," sighed Kevin, as he shuffled his papers.

"Tell you what, why not send him a box of chocolates and inject them with that potion that my wife-to-be has invented?"

"You mean that stuff that will knock the stuffing out of you?" the dear Papa smiled, "persuade you to be a peaceful young man. That could be a ripping idea, me boy. Mind you," he paused, "that is conduct not quite in line with Catholic Wesleyan Methodist methods of conduct. I do have a little incy-wincy smidgeon of conscience, you know?"

"Dad!" he became insistent, "when can I marry Jemima?"

"What do you want to marry her for, me boy? She's even more raving mad than her wee Daddy. Why don't you go in for a nice Oogie girly? They're allowed to get married in their early teens."

"So why can't Jemima and I get married in our early teens?" he persisted.

And so it went on.

•

Derek Normbrain, now well into his dotage, would spend most of his time in the lab with Larry. He had given up trying to moderate the lunatic ideas that Larry kept dreaming up. It was his wife who regularly came in and put the lid on one scheme after another. But it was Jimmy who was having a fine old time of it, not so much for his larcenous impulses, but another notion that came to preoccupy his mind. It was that of female company. It had become obvious to Jimmy the Whizz that it was legal in that country to have more than one wife, and there did not appear to be any limit on the quantity thereof. The result was that he accumulated an entire harem.

"Darling," cooed Ton-Ton, "I think Fee-fee is having another baby. I'd like to have another one too."

"Haven't you got enough on your hands already… isn't it three you've got now, sweetheart?"

"But I'm your favourite wife, or I'm supposed to be," she sulked, caressing his face.

Jimmy was beginning to regret having designated Ton-Ton as his favourite wife, and had the urge to stipulate that there should be no favourites. But the girls would have none of it. They had the idea that the one that produced the highest number of babies ought to be the top dog (we'd better not say 'bitch').

"And Jim," she cooed at him, "you pinched Coo-Coo's necklace the other day? That was naughty, wasn 't it? Why did you do that, after all the things we said on the subject?"

"Simple really," he sighed, "since she hasn't got a wallet, or earrings or bracelets or a nose ring, there wasn't much choice. OK; here it is back again."

"And you really must control that urge to pinch things, Jim, or I shall report you to that Mrs. Robinson again. She knows how to sort you out."

"Not 'arf," admitted Jim. But the positive side of Jim's polygamy was that he was so absorbed with romancing with his wives that his tendency to pinch things somehow got sidelined, at least, almost completely. He was even inclined not to pinch the girl's bottoms.

Like all good things, there has to be an end to it somewhere. That became increasingly obvious in the case of that dear old Catholic Wesleyan Methodist Majesty, King Jaja himself. He was now well advanced in years and very frail. Even so, the occasional burst of the Boogie-woogie could be heard penetrating to the uttermost recesses of the Palace, and that infectious grin kept everyone happy. But he came to his last gasp at the age of 90, with his Queen and Prince Baba in attendance. He requested the presence of Kevin Kerry and his rascally son, Seamus.

"Kevin, I'm about to move on to the next world, dear friend. Will you be a faithful Prime Minister to my son, when he becomes the next king? And your son, he too will make a lovely Prime Minister one day, bless him!"

"Leave it to me, your Majesty," promised Kevin, "everything will be as nice as pie."

"And Kevin, can you tell me just one more of your corny jokes, to finish me off?"

"Oh heck!" he sighed, "at a time like this." But he recalled that Jaja was always a jolly fellow and never failed to laugh his socks off, at even at the weakest joke. Not that he ever wore socks, the climate being so congenial. "Seamus; can you think of a joke?"

"Yes Dad," he chirped, "one of your worst coming up. There was a bus in London town, and the conductor spotted a man that had not paid his fare. So he went up to him and said, in his Cockney accent, the best I can do, imitating Jimmy, 'Ye'll laft ter piey.'" The man, who turned out to be a

Yorkshire chap, replied, 'what me? I never left a pie. I'm too greedy for that.' But the conductor rattled his money pouch and repeated, 'Piey! Cough up, mate.' But the man said, 'I can't cough it up, since I haven't eaten it yet.' The conductor got nastier, 'yer fare, mate,' and rattled the money pouch. 'I'm always fair with everyone,' retorted the man, and so it went on, but neither of them got the ticket."

"Shut up!" hissed Mrs. Kerry in his ear.

"Oh leave him alone, Betty," chuckled the King, "he's a lovely lad and a credit to you both. I think that joke is really splendid. They could hear him laughing himself silly until he finally departed this life.

It came to the big royal funeral, as King Jaja was interred in his ancestors' mausoleum, with all due honours. The whole nation was not in mourning, since they believed unfailingly that Jaja had been their mainstay for so many years and had moved on to a better world with Our Lord. Diplomats came from far and near, including King Chu-Chu his old pal from Eton. The other reason for not mourning was that Baba was now the new king, which meant a new chapter in the history of Oogie-googie Land. There were fears that the Boogie-woogie would never be heard again in the halls of power, but that was a mistaken notion, for one of Jaja's daughters was able to do a creditable reproduction of jazzy music on that old Bechstein. And so, as the coffin slid into its place in the royal vaults, the strains of '*Is you is or is you ain't*' followed him to his final resting place.

All the emissaries from different countries took a turn at having a word with Kevin Kerry in his office. Betty Kerry was right beside him. The chap from Ireland intrigued Kevin.

"In Doublin's fair city," he began songfully, "let me introduce meeself, I'm Dougal McPhale from County Donegal."

"I see yer didn't bring yer favourite leprechaun with ye," Kevin teased with his heavy brogue.

The man's eyes nearly popped out of his head. "Well be Jabers and Begorrah!" he exploded, "an Irishman in charge of things in Oogie-googie Land. Whatever next!"

"I can tell yer what next, Dougal, my son, Seamus; he'll be the next one in this chair. King Jaja appointed him as my successor, so he has an assured future. Now let me see, yer say yer a McPhale. Now my mother was a McPhale. Yer might just be a cousin of mine…" and so it went on.

"And are ye not going to pay us a visit in the Emerald Isle?" Dougal put his foot in it.

"Sorry cousin," spluttered Kevin, "definitely not; my wife won't let me." Betty nodded emphatically. Dougal was left wondering why. But we all know the reason, don't we?!

•

The final visitor was a cardinal from the Vatican. They were unsure about the religious set-up in Oogie Land, but since Jaja was dubbed 'his most Catholic Wesleyan Methodist Majesty, they decided that nothing would be lost if an investigation were to take place.

"We are most impressed with you, Mr. Kerry," congratulated the cardinal, "I was at that peace conference when you got Mr. Chom and Mr. Flam to stop being silly. You have really made a great difference to world politics. You are of course, a Roman Catholic?"

"I would say that would be debatable," Kevin eyed his wife, "you see, in this country, Protestant and Catholic have managed to stop being silly about their differences. My wife, here, is a rip roaring Evangelical."

"How do you manage that?" came the inevitable question.

"It's not that difficult really," interrupted Betty, "we both love each other fit to bust, and more importantly, we all love God, and Jesus and Saint Mary. How about that for a basis for Christian Unity? This country, Oogie Land, has managed to combine the best elements of Protestant and Catholic, under the leadership of dear old King Jaja, and his son, Baba will continue this tradition. We all love each other, even if my son Seamus fancies the occasional punch-up!" she pulled a face.

"Wow!" gasped the cardinal, "that must be an achievement. Now," he came over all conspiratorial, "what I am going to say must not go beyond these walls…" he put his finger to his mouth…"I am so pleased to hear about this. It is completely idiotic for Christian people to have silly arguments. We need unity, and we can have it in spite of various differences of opinion. Sadly there are people at the Vatican and amongst your Protestants, that cannot cope with that idea. I have the greatest admiration for you in this country. Long may it last."

•

Preparations for the Coronation were well under way. Sally had been especially requested to play her violin as part of the ceremony. The Cardinal decided to stay over as representing the Roman Catholic church. As usual, Larry and his daughter were deeply immersed in their researches in the laboratory. They could both see the masses of people gathering for the major event, an open air gathering with a throne elevated on a dais for all to see. But neither of them seemed even slightly curious, since they were totally absorbed in their tinkering with chemicals.

Seamus Kerry appeared in his best suit. "Come on, you two, hurry up," he cried, "you've got front line seats and here you are faffing about with your test tubes."

"I can't hurry this experiment," remarked Larry, vacantly.

"Uncle Larry!" the boy insisted, "Auntie Sally will go mad at you."

Jemima sniggered as she desisted from her fiddling. "I'm coming, Seamus," she ran after him, "Just let me take off this lab coat." Underneath it she had on her very best dress. This had a remarkable effect on Master Kerry; she was drop-dead gorgeous. "Daddy! Come on," she shouted through the door.

The ceremony was well in advance now. Sally Robinson was now asked to play her violin. It was amplified all over the parade ground. Everyone was transfixed by the entrancing tone and beauty of it. She did not notice that the Cardinal was particularly taken by the sound of it. A few minutes later, the crown was placed on the head of King Baba the Umpteenth (plus a few more). They had lost count of how many king Babas there had been, stretching back many centuries to the Stone Age, but who cared? He was the man of the moment.

"Where's Dad?" insisted Sally in her daughter's ear.

"I told him to come," she whispered, "silly ass was still messing about with some fancy potion. Oh! Here he comes," she pointed, "better late than never."

The cardinal leant over and peered thoughtfully at Sally's violin. Amidst the cheering and flag-waving, he asked her, "where did you get that violin, my dear?"

"It's been in my family for many generations," she admitted, "a bloke offered me fifty quid for it once. I couldn't possibly part with it. Family heirloom."

"I'm glad you didn't part with it," the prelate smiled. "I suppose he told you it wasn't a Stradivarius?"

"Yes, so he said."

"No, my dear, but it's almost certainly a lot more valuable than that. Unless I'm mistaken, it's an Amati."

"A whatty?"

"An Amati. He was another violin maker at the same time, and they are even rarer now. It is probably worth a lot more than a Strad. So guard it with your life."

Sally was completely staggered and incredibly grateful for the information. She cuddled her instrument and gave it a kiss. As Larry Robinson slid up to her, she decided to give him a kiss as well.

"Well done, Daddy," congratulated Jemima, "I knew you could spare us a minute or two from your funny looking potion. Did you remember to switch off the gas before you came out?"

"What? Oh erm…" The expert went pale, as he could not recall taking a simple precaution like that. A naughty word dropped out of his mouth, which was a rare occurrence for one of normally modest and clean speech.

"Larry," his wife snapped, "not in front of the children… or the cardinal."

"Oh hello!" gasped Larry, "with a dress like that on, anyone would think you were in the red."

Seamus burst out laughing; his mother clipped his left ear. They watched as dignitaries from all over the world advanced on King Baba and offered their best wishes. He was wearing the Oogie crown, an item of regalia centuries old, so old in fact that no one really knew how antique it was.

But the ceremony shuddered to an abrupt halt, as a rumbling and roaring issued forth from the laboratory. Everyone turned and watched with apprehension.

BANG!!!!! An enormous explosion burst all the windows out and shattered the building.

"Oooooops!" cheeked Seamus, giving Jemima a sly kiss on the cheek.

"I thought they didn't have Guy Fawkes in this country," puzzled Dougal McPhale.

Bits of laboratory flew up into the air, test tubes, pipettes, Bunsen burners, you name it. People ran for cover, but King Baba stood his ground, or rather retained his seated position on his throne. Mercifully, there was no one in the building at the time. But one thing was in the building; it was Larry's stock of permutations on the wheatato. Would you believe it? A sizeable chunk of it sailed through the air and landed with a splodge right on top of Baba's crown.

"Now look what you've done, Robinson," blasted Mrs. Robinson. "That's the end of it for you, young man. Retirement! I insist! And Jemima, you can take up the violin instead of fiddling with chemicals.

"Aw Mummy!" the girl protested.

"Just look how you've messed up the Coronation," she shouted.

But King Baba took of his crown, inspected the leafy lump of splodge stuck to his regalia, and split out laughing, so much that he almost fell off his throne. Everybody caught the mood of the new King, and soon they were all roaring with laughter, which was a good start to all the dancing and fun and games that were to round off the day, and indeed augured well for those long, happy years which were to characterize his reign.